Survivors

ELISABETH NAVRATIL's grandfather, Michel Navratil, and her father and uncle, were aboard the *Titanic* on the night the world's unsinkable ship sank. The story of the tragedy is now very much a part of Elisabeth's own life story, colouring her personal and professional life. Her first job was as a secondary schoolteacher in Paris, but she left teaching to pursue her great love: music. She has always been an avid theatre-goer and now she has realised her dreams of a career in music by becoming an opera director. She has directed works such as *Carmen*, *The Marriage of Figaro* and *Don Giovanni*, and her next project is a production called *Mozart Titanic* – embracing a theme that is very close to her heart.

JOAN DE SOLA PINTO lived in Paris for twelve years where she was a freelance translator and taught English and American law. She now lives on a small farm in Tuscany where, in addition to helping her husband with olive oil production, she paints, makes jewellery and listens to opera as much as possible.

SURVIVORS

ELISABETH NAVRATIL

Translated by
Joan de Sola Pinto

THE O'BRIEN PRESS
DUBLIN

This edition first published 1999 by The O'Brien Press Ltd,
20 Victoria Road, Dublin 6, Ireland.
Tel. +353 1 4923333; Fax. +353 1 4922777
email: books@obrien.ie
website: www.obrien.ie

Originally published in French as *Les Enfants du Titanic*
by Hachette Jeunesse S.A. in 1982,
43 quai de Grenelle, 75905 Paris Cedex 15
Reprinted in 1998

ISBN: 0-86278-590-1

British Library Cataloguing-in-publication Data
Navratil, Elisabeth
Survivors : a true-life Titanic story
1.Navratil (Family) - Juvenile literature
2.Titanic (Ship) - Juvenile literature
2.Shipwrecks - North Atlantic - Ocean - Juvenile literature
I.Title
363.1'23'092

1 2 3 4 5 6 7 8 9 10
99 00 01 02 03 04 05 06 07

The O'Brien Press receives
assistance from

The Arts Council
An Chomhairle Ealaíon

Layout and design: The O'Brien Press Ltd.
Colour separations: C&A Print Services Ltd.
Printing: Cox & Wyman Ltd.

ACKNOWLEDGEMENTS

Many thanks to my husband, Jean Paul Bouillon, and to our friends Madeline and Christian Müller in Onnens who so generously put me up and encouraged the writing of the book. Many thanks to Constance Joly who also encouraged me to rewrite the book and read the manuscript several times, giving me advice about changes.

I offer my admiration and thanks to Jean Jarry, head of IFREMER Toulon, who was in charge of the French team on the Franco-American expedition which found the wreck of the *Titanic* in 1985. And to Paul Henri Nargeolet, who was the first on board the *Nautile* to see the mythical steamship in its magnificent sea cemetery, 3,870 metres down on the ocean bed.

I would like to express my gratitude to Olivier Mendez for the generosity of selflessly sharing his passion for the *Titanic*.

I am also grateful to Sydney Taylor, now deceased, who was the inspiration behind this book.

Cet ouvrage, publié dans le cadre du programme d'aide à la publication, bénéficie du soutien du Ministère des Affaires Etrangères, du Service Culturel de l'Ambassade de France en Irlande.

This book, published within the framework of the Publication Support Programme, has received a grant from the Ministry of Foreign Affairs, through the Cultural Section of the Embassy of France in Ireland.

DEDICATIONS

To the memory of
My grandfather, Michel Navratil
My grandmother, Marcelle Navratil
My uncle, Edmond Navratil
To my father, Michel Navratil
To my husband, Jean-Paul Bouillon
To our children, Carine and David
To my sister, Michèle and my brother, Henri
To all the Navratil relatives

~ CONTENTS ~

CHAPTER 1

A SEA GIANT

AN ELEGANT YOUNG MAN elbows his way along a crowded street in Southampton, towards the embarkation quay for the *Titanic*. He has a serious face, a straight nose, a pale complexion with dark rings under his eyes and a large curly moustache. His name is Michel Navratil. He is twenty-two years old. He has a very small boy on his shoulders and is carrying a baby in his arms. Ignoring the teeming masses around him he fixes his eyes on the bars of black, white and yellow ochre on the near horizon and walks towards them.

It is early in the morning of 10 April 1912, the day of the *Titanic's* maiden voyage. Onlookers crowd around rubbing shoulders with celebrities: English and American millionaires, elegant women clutching their fur muffs with the sad face of a Pekingese or a Pomeranian peeping out, famous journalists, actors and German industrialists. They use valets and maids to push the crowds out of the way and pretend to ignore the envious looks that come their way. It is only a dream for most of the onlookers to take a trip to the United States of America on the finest ship in the world.

Towering menacingly about a hundred metres from where Michel is now standing is an iron wall. It is painted red at the bottom giving the impression that the sea below the waterline is bathed in blood. Above this, pierced with holes at regular intervals, a black mass rises up for dozens of metres and completely blocks out the sky. Lifting his head, Michel can see a large band of yellow ochre and even higher up a huge band of white that shimmers in the sun and overshadows the large warehouses in the port. Suddenly there are several huge resounding blasts from the ship's horn and Edmond, the baby, jumps with fright. Just two years old he is chubby with a round face and curly brown hair. Now his dark eyes are filled with bewilderment as he looks in vain for a familiar face. Michel hugs him even more tightly, and he relaxes.

From his father's shoulders, his elder son Michel, nicknamed Lolo, feels a rush of great excitement at the sight of this immense unforgettable thing that has no name and is as tall as the skyscrapers in his book about America. At the same time, he presses his hands on and off his ears until the great bellowing noises stop. The dark curly haired child with brown eyes and oval face is, like his father, totally absorbed in what is happening around him.

Michel stands still for a moment, a small island at the centre of the huge crowd that surges around him. Even though he is used to the rich clients at his fashion house in Nice, he has never seen so many minks, silver foxes, feathers, and top hats. There are many famous people here, mingling with hundreds of curious onlookers who have gathered together to take part in the event of the young century. Little lines of luxury luggage are being forced through the crowds. Used to the subtle smell of the Mediterranean, the tang of acrid fish, iodine and fresh seaweed now assail his nostrils.

At last the big moment has arrived. Michel is leaving behind him a past he no longer wants. America and her promises of a new life are waiting on the other side of the ocean.

His attention is caught by a loud voice rising above the hullabaloo. A man in his sixties stands head and shoulders above a horde of reporters. It is Stead, the celebrated English journalist, who is famous for having ousted a cabinet minister singlehandedly.

'The *Titanic* will never reach its destination. Remember the *Titan*, the ship that Morgan Robertson wrote about in his novel fourteen years ago? This enormous, floating luxury hotel is unsinkable according to its builders. When they talk about the *Titanic*, the White Star Line says, "Even God cannot sink this ship." It is blasphemy! Drunk on the power of his new technology, Man thinks he is equal to God! But I tell you, like the *Titan*, the *Titanic* will never arrive in New York.'

Always on the lookout for a good story, the journalists take down every word Stead says. Another sensational scoop to look forward to!

Feeling upset, Michel Navratil allows himself to be carried along by the crowd. And yet he is unable to stop the butterflies in his stomach. The painful past, which a moment before he wanted to forget, comes back with a vengeance. As if the wrench from his new country, France, isn't bad enough; as if the regret for the unhappiness he has left behind isn't bad enough. Now this story of gloom and doom comes along to spoil his hopes of happiness in America. Michel stops, frozen in his tracks, and the crowd flows past him like a wave. He hesitates and thinks he would like to turn back but Lolo cannot wait and tugs at his father's hair. Michel, angry at his moment of weakness, walks alongside the massive dark bulk of the *Titanic*.

Two hundred and seventy metres long at the waterline, the sea giant stretches out of sight. From the quayside the four funnels, leaning majestically towards the stern, are invisible. The *Titanic* is the same size as an eleven-storey building, stretching for over a quarter of a kilometre. Hundreds of portholes dot the black side of the ship, and go on and on towards the horizon.

'Wow! What is it daddy?' Lolo asks anxiously. He cannot understand this impressive sight.

'It's the *Titanic*, the sea giant I've told you about. It's taking us to New York on the other side of the ocean'.

This ship is a symbol for Michel. He feels sure his worries will be forgotten once he is on board amongst the privileged passengers of the *Titanic*'s maiden voyage.[1] He puts Momon and Lolo on the ground and all three of them survey the sunny quayside, amused by the sight of all the wealthy passengers. They are the sort of people who cannot move without a fleet of maids, valets, secretaries, private advisers, and governesses who themselves would fill a larger than average ship and who now dance around their masters and mistresses creating chaos.

The port is buzzing with activity. Dozens of cranes are lifting luggage on board as well as hundreds of tonnes of supplies needed for the voyage. Michel, who had carefully read the brochure he received when he bought the tickets in Monte Carlo, explains to his sons how in order to feed the 2222 people travelling on the ship, 60 tonnes of beef, 20 tonnes of potatoes, 10 tonnes of vegetables, 500 kilos of sausages, 250 kilos of tea, 40,000 eggs, 600 pots of jam, 12 tonnes of fish, 250 kilos of bananas, 20 kilos of smoked salmon, 3 tonnes of lamb, 2,500 chickens, 6000 bottles of wine, 3000 bottles of spirits, 6000 litres of beer and 4000 litres of milk have to be loaded!

While listening to all this Lolo becomes intrigued by the sight of sacks of potatoes being hoisted up by a crane not far away. Without his father noticing he goes and sits on one of the sacks so he can have a better view. Suddenly he feels himself being lifted up into the air and grabs a rope. The dockers see him and laugh.

'Look at the acrobat! He's a real clown, that lad!'

They immediately reverse the manoeuvre and the sack is let down gently. Michel, scared out of his wits, rushes over, grabs Lolo roughly by the hand, and pulls him in silence towards the embarkation area.

It's a good job their luggage has been sent on ahead. The crowd on the quayside makes it very difficult to reach the ship.

Michel now hoists Momon onto his shoulders leaving his hands free to hold the tickets and passport in one and Lolo in the other. Poor Lolo feels suffocated by the tall grownups and can't even see their faces above him.

At last they reach the steps of the gangway and they start to climb up. From this height they have a good view of the crowds on the quayside. Most passengers are leaving behind relatives and friends who are waving goodbye. But nobody is waving to the three Navratils. Michel feels lost and alone. Nobody knows about this voyage with his two small children. What if something happens to him?

The queue on the gangway comes to a halt and to pass the time, Lolo tells Momon, who Michel has put on the step next to him, a little story. A woman standing near Michel is fighting back her tears. Suddenly a piercing wail comes from the quayside, a few metres below, and a young girl aged about fourteen, tears herself away from her father, cuts through the crowd, runs up the gangway, pushing everyone aside, and joins the woman standing near Michel.

'Don't go, Mother, I know you'll never come back! You're all going to die! The ship's going to sink!'

Mrs Hoghes hugs her daughter and tries to calm her down. She has just been taken on by the White Star Line as a chambermaid on the *Titanic*. Her wages will be much better than on the *Mauritania* where she used to work. But her daughter, Rosalind, is convinced that this job will cost her her life.

'Mother, I can't let you leave without telling you about my dream! You must listen to me!'

'Tell me about it, my love!' says Mrs Hoghes gently wiping away the girl's tears.

In between sobs, Rosalind's dream is revealed:

Two days earlier, on Easter Sunday, she was having an afternoon rest when she dreamed that from her bedroom window overlooking Trentham Park in London, she saw a huge ship slowly rising out of the ground. A crowd of people were panicking and running from one side of the ship to the other. She could hear children crying and screaming. Then the ship keeled over. After that there was complete silence apart from distant shouts of frightened people whose voices were very clear and sharp. There was not a breath of wind and yet the light was shimmering as it does on a mountain under the stars on a cold moonless night. All of a sudden there was a terrible cracking sound and the giant ship broke in two right down the middle, sending people toppling into the abyss and tipping everything out of the ship with a tremendous noise. The ground swallowed up the front of the ship leaving the back pointing up to the sky like a tragic statue. It stayed still for a few moments and then thrust itself rapidly into the half open earth of the square, crushing hedges and trees in its path.

Rosalind had woken up in a terrified state but hadn't dared beg her mother not to go on the *Titanic*.

Now that she had been able to tell her mother about her dream she waited anxiously for a reply. Mrs Hoghes tried to comfort her, 'But it's only a dream, my darling; there's no need to get yourself in such a state about it! Calm down, nothing is going to happen to me.'

Desperate because she hadn't managed to convince her mother about the danger she was in, Rosalind pulls at her hand with all her strength, trying to drag her down the gangway back onto the quayside.

Mr Hoghes who had watched what was happening from down below, comes and pulls Rosalind from his wife's arms, because she is obviously becoming very upset by their daughter's premonition.

Rosalind's convincing tone, the intensity of her grief, combined with Mr Hoghes' somewhat brutal handling of the situation have deeply disturbed Mrs Hoghes. She fumbles nervously in her handbag without managing to hide how upset she is, and blows her nose noisily.

Michel couldn't help overhearing the young girl's story. He glances anxiously at Lolo who is telling Momon a story about Little Nemo, his favourite hero. Let's hope the child didn't hear anything!

Rosalind's tears and her vivid dream have made a deep impression on the young father. What if the girl was right?

Michel questioned himself again as he had done several times since he left Nice. What if his false passport had been pointed out to the immigration authorities? Am I really setting off on an exciting voyage he asks himself climbing the gangway onto the *Titanic*, or am I going to be taken straight to prison by the police? No, that would be too awful. Shivering a little Michel hoists Momon on to his shoulders again and Momon grabs hold of his hair.

'Daddy,' a quivering little voice pipes up loudly so as to be heard, 'why did that girl cry so much with her mummy? Are we really going to die?'

So, despite appearances, Lolo had heard Rosalind talking about her dream. Michel squeezes his hand tightly and reassures him, 'Nobody's going to die, Lolo. Everyone knows the *Titanic* is unsinkable.'

Lolo is deep in thought. Children are familiar with the idea of death. Lolo has thought a lot about what his mother once told him, that after death there is another life which is much more beautiful and nearer to God. She had said that death is nothing more than a door opening into another life. Lolo wasn't afraid of death. But, at his age, the idea of being without even one parent is frightening. The fact that they might disappear forever had never occurred to him. The idea of his own death is one thing. The death of those close to him is another. Suddenly Lolo is very anxious. He had never been separated from his mother for so long. Perhaps she is dead and that is why she's not here?

'Mummy, Mummy, where are you? I need you so much!'

Michel is quite overcome and bends down.

'Look, don't worry, Mummy's fine and you'll see her soon.'

There I go, he says to himself; I'm lying to him again.

His obsession returns: to leave France and to take the children as far away as possible from their mother's clutches. But will the ocean really separate them from Marcelle? My God! Why is it taking so long to get on board? Michel looks around him. Nothing and no one is moving.

Michel cannot stand this waiting any longer. He suddenly gets the urge to confess his secrets to the people around him. Anything rather than putting up with this standing about.

I think I'm going crazy. It must be anxiety, he says to himself. Just at that moment, the queue starts to move and Michel breathes a sigh of relief. Suddenly he feels Lolo's little hand pressing against his. He lowers his head. The child smiles up at him through his tears. Michel smiles back. No, he is not alone, the children are here. His most treasured possessions are with him. This gives him courage. He now feels ready for this voyage on which he has pinned all his hopes.

CHAPTER 2

A FLOATING TOWN

'YOUR PASSPORT please, sir!'

Michel has reached the top of the gangway and is holding his passport and three second-class tickets. Haunted by the fear of being found out, he trembles slightly as he carefully watches the petty officers check the identities of passengers with their tickets. He notices one of them walking off with his passport! Michel feels dizzy and holds on to the rail. He is waiting for the worst: they are going to discover his passport is stolen! Lolo, fascinated by the blue and white uniforms, stares at the petty officers. Suddenly he hears a vibration, a deafening rumbling coming from the side of the big ship. He asks his father several times about the noise but Michel is too preoccupied to pay attention to Lolo. It is only after Michel's sleeve has been tugged several times that the little boy gets a reply: the *Titanic*'s engines are being started up in preparation for the ship to move off.

Time is passing slowly. Why are they just standing here? Behind them people are pushing and shoving, impatient to embark. The child looks at his father who doesn't seem to be very well. Michel's hand is trembling and Lolo has never seen him in this state before. Almost immediately however, Lolo's attention is caught by the opening refrains of a waltz coming from high above him. He closes his eyes and is back in the teashop of the Negresco hotel in Nice with his mother. Precious memories that he had almost forgotten come rushing back. The music he can hear now is being played by the *Titanic*'s orchestra and they are giving their first concert on the upper deck to welcome passengers on board.

Michel is anxious and cannot stand still. He looks at the quayside, the people, and his children, lifts Edmond up, puts him down again, and goes through his wallet – for no reason at all. Finally, the petty officer returns and, with a big smile, gives him back his passport.

'Welcome on board the *Titanic*, Mr Hoffmann! We hope you have a very happy trip!'

The name Hoffmann sounds like heavenly music in Michel's ears. The petty officer didn't suspect that there was anything unusual about the passport. Just then, another officer bends down towards the children and hands Momon a model of the *Titanic*. Momon is very happy with his unexpected present. The petty officer also gives Lolo a beautiful miniature Bugatti. But Michel is not keen to hang around for too long so he quickly thanks the officer and rather brusquely takes the children by the hand. The three Navratils are finally on board the *Titanic*.

Lolo is very impatient and strides off leaving his father trailing behind. A steward takes charge of them and leads them through an unbelievable maze of stairways and corridors. They climb up ten floors on the beautiful teak staircase from the third class to the front of the ship and come out on the boat deck, high up on the ship. The steward crosses the vast open air deck, followed by the little family, who are very impressed by the sight of the immense funnels at close quarters. All the strength of the sea giant's engines seemed to be concentrated in the curling grey plumes of smoke coming out of the funnels. Lolo pulls at his father's sleeve and points to the fourth one that isn't smoking. The steward explains it is only for show.

Lolo is interested in the small boats suspended from winches and the steward explains that they are used in an emergency and that each boat is hung on an immense davit before being lowered into the water.

They are now in front of a kind of little white house with arched windows. The door leads to the second-class part of the ship. Strangely enough, they have to go down three floors again, via a beautifully decorated staircase covered in plush red carpet, which deadens the sound of people walking on it. The waxed wooden banisters are a complex design of very detailed curls and curves. L 86. 018 | J 363. 123092

'You are on D deck, Mr Hoffmann. You are in a double cabin and I will fix you up with an extra bed for the smaller boy.'

The thick carpets in the corridors and on the staircase make walking very comfortable. The cabin doors are light coloured wood and between each one of them is a large mirror.

The steward stops outside cabin twenty-six. 'Here we are!' He says as he opens the big door. 'Allow me to go in first.'

Michel feels as if the heavy weight resting on him since Sunday has been lifted off his shoulders. He goes straight to the central window and opens the porthole a little. It is seventy-five centimetres in diameter and from down below it looks tiny. But everything here is enormous compared with the *Fécamp* that brought the Navratils from Calais to Dover.

Leaning against the porthole, Michel relives the journey of the previous two days: the secret departure from Nice, the drawn curtains in the compartment, the awful anguish whenever a train steward opened the door to see if they wanted anything. He was constantly waiting to be arrested by the police for having stolen a passport as well as for kidnapping Lolo and Momon.

On Easter Sunday, 8 April, Michel had lunched as usual with his two children at his friend's house, Michel and Emma Hoffmann. After the meal, over coffee, he had begged Michel Hoffmann, on some pretext or other, to lend him his passport. After a walk in the woods above Cimiez, the Navratils had left.

But instead of taking the children back to their mother, Michel had gone to the railway station, collected some luggage from the left luggage office and all three of them had taken the night express from Nice to London, via Calais. Michel was leaving Nice forever. Without a word of explanation he was abandoning his wife. He had taken on his best friend's identity in order to escape from anyone who might follow him. He was going to make a new life in America.

Their arrival in Calais had been very stressful for Michel. Terrified in case the real Hoffmann might have alerted the police about his missing passport, he was waiting to be arrested. He had hurriedly dragged the children onto the *Fécamp*, the ferryboat to Dover, and they had then taken an express train to London. After a good night's rest they had caught one of the special boat trains, laid on for *Titanic* passengers, to Southampton. Michel had reckoned this was the quickest way to reach the ship but in fact it would have been far better to go straight to Cherbourg where the *Titanic* was to pick up more passengers before crossing the Atlantic.

They had left Calais on the *Fécamp* on a calm sea but soon the wind had got up and the children had begun to feel seasick. Michel had spent much of the trip leaning over the rail of the ferryboat, holding one or other of the children over the hostile dark sea. At last the children had gone to sleep but their sickness had made him feel worn out. Lying down, he had hoped the feeling would pass but he had been completely overwhelmed by it all. Later the sea had become calm again and the light broke through the dark clouds and caught the iridescent foam. Michel had felt revived by the view of the jagged outline of the white cliffs of Dover. The grassy slopes that fell gently towards the sea seemed very close. But then, for a moment, he thought he could see his wife, Marcelle, waiting for them on the shore; a tragic figure, deathly pale with arms stretched out towards her children. He closed his eyes but the hallucination was still there. He was eaten away by the silent agony of remorse. Whatever her faults had been, he had no right to inflict such suffering and worry on her. He had congratulated himself on having taken the children away from her influence, but to have abandoned her without explanation was very ruthless!

The train journey to London and the night they had spent there hadn't managed to rid Michel of this ghost of Marcelle. Because he and Marcelle had been immigrant workers in Nice and had no birth certificates, it wasn't possible to get married there, so they had gone to London to get married. He would never forget their honeymoon in the same little hotel where the three of them were now spending the night. If only the happiness they had felt then had not disappeared so quickly!

Soon the children's laughter brings Michel back to the present. Closing the porthole, he turns towards them and sees Momon, oblivious of his surroundings, playing with his *Titanic* model while Lolo is gleefully exploring their spacious cabin.

The cabin is as comfortable as a suite in a five star luxury hotel. The mahogany beds with their soft mattresses are typical examples of turn-of-the-century design and the thick curtains are a floral print in autumnal colours. Lolo, examining the bathroom, admires the white porcelain washbasin decorated with a long intertwining lily motif.

The shelves above are stacked up with tubes of toothpaste, round tumblers and a variety of different shaped soaps scented with flowers from Nice. The soft thick towels with long fringes, smelling of lavender, are printed with the name *Titanic*. A glass panel separates the toilet from the rest of the bathroom and Lolo switches on the light. It's electric![1]

Momon looks up and joins his brother. His face lights up and he laughs with delight while admiring the glass panel where a solitary white swan glides on a square of water. A family of

Japanese ducks is in the background. The males are blond, gold, and red with a peacock blue crest on their heads while the females are speckled brown and yellow fringed with black and white. A wise snake crosses a large forest of smooth light-coloured tree trunks, shining emerald green leaves and mysterious scarlet fruit. Lolo is fascinated and taking his brother's hand they stand together bewitched by the fairy-like images on the panel. Suddenly Momon grabs his *Titanic* model and runs out of the bathroom to the settee as fast as his little legs can carry him. He climbs up, squealing with delight.

Michel feels that three hours rather than only one has passed since they boarded the ship. It is nine o'clock, the gangways are about to be pulled up and Lolo, standing on a chair by the porthole, looks at the quayside. The departure of the ship is imminent. At that moment, a group of workmen come running along the quay frantically waving their arms.

'Daddy! Come and see!'

Michel opens the porthole and leans over holding Lolo.

'Wait for us! Wait for us!'

The workmen are obviously part of the crew but they have arrived just after the gangways have been ordered to be lifted. The officer in charge leans over the side and shouts at them. 'Half an hour late! You can go home, we don't need your services. We don't want lazy folk like you on board the *Titanic*.'

The men on the quayside protest loudly and beg to be allowed on board but it is no use, the *Titanic* is leaving without them. Some of them hang around shouting and waving their fists until they are escorted off the quayside by security guards.

The rumbling noise Lolo had heard when he was on the gangway had more or less died down but nevertheless there is still some vibration in the bulkheads. It is very light and fills the cabin with a rhythm rather like a heart beat. Sitting on an armchair with Lolo on his knee, Michel re-reads the White Star

Line brochure and translates it from English into French in a high-pitched voice.

> The *Titanic* is the largest ship that has ever been built: 270 metres long, 28 metres wide, 18½ from the water line to the upper deck, and 53 metres to the top of the funnels. It is as high as an eleven-storey house and as long as a road. One of its propellers weighs 22,000 kilos and it has a tonnage of 46,328 tonnes. It contains the equivalent of an entire town, with houses, shops, a theatre, bars, restaurants, a casino and accommodates 2,222 people, 680 of which are officers and crew.

Lolo listens to his father with great interest and it makes him laugh. Then he thinks silently for a minute about what his father had said and asks, 'What's the Captain's name?'

'Captain Smith and we'll certainly meet him sometime when we're having a walk around the ship.'

'Oh! Let's go for a walk now! Perhaps we'll see him!'

Michel looks at his watch and sees that it's nearly ten o'clock. The *Titanic* will soon be on its way. Just at that moment the steward knocks at the door with a folding bed for Edmond and puts it near Lolo's bed. Until now little Edmond has been very quiet, absorbed with his model ship which he has been sailing all over the ocean of the soft settee. He is capable of playing for hours on end with toys like this, imagining that he is on some adventurous voyage. He stops playing when he sees his bed and gets on it while Michel goes into the bathroom to look at himself in the mirror. He carefully trims his moustache and removes his side parting by brushing his hair back. His beard is showing several days growth. He puts on an English style bowler hat and studies himself in the mirror. He feels different and is now confident enough to take on his new identity. Just then there's a knock at the door and the steward suggests they go on the tour of the ship that has been organised for the second-class passengers. The Navratils follow him and the children pester him with questions that he does his best to answer.

First though, the steward has to stop to wait for some passengers in the neighbouring cabins who are joining the tour of the ship. There's an American couple, Mr and Mrs Caldwell with their baby and a young Italian girl, Mirella Cesarese. An English gentleman offers Mirella his arm, as if he is quite used to being an escort for unaccompanied young ladies on transatlantic trips. She's very relaxed and laughs at his attempt to speak Italian with her even though she speaks perfect English. She shakes her long brown curls.

'*Dio, che bei bambini!*' she exclaims when she sees Lolo and Momon.

'*Buon giorno signorina,*' replies Michel.

'*Lei permette?*'

Without waiting for a reply she leans over, kisses the children and lifts Momon into her arms.

The little group getting increasingly bigger follows the steward towards the belly of the ship. At first they take the same route they had taken when they arrived but this time it is in the opposite direction. The carpet is as soft as ever and the large staircase, leading to the upper deck with its bronze cherubim guarding the bottom of the handrail, is also as grand as ever. No other transatlantic ship offers the same standard of luxury to its second-class passengers. Even the *Olympic* isn't as luxurious as this and its floors are covered in a vulgar linoleum, Michel explains to the children, 'You see how beautiful everything here is! And we're only in second class. In first class the richness of the decor is more than you can imagine!'

'Who's in the first class?' asks Lolo.

'Anyone who has a lot of money to spend.'

'Ah yes!' says Lolo 'Like the beautiful lady who made me feel better when I fell over in the train.'

'Which beautiful lady?' asks his father. 'You never told me about anything that happened on the train.'

'I was running along the corridor and I fell over in front of the door of her compartment just as she was coming out. Because I hurt myself she helped me get up and took me into her compartment. It was nearly as pretty as our cabin here on the ship. She gave me some chocolates and I even brought some for Momon and when I left she gave me a kiss.'

'Do you know her name?'

'No, I couldn't understand what she was saying 'cos she was speaking English like Charles, with an old gentleman who loves her a lot. I'd like to see her again very much.'

Meanwhile the tour of the ship continues.

'We are now on the same level as B deck,' says the steward. 'You can see the smoking room and the bars on your right and on your left, an à la carte restaurant that you may use. You also have a covered deck at your disposal. Strictly speaking your dining room is on D deck and you'll find a large and very well-stocked library on C deck. Since you don't have access to A deck we're going straight to the upper deck where we'll see the ship casting off. The journalists are just leaving the ship.'

A huge noisy crowd is on the promenade deck and Michel has difficulty in reaching the ship's rail. The children, afraid they might be too late to see the ship casting off, shout excitedly. The rush of water produced by the propellers just turning under low power splashes the crowd of onlookers on the quayside and they laugh as they run out of the way. With the dignity of a volcanic eruption, the funnels send a jet of steam skywards and let out blasts at regular intervals equivalent to twenty fog horns going off at the same time. A wonderful sense of freedom envelops Michel. He feels as if he wouldn't change places with an emperor.

Leaning over the rail, he watches the manoeuvres on the lower deck with interest. On both the portside and starboard a group of sailors are casting off and officers are coming and going shouting orders that are sometimes contradictory.[2]

The casting off is done as well as can be expected and soon the ship is approaching the channel that leads to the open sea. Down below tiny flotillas of boats dance on the water. Two tugboats look so ridiculously small that the children cannot believe they are able to tow the large ship. The boats are roped to the stern, which the children think is the bow because the Atlantic is still behind them.

'There are two tugs at the stern because if the engines were on full power the force of the water would sink all the boats in the area,' explains Michel.

At this moment a large wave coming from the huge hull of the ship reaches the quayside.

'Look over there!' shouts Lolo. 'The water's flooding all over the quayside.'

In fact the wave splashes the crowd who have to run away fast to escape getting wet. Several boats tied up at the quayside break loose from their moorings, their heavy chains waving through the air and it's a miracle that no one is injured or killed. But the children are too far away to be in danger.

It seems to Lolo that the ship is slowing down, or even coming to a stop.

'What's happening? We're not moving!'

The casting off manoeuvre is now over and the ship, having been turned round is ready to go on its way.

Michel points out the third class part of the *Titanic* on the two lower decks, E and F. And then the first class at the centre of the ship where there is hardly any noise from the engines and where the pitch and roll of the ship is less noticeable. Lolo is indignant about the poorer people being relegated to the waterline right next to the engines. But Michel explains how the immigrants and their families, who are going to America to find work, are much better off in the third class of the *Titanic* than on any other transatlantic ship where they are very badly treated and they pay the same price as here. He says on the other ships, third-class passengers have to sleep in the open air on the floor of the deck above the engine room where there is a deafening noise. They don't have bathroom facilities, the food is disgusting and most of the time they don't even have knives and forks.

'But that's terrible, Daddy!'

Michel tells him about how on this ship third-class passengers have cabins and their own dining room with very good food. He also explains they have the same kind of rooms (as well as a promenade deck), as are found in the first class except they are smaller and much less luxurious.

'I'd really like to see it all.'

'Of course, Lolo, we'll go tomorrow.'

Slowly and smoothly the *Titanic* follows the channel out of Southampton until it reaches the point where two ships, the *Oceanic* and the *New York* are anchored. Captain Smith gives orders for the turbines to be started up but he has misjudged the force of the rush of water the propellers produce. Up to now they have only been turning slowly, but on full power the strong back wash they cause makes the *New York* break loose from her moorings and she starts to drift towards the *Titanic*. The children are terrified to see the ship coming towards them with its crew, unable to do anything about the situation, panicking and shouting.

'The little ship's going to hurt ours!' shouts Lolo.

Without replying Michel picks up both the children and, with a wild look in his eyes, watches as the *New York* comes straight towards them. The passengers wait for the inevitable collision but something unimaginable happens. Just as the *New York* is only a few metres from the *Titanic's* hull, the little transatlantic ship, which would have been completely crushed by the colossal *Titanic*, moves away dancing like a nutshell in its wake. Everyone sighs with relief and the passengers on the *Titanic* clap their hands with joy. Three deafening blasts are heard from the *Titanic's* horn and the enormous ship continues on its way.

From on high, Michel looks back at the long trail of swirling foam stretching as far as the eye can see behind the ship. It's still quite a long way to the open sea but the port pilot, George Bowyer, in whom Captain Smith has every confidence, leads the ship along the narrow channel with great care. The big black ship and its slender white and yellow streamlined funnels seem to cut the air in two. The cold cloudless sky, with the spring sun already high in the heavens, creates a vision that is so beautiful that it seems unreal. Michel feels somewhat unreal too. The children are running around among the passengers shouting in high-pitched voices. It is as if he is going to the other side of the world when, in fact, the ship is at the moment going towards France, almost the same route they took the night before last, but in reverse and about a hundred miles[3] further north.

Reaching the open sea in Osborne bay, the *Titanic* is on course for Cherbourg where more passengers will embark. The Isle of White coastline looms up in the twilight. White sandy beaches, villages dotted about in green valleys and clumps of dark trees can just about be seen.

The incident with the *New York* had disturbed some of the passengers. Without being aware of it they made a connection between the name of the ship and the name of the city and interpreted it as a bad omen. Michel overhears a man speaking to Margaret Hays, an elegant young woman from first class, who listens quietly to his words.

'Margaret, do you value your life?'

'What a question, sir, you must be joking,' she replies, looking at him with astonishment.

'Well then, believe me, you should get off in Cherbourg. This ship is going to sink!'

Margaret smiles and says she isn't superstitious. Later however, she would tell people how the man who had given her this advice had got off the ship in Cherbourg.

CHAPTER 3

CHERBOURG

IT IS 12.30 and the lunch bell is ringing on the promenade deck. The second-class dining room, which seats four hundred, is immediately above the library on D deck, not far from the Navratils' cabin

Reaching B deck Michel is just about to go down the staircase when Lolo, who is running in front of him, points out the wrought iron door of the lift. It stops near the beautifully sculpted doors of the dining room, so immense that the children cannot see the far end of it. A French headwaiter welcomes them and leads them through rows of seemingly endless tables to a table for eight where their neighbours from adjoining cabins are seated. Michel takes off his hat, greets them and sits down to the left of Mirella Cesarese.

During the next few minutes Lolo is far too busy to talk to anyone. Turning his head and stretching his neck he tries to see beyond the nearby tables where white napkins stretch as far as the eye can see. He watches waiters wheeling and bending as if doing a ballet dance around the little islands of diners. He can see large comfortable benches standing back to back marking out different areas of the room as well as giving a little privacy, and chairs with high-convoluted backs stuffed with horsehair and covered in red plush velvet. The painted stucco ceiling catches his eye and giggling, he shows Momon a bearded Neptune surrounded by chubby nymphs who all seem to be beckoning them to play in the blue water fringed with foamy waves.

Michel feels very relaxed during lunch. Because he speaks very good English, conversation is quite easy and he readily answers questions about his origins and the reasons why he is emigrating to America. He avoids answering some embarrassing questions about Marcelle. He pretends her work requires her to be in Nice until June and she will be joining them in New York afterwards. 'Oh Daddy, is it true that mummy is joining us?' butts in Lolo, in a little trembling voice.

Michel doesn't dare tell him the truth but he sees that Lolo wants him to be honest. He has no intention, however, of ever returning the children to their mother. On that, his mind is firmly made up.

Mirella, sensing that Lolo is upset spontaneously speaks to him in Italian, just as Marcelle has always done, and curiously enough she has the same tone of voice and the same Genoan accent as his mummy.

'*Ma certemente è vero, bambino mio, la tua cara mamma non puo abandonnarti.*'

This cheers him up and at the same time allows Michel to avoid having to lie again.

'You come from Genoa, don't you?' says Michel quickly.

'Ah! You've guessed correctly, probably because you recognise my accent.'

'Yes, I know the Genoese accent well. Are you emigrating to the United States?'

'Not yet. My aunt and uncle have invited me to spend a month's holiday with them in Philadelphia.'

'What do they do?'

'They opened a shoe shop in 1890, selling Italian shoes. They're paying my return passage because they would like me to manage a new branch that they're opening in Washington but I want to spend some time there before I commit myself to completely changing my life.'

How wise she is, thinks Michel who often leaps, usually with disastrous consequences, before he looks.

The young Englishman sitting opposite Mirella is called Trevor Pritchard. With his mop of flaxen hair, pale blue eyes, freckled turned-up nose and angular chin, he is a funny contrast to the young Italian girl. He's a physics graduate from Trinity College, Cambridge and he's going to be working for the new Marconi Telephone Company in New York because he wants to have a period of training before he starts his career back in England.

'Would you believe it? One of my friends from university is working on the *Titanic* as a radio engineer! He was the one who gave me the idea to come on this inaugural trip. I'll probably give him some help if Captain Smith agrees to it.'

At this point, the man next to him, Albert Caldwell, sitting opposite his young wife Sylvia and their one-year-old baby, interrupts his flow of conversation. 'As for us, we were simply tempted by an attractive poster advertising the *Titanic*. After several years in Bangkok where I taught at a Christian College, we decided to leave Thailand and go back to the United States for good.'

'We got a boat to Naples and spent a wonderful two-month holiday there,' Sylvia added. 'Albert was just about to reserve tickets for New York on the *Oceanic* when I saw a poster advertising the maiden voyage of the *Titanic*, the first unsinkable ship. There was only one cabin left in second class and it didn't cost much more so we couldn't resist it.'

The conversation during this first lunch centres around science and technology, two subjects very dear to the modern world of America and reflected in the conception and building of the *Titanic*. Albert points out that without the investment of the current owner of the White Star Line (which was originally English-owned but taken over by the American financier,

Pierpont Morgan, in 1900), the new sea giant would never have been built.

'But,' says Trevor 'the ship is British and not American.'

'Yes, but like the *Olympic* it was actually built in Belfast, not in England. The Irish shipyard is famous for its excellent workmanship.'

Much to Michel's annoyance, the conversation is becoming argumentative but the arrival of the first course saves the day. The White Star Line has decided the first meal on board should be a special occasion and has laid on a feast for the passengers. After the hors-d'oeuvres they are served with creamed vegetables, buttered pike from the Loire, duckling with olives, asparagus salad, fresh garden peas, cake and ice-cream topped with a fruit sauce, Sancerre wine and Veuve-Clicot champagne.

Albert's stories of their experiences in Bangkok capture everyone's imagination and Sylvie waxes lyrical about Naples and Venice. Listening to this interesting conversation makes Michel forget about his worries.

Lolo and Momon feel bored. They're not very keen on the fancy menu and the food tastes strange. Noticing their plates are still full, the headwaiter brings them two fried eggs with mashed potatoes and a salad, all served on a huge silver platter. Lolo can't believe his eyes. Since the beginning of the meal he has been fantasizing about his favourite lunch and suddenly, by magic, there it is in front of him. Momon has already eaten his second egg by the time Lolo finally breaks into the first one with his fork. What a pity to spoil the carefully arranged wonderful food!

It is after four o'clock when they finish lunch. The children's patience has been sorely tried by sitting for such a long time and they are in need of exercise. The Caldwells return to their cabin while Mirella, Trevor, Michel and the children decide to go out on deck.

The second class has two decks, one at level C around three

sides of the library, and the other, on deck B running along the à la carte restaurant and the smoking lounge. Here, as in first class, the side of the ship is mostly glass to allow the sun to stream in. Today it is nice and warm compared with the freezing wind in the English Channel the previous day. While the children play on the deck, Michel, Pritchard and Mirella stand by a window silently watching the little white waves far beneath them. There's no sensation of pitching and rolling and Michel thinks about the *Great Eastern*, the ship in Jules Verne's novel *A Floating Town*, whose engines vibrate so much that travelling becomes a nightmare. What fantastic progress has been made in fifty years! The silence on the *Titanic* is very noticeable and it seems as if unknown supernatural forces are pulling it. Michel, Pritchard and Mirella look at each other sharing the same feelings of admiration for the silent ship.

Suddenly Mirella goes off along the corridor to meet the little ones. At eighteen she relates easily both to children and adults. By the time she rejoins Michel and Pritchard, holding a child in each hand, there is a shrill whistling coming from the funnels. The Titanic is now approaching Cherbourg. Outlined in the distance are the cliffs, which are just north of the town.

Michel remembers another test lies in wait for him. He must keep out of the way, while the ship makes a port of call at Cherbourg, because if his friend, Hoffmann, has reported his stolen passport to the police, inquiries may be made. It could mean goodbye to America! Mirella asks if she can look after the children until it's time for dinner. Michel hesitates for a moment but she pleads with him and in the end he agrees. Pritchard and he wander along the corridors of D deck until they find their cabins. Once inside his, Michel collapses onto the bed and almost immediately falls asleep.

Mirella and the children go to the library. It is a big room with bookshelves forming little alcoves where readers can easily be alone. Lolo loves books and he wastes no time in finding the children's section where he furiously rummages around. He has almost learned to read recently, practically all by himself, with a book illustrated by Benjamin Rabier, a present from his mother. He can't read properly yet, but he knows his alphabet and with pictures to help him he can guess what the words are.

He soon finds the most recent edition of his favourite stories, *Little Nemo in Slumberland*, under a pile of large books. Little Nemo is his age and he shares the same dreams. Even Lolo's bed looks like his. He is so absorbed in the book he doesn't hear a series of whistle blasts announcing the ship's arrival in Cherbourg. Mirella suggests they go up on deck to have a look at the port but he is reluctant to leave his newly found book and refuses to go.

'Come on, you can come back later, don't worry, the book will wait for you. Look, I'll put it behind the other books so nobody will see it and take it away.'

Lolo won't move so she says in a soft pleading voice, 'I've forgotten how to get upstairs, would you show me the way?'

Lolo gets up immediately. For someone of his age he has an amazing sense of direction. He knows the difference between right and left and can instinctively find his way to places that even sometimes an adult is at a loss to find. He can already recognise the corridor where their cabin is because he has noticed the mirrors are oval, whereas on other corridors they are rectangular. He easily finds the way upstairs. Trevor, who they meet on the way, and Mirella, holding Momon's hand, follow Lolo.

It's nearly seven o'clock and it's getting dark. Because the *Titanic* is too big to go into the port at Cherbourg, she is anchored in the deeper water of the harbour and two boats, the *Nomadic* and the *Traffic*, are to bring passengers to her.

Waking up with a start, Michel leans out of the porthole to see if he can make out who is coming on board. There are several men in uniform. Are they the police? Are they looking for him? He breaks out in a cold sweat and sits in an armchair waiting for the worst to happen. A quarter and then a half-hour pass and nothing happens. He brushes aside his fears and gets up. Better not to stay in his cabin. Better to go and mingle with the crowds on deck. Taking a deep breath he closes the cabin door and walks casually up to the top deck.

He watches as the *Nomadic*[1] draws alongside the *Titanic*. He sees gangways being thrown from F and G deck on to her top deck. There are a lot of sailors running to and fro, carrying sacks of post on their shoulders. It is almost too dark to see anything but Michel can just make out a group of men in uniform who are coming in his direction. He turns and sees some people whose faces are lit up from time to time by a blinding flash. The place is swamped with journalists taking photographs and the uniformed men turn out to be from the French merchant navy! Saved again!

Lolo, meanwhile, is not far away. He is looking at the twinkling lights in the town ahead. He watches, fascinated by the comings and goings of the two small boats and hangs over the rail to get a better view of the cranes loading fresh supplies onto the *Titanic*. He can hear the sailors' rough voices and the officers in charge of the manoeuvres shouting orders to them. He turns round at the sound of some deep voices. Lit up by a spotlight are three men in uniform covered in braid. Behind are about twenty journalists from the big French daily newspapers: *Le Temps*, *Le Matin*, *Le Figaro* and others. A reporter from *L'Illustration* holds everything up because he's having problems with his big wooden tripod and everyone is shouting loudly in French.

'Lolo, look,' says Trevor. 'There's Captain Smith and you can also see his second-in-command, Wilde, as well as the first officer, Murdoch. They're showing the journalists round the ship. By next week all their readers will know the *Titanic* almost as well as you and I.'

Lolo is green with envy because he wants to talk to the Captain too and as the group moves away he grabs Trevor by the hand.

'Shall we follow them? There are so many people nobody will notice us!'

Trevor consults Mirella.

'Lolo knows what he wants all right and knows how to get it!' she says. 'Let's go, we haven't got anything to lose.'

Thus, for the first time since he got on the ship, the mysteries of the first class are going to be revealed to Lolo. He is not at all pleased with the idea of part of the ship being out of bounds for him and has hoped to find a way around the problem.

Actually, access is very easy. Going from the à la carte restaurant via the second-class smoking lounge you come to a circular lounge and there on the other side is a grand staircase going up to the first class.

Just as Mirella, Trevor, and the children are crossing the circular lounge, Lord Ismay, the president of the White Star Line, comes down the wide staircase to meet the journalists. On tables covered with damask table cloths initialled with the company's name, flutes of champagne await the journalists who are in ecstasy over the rather pretentious large clock, identical to the one on the *Olympic,* that is a symbol of the White Star Line's prosperity. It is encased in one of the oak panels forming the wall where the big staircase divides into two. The stairs are very wide and there is a large central banister. Framed by four fluted pillars and two arched sculpted garlands, the clock is set into a big rectangle with an overhanging ornate cornice. It is supported by two bas-reliefs representing Glory and Honour. The clock is a perfect symbol of the Blue Ribbon that the White Star Line hopes to take from Cunard – their rival company.

Momon's getting impatient and isn't at all interested in taking part in the reception. They all go back to the area they are supposed to be in and go to the second-class dining room where dinner is being served. Despite having arranged to meet Michel there, they find he hasn't arrived yet.

Without anyone being aware of it, the engines start up half way through dinner and the ship gets underway. A smiling Michel announces this when he eventually joins them at the table. He feels fine after his long rest and after dinner, when the children are asleep, he intends to play bridge with his young friends, Mirella and Trevor, as long as they can find a fourth person. But where will they find someone? Perhaps in the smoking lounge or in the ladies' lounge? They laugh about the latter idea because the ladies' lounge is always empty. The majority of women on the *Titanic* have no desire to be closeted away in the lounge specially reserved for them. Some of them take delight in shocking people by going into the smoking lounge, originally designed to be for men only. It is, after all, the beginning of the twentieth century and society's rules changing all the time.

CHAPTER 4

THE PALM GARDEN

IT IS TEN O'CLOCK in the morning and Michel is slowly waking up. For a moment he doesn't know where he is. Then he recalls the events of the previous day when the ship had called into Cherbourg. He thought about how anxious he had been, and then about how much he had enjoyed playing bridge in the second-class smoking lounge in the evening. He feels the same sense of freedom as he did when the ship left Southampton. The children are still sleeping peacefully, a smile on their lips. No one would ever imagine they were victims of a kidnapper.

Not having any particular need to get up, Michel stretches his arms and legs and delights in the pleasure of being able to lie in bed a little longer than usual. He's very relaxed and the stress and anxiety of yesterday now seem almost ridiculous to him. He asks himself how he could have possibly got into such a state. He had felt like a common criminal. He is comfortable with his pseudonym and the millionaires on the ship no longer seem to be part of another world. He feels an affinity with people who have started off with nothing and built up a fortune for themselves. The Straus couple, for example,[1] for whom he had designed clothes whenever they spent winters at the famous Negresco hotel in Nice.

Isidor and Ida Straus were a legendary couple in their world where people's marriages were often troubled. When they came to Michel's fashion house for fittings, their kind natures and lack of pretentiousness made it easy for a friendship to develop. The couple were a role model for him. Just like Isidor at the beginning of his career, Michel too is aware of his talents and is determined to build up a clientele in New York based on his gift for fashion design. He too hopes to make a fortune for himself. He isn't worried about being in competition with Madame Lucile (Lady Duff Gordon's first name) and other famous fashion designers. After all, the fashion house business is a new phenomenon, as new as the century in fact, and the Americans were always behind the French in fashion. Although a long way from Paris, Michel had always kept up to date with what was going on in the fashion world and knows the business very well. The market is huge and there is still an immense amount of untapped territory on the West Coast of America. He feels like a pioneer. Forget the Nice failure, at twenty-two he has his whole life before him, even though he had already established a business and started a family by the time he was eighteen!

If Michel had really reflected on his life up to now he would have seen a behaviour pattern bringing a lot of happiness, but also a lot of pain. Leaving Nice in secret and separating the children from their mother had been impulsive. He often found it difficult to control his impulsive urges. He was restless by nature. A constant desire for change was what had taken him to the sunny south of France. He was only fifteen when he had run away from Presbourg, to the Bay of Angels in Nice, leaving behind his parents and brothers and sisters. He had quickly prospered there. But it was as if, once he had achieved something he desired, he had to destroy it. His wanderlust had led him to this present situation. He was involving the children in an adventure without paying any attention to the dangers that might lie ahead.

Michel catches sight of his reflection in the mirror. At first he hardly recognises himself. His newly grown beard makes his face seem wider and gives him a military look. His long hair falls in strands over his forehead making him look younger. He misses his long moustache, carefully curled with hot tongs each morning, giving him such a distinguished look, but decides he will let it grow again once he is in New York.

After bathing he uses some lime-scented aftershave and puts on a corduroy suit with a large jacket that has a tight waist. It makes him look rather bohemian, like a painter. He stands back admiring himself in the mirror. Yes! He is no longer Michel Navratil he is definitely Michel Hoffmann on the *Titanic*. The children do not know their surname or even their proper first names; they only know their nicknames so there's no danger of them revealing their true identity!

Half an hour later the three Hoffmanns are off on an adventure in the floating town. They're exploring everywhere they're allowed to go on D, C, and B deck. They discover a real shopping street with every imaginable kind of shop. There's a delicatessen, a hairdresser's, a bookshop, a sweet shop, a leather shop, a shoe shop, a jeweller's and a beauty shop. They are pretty small but very well stocked. It feels rather strange, but at the same time quite familiar, to wander around looking in shop windows as they would in Nice. This is the first time that a ship has such luxurious facilities and the Hoffmanns find it fascinating.

Michel has very little money on him because he has given his savings, which is his little nest egg, to the purser, MacElroy, to put in a safe. He feels in his pocket and finds enough change to buy the children a packet of biscuits.

'Daddy, if there were robbers here they could attack these little shops and ask for the money that's in the till.'

'Oh yes! And hold up the bank like they do in the Wild West,' replies Michel laughing at Lolo's vivid imagination. 'Let's go quickly before the robbers arrive or else you might have to give them your biscuits!'

They run along the 'road' towards the upper deck. They go

along a white corridor, up a red staircase, along another white corridor, up another red staircase and lastly, because it is good fun, they take the electric lift.

The upper deck at this hour, still too early for the majority of passengers, who like going to bed late, seems somewhat unreal. Seen from the stern,[2] it is 270 metres long and is very white, very new, and very shiny. There is still a smell of new paint in the air because the ship had only left the shipyard in Belfast twelve days earlier. The streamlined funnels leaning towards the stern, as if they've been bent by the wind, haven't had time to get dirty. Looking at them produces the same sense of dizziness as people feel when they see the leaning Tower of Pisa.

'Daddy, Momon, come and look!'

Lolo is in front of a small door that is open. It's the ship's gymnasium, created by the architect-engineer of the *Titanic*, Thomas Andrews, and was a great success with the journalists. It is full of bizarre-looking machines designed to provide exercise for passengers who suffer from over-eating during the voyage. Michel and the children are the only ones there and they have lots of fun having a go on all the machines.

After a while Michel looks at his watch, a present from Marcelle on his last birthday. It's 11.30am and there's still an hour before lunch – just enough time to go to the library to read the daily newspaper mentioned in the *Titanic*'s brochure. It is printed on board and gives news from the United States via the Marconi radio as well as information and gossip about life on the ship.

He had only hurriedly looked at the first edition and decides he would like to read it properly. Lolo, overjoyed with the idea of finding his Little Nemo book, leads his father straight to the children's section, and shows him the book, still hidden away behind a row of picture books.

Lolo is immediately plunged into the world of Little Nemo

and his search for the beautiful princess. But after a few minutes he is overcome with her likeness to his mummy and, gazing into space, is lost in a daydream.

Suddenly he feels restless, as if he's got ants in his pants. He glances at Momon who's looking at a book near his daddy, and runs like lightning up the stairs leading to the second-class smoking lounge. He then calmly crosses the dining room where waiters are laying the tables and climbs the majestic staircase going up to the first class. He sticks his tongue out at Glory and Honour, because he hates them, just as the large clock strikes twelve. He finally reaches the first-class promenade deck where people are sunning themselves in deckchairs. Then walking alongside the smoking lounge, he thinks he sees, by one of the windows, the old man with a white beard, who was shouting at the group of journalists in Southampton. Not feeling in the least bit intimidated, he goes on until he finds the Palm Garden, which is just what he's looking for. No doubt because it reminded him of the teashop in the hotel Negresco, the name had sounded magic when he had heard it the day before.

Suddenly he feels shy and scared of being looked at and hesitates before going into the enchanted garden. The enormous palms reach the ceiling and get their light from a glass roof supported by green wrought-iron pillars covered with climbing plants. Basketwork chairs and tables fill the room where a lot of mainly young people are having drinks and ice cream. The sight of a wide-eyed Lolo, creeping in, fills the room with laughter.

Fascinated by the place, Lolo searches the room hoping to find his princess. Surely his mummy must be here amongst all these beautiful women with their pale delicate skin, pretty eyes and curly brown hair. He goes underneath the overhanging palms and stops at every table to examine the young women. They are very amused by him.

He is extremely disappointed not to find his mummy. He stands against the veranda window with his eyes closed and his hands tightly shut, fighting back tears. It is suddenly too much for him and he bursts into tears with the word 'mummy' quivering on his lips with each great sob.

He feels himself being lifted up and finds he is in the arms of an old man. Stead had been intrigued by this little solitary figure walking past the smoking lounge with such a look of determination on his face. He thought he had seen him before. Then the image of a young man with two little boys in the next compartment to his on the boat train from Southampton flashed into his mind. As he was going along the corridor in the train he had seen Lolo opening a compartment door and remembered the little boy's father had snapped at the child and slammed the door shut.

Stead suspected there must have been some trouble in this family travelling without a mother. The child's strange behaviour today rather verified those suspicions. He questions Lolo, who is now clinging to his neck, in a gentle, paternal way. Speaking French very softly Stead's warm voice makes Lolo feel better and he stops crying. He tells Stead about running out of the library, where his brother was with his daddy, so he could find his mummy. As Stead leaves the veranda with Lolo, intending to return him to his father, he bumps into his friend, Charles Bedford. They are in neighbouring suites in first class. By coincidence, Charles is a close friend of Michel Navratil, and is in fact Momon's godfather.

Charles had first met Michel while on business in Presbourg.[3] He had ordered an overcoat from Michel's boss and during a fitting for it, had noticed the young apprentice, Michel, spoke English. It was the start of a close friendship between them despite an age difference of about forty years.

Two years later in Nice, they bumped into each other by

chance on the Promenade des Anglais. Charles, escaping from the cold London weather, was wintering in Nice. Michel was strolling along the promenade with Marcelle – then his fiancée – by his side.

Charles had been struck by Marcelle's beauty. She was a fifteen-year-old Italian with ebony hair and a lovely smile. Everyone admired her both for her youthful looks and elegant feminine figure. Her family from Genoa had recently emigrated to Nice. Somewhat against her will, she had been found work, as an apprentice dressmaker, in the fashion house where Michel was the head tailor.

Charles had decided to help the young couple who, unhappy with the monotonous work in the fashion house, wanted to open their own business. He had loaned Michel enough money to open his own fashion house at 26 rue de France in Nice. He was a witness at their wedding in London and Michel was very grateful to him for his help. He managed to repay Charles pretty quickly because he soon became much sought after by people in Nice. This young eighteen-year-old designer created Paul Poiret models! The business prospered and Marcelle gave up working at the fashion house in order to look after the children. She started taking piano and singing lessons and showed a great deal of musical talent.

Towards the end of 1911, a short time before the young couple separated, Charles had become very concerned about Michel. He had lost interest in his business. He had a wonderful winter collection ready and was attracting a lot of customers, but he had started leaving his junior staff in charge. His clients were not at all happy about this. They wanted personal attention from the young dynamic Michel. Clients gradually stopped patronising his fashion house and he started losing money. Michel Hoffmann, Navratil's head tailor, had prevented the business from going completely bankrupt by buying it from him.

Michel's private worries centred round the fact that his wife, Marcelle, was having an affair with one of his best friends. Naturally, he was very upset.

Charles Bedford had learned about the young couple's separation but had had no contact with them since then. Now, suddenly, he finds himself standing next to Stead on the *Titanic*, holding Lolo in his arms.

'Charles!' shouts Lolo.

'Lolo, it's you? Here? What are you doing all alone? Where are your parents?'

Lolo puts out his arms and Bedford takes him from Stead. He can see big tears on Lolo's cheeks.

'I'm looking for Mummy but I'm stupid! She's not even on the ship!'

'There's something strange going on here,' says Charles looking at Stead. Stead says nothing but obviously shares the same view of the situation.

'I propose the following, my dear Bedford, I'll take our little friend for an ice cream or a fruit juice while you go and look for his father. Perhaps you can explain the situation to him? Take your time, there's no hurry.'

Bedford readily agrees. Stead's intuition is sometimes unsettling: it's as if he can read your mind better than you can. Some people find it uncomfortable and so he has few friends. However, those he does have are very loyal. If need be, they will defend him as fiercely as he defends them.

Bedford is one such friend. Stead appreciates and values this close friendship, so rare to find in the circles in which they move. He likes the spirit of this self-educated aristocrat who travels the world studying people and society rather than wasting his fortune on gambling. They have a deep understanding of each other because they have a lot in common.

Lolo eagerly follows his new-found friend, Stead. Bedford

can see them at a table near a north-facing bay window overlooking the ocean, with its white foamy waves stretching to infinity. Lolo seems to have forgotten how upset he has been and is chatting away happily with Stead. Charles goes off to find Michel.

He discovers him clutching Momon, wandering around B deck looking for Lolo. Michel is unrecognisable in his corduroy suit, with wild-looking hair and a beard. Charles hesitates for a moment, hardly knowing him. He looks completely different and is obviously very anxious, biting his lips and chewing his fingernails.

Michel doesn't see Charles until he is about two metres from him. With a look of complete disbelief, he suddenly comes to a halt, thinking it's another ghost!

'It's me Michel! You're not dreaming! I must just tell you that Lolo is safe and sound with my friend the journalist, Stead. They're in the Palm Garden. And now tell me, how come you're here?'

Michel hesitates before answering. Lolo's disappearance has made him feel guiltier than ever about lying to the children. It has really brought home to him the fact that Marcelle, hundreds of miles away, will be suffering terribly. What a relief to find Charles! He begins to pour his heart out.

'Charles, I've left Nice for good. I intend to get established in New York.'

'But why have you got the children with you? Where's Marcelle?'

'With her lover, our mutual friend, Marquis Rey de Villarey!'

'You must be joking Michel. The Marquis is a gentleman of honour. He would never do such a thing as to take a mother from her children or a wife from her husband. And isn't he Momon's godfather?'

'Yes he is, but that didn't stop him from seducing Marcelle!'

'Seducing Marcelle? Are you sure? Don't tell me that he's living with her. I don't believe it!'

'No, you're right. Marcelle is still living at home. I asked for a separation and left.'

'But Marcelle loves you and is obsessed with the children. Look, the Marquis is nothing but a passing fancy. She can't want a divorce!'

'It's me who has asked for a divorce. After she confessed to this liaison with Rey de Villarey, the house became a living hell. We couldn't stop arguing. I had to leave. When the separation was made legal last February, she was given custody of the children until the divorce comes through. I was disgusted with this decision. For obvious reasons, Marcelle was often absent, and most of the time she used to leave the children with Angelina, her mother, who let them do anything they wanted. She completely spoiled them, they were taught all kinds of bad habits and since I only had the right to see them on Sundays, I had no way of doing anything about it. To make things worse she never stopped telling me it was my fault for not having been stricter with Marcelle! I suppose I should have kept a better eye on her. A young woman as beautiful as a princess needs a chaperone and shouldn't be allowed to spend her time flirting.'

'But Marcelle never flirted. She worked hard with her music. You know how confident her teacher was about her having a great career as a singer.'

'Yes, but I didn't want to listen to all that. It would have ruined my reputation in Nice. Rey de Villarey encouraged her to disobey my wishes and, to crown it all, Marcelle didn't tell her mother I had left the house because of her infidelity. So you see, I had no choice about the children; I had to take them with me to get them away from Marcelle and her mother's bad influence. I want them to have a good education. Marcelle used to talk about teaching them herself but there's no question about it, they're going to get a good education and have a successful career like their father!'

'But Michel! I don't understand you! How could you have done something so serious without first giving it a lot of thought and discussing it with friends?'

'Charles, as I said, I didn't have any choice. I'm travelling under a false name. I took Hoffmann's passport and will send it back to him when we get to New York. Believe me, I'm not very proud of myself, but it was the only thing to do. Marcelle would never have let me take the children if I'd told her I wanted to emigrate to America.'

'But perhaps she would have come with you.'

Charles knew Marcelle and he knew she would never have consented to the children going very far from her. She must have been going through great misery to betray her husband in this way. No doubt Michel's intolerant behaviour must have pushed her beyond her limits.

'What bothers me now is what has happened to the letter I wrote to my wife from London telling her we were going on the *Titanic*. I didn't want to write earlier or else she would have reported me to the police.'

'I'm sure she would have!'

'I promised to be in contact with her as soon as I established a new life for myself. I didn't have time to post the letter. I gave it to the chambermaid at the hotel in London where we stayed the night. I gave her a big tip and she promised to post it the same day.'

'Well there's no point in worrying about it now. There's no reason why she wouldn't have posted it.'

Neither Bedford nor Michel was really convinced but they don't say anymore about it, the first out of a sense of discretion and the latter out of a sense of helplessness.

Michel falls silent and Bedford refrains from continuing the conversation. He doesn't think he has the right to interfere in his friend's destiny, even in the face of such blatant irresponsibility. Michel finds it hard to look Charles in the eye but, all the same, he knows his secrets will be safe with him.

Momon feels neglected and tugs at his father's sleeve. He wants to find his brother, which prompts the two men to go off to the Palm Garden. They find Lolo still happily chattering away with Stead.

It is about two hours later when the Hoffmanns leave the lunch table. Trevor has suggested taking Lolo to the radio cabin to see his friend, Harold Bride, the second radio officer. Lolo is very pleased with this idea. Mirella is keen on playing with Momon and Michel is very grateful for the opportunity to be alone for a while. Knowing the children are in good hands, he goes to the cabin to try and sort out his thoughts.

CHAPTER 5

LITTLE LIGHTS IN QUEENSTOWN

THE RADIO ROOM is at the front of the upper deck and is made up of three adjoining rooms. In the first there is a receiving set, a worktable and some control panels. The second room holds a transmitter while the third is simply an ordinary cabin. At the moment Bride is off duty. He is pleased to see Trevor who has taken the liberty of bringing Lolo along with him. Bride smiles when he sees the little boy and invites them both into the first room where he gives them a general outline of the radio room and how it functions.

Both the *Titanic* and the *Olympic* use the Marconi wireless system. They are the most modern and the best equipped ships in the world, capable of sending and receiving messages up to between 250 and 400 nautical miles during the day and about 2,000 at night. The Marconi system is not the only one used at this time; Telefunken, Lee de Forest and United Wireless are all competitors in the field. By 1912 the competition is such that no two systems can communicate together apart from in an emergency. Sometimes the operators play the sorcerer's apprentice and disrupt a rival transmitting system without paying any heed to the possible consequences!

Trevor is very kind and tries to simplify Bride's explanations for Lolo who finds it very difficult to understand what an electromagnetic wave is. Bride slips out of the room for a moment. He returns to take them next door where Phillips is in the process of sending a message. Trevor and Lolo approach Phillips very quietly and Lolo watches the strange things he is doing. He doesn't understand what on earth is going on. The receiver is tapping out Morse code with short sharp sounds in every imaginable combination. Lolo is thrilled with the ti-ti-ta and the ti-ta-ta-ti noises and watches as the young man writes down the message letter by letter. Bride, Trevor, and Lolo leave Phillips to get on with his work and go outside where the two men explain the Morse code alphabet to Lolo. It fascinates him even more that the printed alphabet that he so recently learned at home.

Sitting on folding chairs, Bride and Trevor have a chat while Lolo taps out a fantasy ti-ti-ta-ta message on his knees.

'What's life like on board the *Titanic*?' asks Trevor.

'Quite difficult really. Like all radio operators, we don't have officer status so we can't take advantage of using the officers' mess. We are more or less left on our own in our cabins. We're supposed to work in shifts but I can see us sometimes having to work together for twenty-four hours at a time! The radio is so busy. At times it becomes exhausting.'

This is certainly how it is on the *Titanic* where rich passengers want to send and receive private messages. Businessmen, bankers, and politicians want to keep up with their business empires and their finances. They wheel and deal like they do in their offices in London or New York. Telecommunications is at this time, seventy-five years before portable computers and the Internet, very important and rapidly changing for the better. Both Bride and Trevor are very aware of the importance of their work. They know a great future lies ahead for them, in this era of communication development.

As Trevor is getting up to leave with Lolo, an impressive looking fellow comes along. It's Thomas Andrews, the engineer-architect of this floating town. He's a well-built man with a large square chin, a receding hairline, and big bushy eyebrows that accentuate his shy eyes. He has a particular liking for Bride and has recommended him to Captain Smith. Lolo's 'Morse code' tapping catches his eye and, smiling at him, he asks what he is doing. Lolo, not at all frightened of this large man, immediately starts asking him questions. When he finds out who he is, he doesn't hesitate to proclaim his admiration for the finest ship in the world. Lolo listens attentively to Andrews talking to Bride about having to go and inspect the watertight compartments and the boilers next day. He butts in, begging Andrews to take him along. Amused by this unusual little boy, Andrews agrees, and arranges to meet him at ten o'clock the next morning here, at the radio room.

It's five o'clock in the afternoon when the Irish coast looms up in the distance. The *Titanic* gets ready to make its last port of call before crossing the North Atlantic. The ship will dock at the port of Queenstown where a hundred and thirty passengers, mainly emigrants, will embark along with over a thousand sacks of post.

While the children play ball, Michel looks over the side of the ship admiring the green translucent water far below. Lord Bedford joins him. He suggests they go to the reading room in first class where they will get a wonderful view of the Irish coastline through the large windows.

While climbing the staircase up to first class they pass a stunning-looking woman. Judging by her looks and her clothes, she must be a film star. Her white gloves come up to her elbows and in her right hand she's holding a long cigarette holder with a thin cigar in the end of it. Her hair is bobbed short like a boy and there are two kiss curls on each cheek. She's wearing a beautiful flimsy white dress with a bloused bodice hanging over a tight skirt, showing off her slim legs. A long black silk scarf wound round her neck floats down her back touching the hem of her dress. Michel immediately recognises her outfit as one of Paul

Poiret's latest designs. As she reaches Michel's level on the staircase, she turns her head towards him. She speaks in French with a strong American accent, obviously certain it will have an impact on him.

'Excuse me but do you know by any chance when this place arrives in New York?'

'On 17 April, God willing.'

'Really? So quickly! How surprising, I would never have thought it!'

With this she goes dreamily down the stairs without turning her head. She is one of the most famous silent film stars in America, Dorothy Gibson.[1]

'D'you know her?' asks Bedford.

'Not in the least! But she's right about it being a 'place,' it's more like being in a town than on a ship.'

When they reach the reading room there are no chairs vacant. But, just as the two men start to go in search of some, Lolo sees an old couple gathering up their things. They look as if they are leaving.

'Daddy, Charles! Look! There are some chairs!'

They go towards the chairs the couple are vacating.

'What a surprise you being here, Mr Navratil! What a mysterious man you are! You design a wardrobe for our Atlantic crossing on the *Titanic* and never even say one word about being on the ship yourself!'

The loud voice echoes around the reading room like an announcement in a railway station. Most of the people in the room turn their heads and smile. At the sound of his real name, Michel thinks his heart is going to stop beating! After the initial shock, he looks furtively at the passengers around him. Luckily there's nobody here he knows. He now thinks he should never have accepted Bedford's invitation to come into first class. He should have realised he might bump into the Straus couple.

After all, it was from them he got the idea of taking the *Titanic* to New York.

Isidor and Ida Straus had boarded the ship in Cherbourg. First-class passengers who often crossed the Atlantic knew them very well.

'My dear friend,' smiles Ida Straus. 'We wear only your clothes and we like them very much and yet you don't have the grace to tell us why you are on the ship? Did you decide at the last minute or had you already decided, the last time you saw us?'

'To be honest, my dear lady, it's thanks to you both that I am here. Don't you remember how I asked you about the *Titanic*? I even asked you where the tickets were being sold. I made the decision to go to New York a little later.'

'So,' insists Isidor. 'Tell us all about it!'

Michel, amazed at how relaxed he feels, quickly tells them his story, omitting, of course, details about Marcelle.

Isidor is impressed with his young friend's decision-making and cannot help but think his plans for the future will be very successful.

'Believe me, I think you made the right decision to leave Nice. I know you well and I know you'll go a long way. I'll do everything I can to help you. Perhaps you might be interested in designing ready-to-wear luxury clothes for our Macy's department stores?'

Michel is lost for words at such kindness and it shows on his face. He tries to thank the Strauses.

'Dear sir,' interrupts Ida. 'We are more than happy to do for a young talented man what others have done for us for more than forty years!'

At that moment, Lolo and Momon, who had gone off to run around on deck, return.

'Oh! And your family is with you! Come and give me a kiss my darlings! Where's your Mummy?'

'In Nice!' replies Lolo, very happy to kiss such a nice old lady who feels so soft and smells of perfume. 'But she's going to join us soon in America!'

The Straus couple move on, leaving their chairs for Michel and Charles. Dusk fall over the ocean and turns the sky purple in the west. The emerald water flows in mysterious currents, circling and crossing each other, around the ship. The sky slowly darkens and the little lights of Queenstown twinkle faintly in the distance. The reading room is quiet now.

Lolo sits on Michel's knee and watches the dark strip of coast rapidly coming towards them. Momon quietly plays with the little car Lolo had been given when they got on the ship.

'So this is Ireland,' says Michel softly.

He can just make out the rocky coastline dotted with deep sandy bays and crowned, to the east of the port of Queenstown, by a ruined castle and to the west, by a church, also in ruins. Along the eastern promontory there is a fortress whose walls go down to the sea and a little further to the west, facing it, there's another one. The entrance to the port between these two points is full of small fishing boats.

Soon the *Titanic* slows down. Her engines come to a stop, and the pilot, who is going to guide the ship between the rocks, comes on board. Anchored two miles from the port, Lolo is about to see the same performance as he saw in Cherbourg. Little Irish boats come and go bringing passengers, post and different kinds of supplies. Again, journalists are shown around the ship. They marvel at the modern engineering used in the construction of the *Titanic*.

Bedford has already left the reading room and the Hoffmanns are now almost alone looking at the port slowly disappearing into the darkness. Edmond has gone to sleep in his father's arms and Lolo now sits in the chair where Charles had been sitting. He's so quiet he appears to be asleep but his eyes get bigger and bigger at the marvellous sights he can see outside. Perhaps this town doesn't exist; perhaps it's simply a vision and appears only once every hundred years to those who deserve it. Tomorrow it will disappear and float with time towards the future.

A long way from Lolo's poetic daydreams, Michel is thinking about the Straus proposition. He knew it wasn't an empty gesture. Designing for Macy's department stores! A guaranteed fortune ahead of him! He almost feels dizzy at the thought of it. It's not the time to build castles in the air nor, more to the point, in America! But why let such a great opportunity slip away? Keep calm. Better to reflect on things for two or three days before talking about it again to Isidor and Ida. Don't force anything and above all, he must ask them to respect his assumed name.

Without wanting it to happen, he starts thinking about Nice, and the distress the people there inevitably must be feeling at the moment. He pictures Antonio, the grandfather, explosively angry at being deprived of his grandchildren, Angelina's pain, and Marcelle's silent distress. He senses Marcelle has not received his letter and will never receive it. The chambermaid in London broke her promise and Marcelle will be thinking the worst; he has committed a criminal act. Time passing with no news of the children will erode her hopes. Michel suddenly thinks she is perhaps too fragile to survive this drama. She might fall into a state of depression and even kill herself. Then he would be the person responsible; he would be the murderer. Will she be able to hang on until they get to New York from where Michel will send her a telegram? Will it be too late?

The image of Marcelle on the verge of suicide is suddenly overshadowed in Michel's imagination by that irritating, intolerable idiot, Marquis Rey de Villarey.

'And to think it was I who suggested he should be little Momon's godfather!'

Then he had the most terrible thought. Momon is just two, and perhaps Villarey was already Marcelle's lover when she became pregnant! Could he be the father? He looks very carefully at the sleeping child's round face. At the moment it's difficult to see whether he resembles Villarey more than Navratil. This insupportable uncertainty doesn't in any way change the love he has for the baby but he feels a great deal of anger welling up inside him. He can't control the feelings of hate that he now has for his former friend, this destroyer of families, this thief of happiness! It's useless to worry about Marcelle, the Marquis will take care of her, he says to himself pitifully. He has now turned the page of a new chapter in his life. The Marcelle chapter is over, finished.

It is totally dark by the time the ship moves off. It turns round slowly, leaving a circle of foam in its wake almost as big as Queenstown.

Michel feels more at ease and gets up from his chair, holding the sleeping baby tenderly in his arms. He calls Lolo softly and he follows his father back to their cabin where Michel puts the sleeping baby on his bed. He and Lolo then make their way to the dining room.

Their table is nearly full. A new companion has joined the little group. Two bottles of champagne sit in their ice buckets waiting to be opened to toast a welcome to the newcomer, a young English professor, Lawrence Beesley. He is going to visit his brother in America.

That evening there is a lot of discussion about Irish emigration. Lawrence is one of the few Irishmen to embark at Queenstown who is travelling in second class. Nearly everyone else joined the other migrants in third class. For the most part they come from the south and west of Ireland. They have sold, with few regrets, their small pieces of land and small businesses or left behind their tied cottages. Some, who have nothing, have left behind only ageing parents. What they all have in common are hopes for a new and better life in the United States of America.

Beesley explains how Queenstown is a wound that Ireland can never heal. For more than a hundred years, the flow of emigrants has never dried up and he says that the youngest and best have left, draining Ireland of its life-blood. Michel knows the problem very well! What else can people do but emigrate when there's no future ahead of them! Even though he hasn't got much money now, he sees long days ahead full of wonderful plans and hopes. He looks forward to starting a new life from zero. Michel feels a warm friendliness towards Lawrence Beesley. Without doubt, this trip on the *Titanic* is going to be a great turning point in his life.

CHAPTER 6

IN THE MONSTER'S BELLY

MICHEL WAKES UP clear-headed on the morning of 12 April. Stretched out on his bed, underneath the wide-open porthole, he has all the time in the world to enjoy the peaceful silence hanging over this extraordinary, luxurious ship. He can hear the gentle lapping of the sea. Eager to be nearer the unreachable pale sky, reflected in the now still ocean, he kneels on the bed and leans out of the porthole. He feels as if he is one of the seagulls he saw the previous day, following the ship, gliding and piercing the air with high-pitched cries. A good night's sleep has convinced him he should take advantage of these peaceful days on the ship to empty his mind of the painful recent events, once and for all. Changing his physical appearance, he realises, is not enough. He has to rid himself of his anger. It has sometimes made him blind to reality and has imprisoned him in a never-ending circle of impulsive action and regret.

Spending so much time with the children at the moment, has made him see them with growing interest. In many ways, Lolo is very much like Marcelle. He has the same emotions, the same tenderness, and gentleness. Little Edmond is still too young to be able to fathom out but Lolo is fast developing into an astonishingly mature child. He has practically taught himself to read. Michel has high hopes for him and wants him to develop a practical approach to life rather than becoming a dreamer. He has decided Lolo should become a very successful businessman. Marcelle, on the other hand, had a great respect for intellectuals and wanted her elder son to become a professor at a university. But Michel thinks he knows what is best for his sons. He is convinced he is doing the right thing by rearing them on his own, away from their mother's influence.

Nevertheless he feels he needs to think these things over in order to reassure himself. He is trying, in his own way, to be objective. He should perhaps admit to himself how Marcelle isn't entirely to blame for what has happened in their lives. She is a sensitive person with a friendly, tender nature and lacks confidence in herself. His temperament must have made him a very difficult person to live with. She probably felt overwhelmed by his contradictory moods. He can be the most generous but also the most selfish of men, the most authoritarian but also the most pliable. Had he allowed her enough freedom? Had he tried to understand her? He should have been the first person to admit he had not really taken enough time and trouble with her. She had wanted to become a classical singer but he had opposed the idea. She knew Michel would never allow her to do anything he disapproved of. Why should he have been so astonished and outraged when she turned to someone who admired her talent and encouraged her to follow an artistic career?

Waking up with the feeling there was too much to do to waste time sleeping, Lolo climbs on to his father's bed. Michel, overjoyed to be interrupted in his sad thoughts, pretends to be asleep so Lolo will move closer to him. Lolo covers him with kisses and giggles loudly because his daddy's beard tickles him. Michel laughs too and Edmond wakes up. It's already eight o'clock and there are lots of things planned for this morning: a Turkish bath, a swim in the swimming pool, breakfast in the third-class dining room not to mention Lolo's appointment with Andrews at ten o'clock.

They see hardly anyone in the second-class corridors but the two third-class dining rooms, which they have to go through in order to get to the Turkish bath, are already half full. There is a mixture of people in third class. Between them they speak at least twenty different languages. The resident interpreter whose job is to help people communicate with the staff on the ship, spends a lot of time helping passengers to communicate with each other! Although people tend to be grouped together according to their social category there is a friendly feeling among the third-class passengers. They are really interested in finding out about each other's way of life. The lively atmosphere in the third-class dining rooms fascinates the three Navratils. Michel feels as much at home here as he does amongst the rich and famous. It occurs to him the only difference between the people here and those in first class, is the former have not yet had the opportunity to make their way in life, while the latter have done so successfully. He wonders how many people here will manage to overcome their difficult beginnings and make a success of their lives. He thinks it is a question of energy and determination. If an individual has faith in themselves, then anything is possible.

The children have already found some playmates and Michel is just about to start talking to someone when Lolo runs up to him.

'Daddy! What about the swimming pool? Let's go and swim then come back here and play!'

Michel thinks it's a good idea but Momon has disappeared so they go off to find him. Lolo soon finds his little brother. Just then a familiar voice calls to them.

'Michel, Lolo, come and join us!'

Mirella and Trevor are sitting with a huge breakfast in front of them. They're with a group of young people who quickly introduce themselves. There are three Irishmen: Daniel Buckley, Martin Callagher, and Carl Johnson; a young man, like Michel, from Bratislava, called Otto Schmidt who is a pianist; and a Norwegian, Olaus Abelseth, who seems to be completely preoccupied with Mirella.

The group had met each other for the first time the evening before when Otto started playing the piano after dinner. They had all danced till after dawn. Nobody had slept and they had waited in the smoking lounge until it was breakfast time. Michel was struck by how different Mirella seemed to be. She was strangely quiet and blushed each time Olaus Abelseth looked at her. It is odd the way the notion of time changes things at sea. What would have taken days or even weeks to accomplish in the realm of love on land, here on board ship, it had taken only hours for a romance to blossom.

After breakfast most of the group go off to their cabins to get some sleep but Trevor, Otto Schmidt and Martin Callagher follow Michel and the children to the Turkish bath.

Once there, Lolo stands rigid, looking around anxiously. As the heat and steam increases, he panics and runs to the door, trying to open it.

'Fire!' he screams and Michel suddenly understands what is happening to his son.

'Look after Edmond and join us at the swimming pool,' he calls to the others. Grabbing his clothes with one hand and Lolo with the other, he runs out into the corridor.

Lolo sobs so much he nearly chokes.

In the swimming pool Michel sits Lolo on his knee and cuddles and rocks him explaining how it is the hot water that makes steam in the Turkish bath and not fire. He feels angry with himself for having taken Lolo there. He should have known what effect it would have on the poor boy. About a year earlier, Lolo had been rescued from a hotel fire. Marcelle had taken him to Vichy, where she was having a course of treatment at the spa, and one evening after she had left him asleep in their room, a fire had broken out. It had been a very traumatic experience for him. Ever since he had been very scared of fire and smoke.

Soon the others appear. Lolo's tears are wiped dry and the Turkish bath incident is forgotten.

The swimming pool is another innovation of the architect-engineer, Andrews, who designed a similar one for the sister ship the *Olympic*. About twenty metres long and five metres wide, the pool is lined with green and blue ceramic tiles. One side is lit by electric lights while the other has portholes overlooking the sea.

While Michel swims with the other adults the children have their first swimming lesson. The instructor pulls the children through the water with a rod attached to a cork belt around their waist. After half an hour the children declare they can now swim as well as the grownups!

Otto and Michel get on very well together. Otto talks about his music studies in Vienna, a place that Michel was very fond of. The conversation brings back memories of when he had been an apprentice in Presbourg and would often go to Vienna. It had been an inspiring place for him.

Trevor and Lolo arrive ten minutes early for their appointment with Andrews. The weather is beautiful and the new paint on the deck gleams, like a mirror reflecting sunlight. It seems to Lolo as if the funnels are smoking much more than they were the day before. There are already traces of soot on the new yellow ochre paint. He points this out to Trevor who says the ship often increases its speed. At the moment the ship is travelling at twenty-one knots[1] and it will almost certainly go faster as the day goes by. The engines are being run in and they cannot be forced, they have to get used to their work. Phillips, taking advantage of a lull in his work, is sitting in a deckchair by the radio room door. He says some of the American millionaires on board have sent bets to New York about the average speed of the *Titanic's* first voyage.

'They've bet thousands of dollars. In fact most of the messages I send are about money. I'm dealing with huge sums of money!'

In the radio room Bride is in the middle of decoding a message and asks Trevor to do it for him. Bride and Lolo watch attentively as he writes down the message, letter by letter until Phillips says in a very deep voice, 'A little boy is wanted!'

Lolo runs towards the door and nearly collides with Andrews. They take the lift to F deck. They have to go about a hundred metres along passageways through the crew's quarters and through the third-class dining rooms, before they reach the turbine room. They are now in the bow of the ship.

It is quite a shock for Lolo to go into this world of engines. The rooms, the same size as the library, extend upward getting narrower and narrower, reaching as far up as B and A decks. They look like swallow holes and Lolo feels suffocated in this confined space. A terrible din reverberates around this area but it is extremely well insulated. Very little noise is heard on the rest of the ship. Immense wheels with cogs are partly boxed in and Lolo is fascinated by the gigantic pistons that go up and down creating a rhythm all their own. Each turbine has an enormous tube on top, running into an adjoining room. There are so many machines in this room; he doesn't know which to look at. Andrews's voice is lost in the noise but he manages to explain to Lolo how the tubes ending up in the engines, come from the preceding rooms where the boilers are. The mechanics looking after the machines don't have to put up with as bad working conditions as the men who work as stokers for the furnaces. The furnaces have to be looked after but they also have to be filled up with coal. The work is terribly hard. A dozen or so men, stripped to the waist because of the intense heat, stand feeding the monstrous mouths of the white-hot furnaces with shovelfuls of coal. Working in temperatures of up to sixty degrees, stokers often pass out because of the heat.

Happily for Lolo, his hand is firmly locked with Andrews's and his fear of fire is under control.

'Look carefully,' says Andrews. 'The pipes you just saw feed those big reservoirs up above. When the water is hot it produces steam. This runs the engines, turning the propellers to make the ship move. It's exactly like the lid of a saucepan moving when the water inside is boiling.'

What a relief it is when they leave this inferno. What a terrible life these men have. Lolo is overawed by it all and thinks to himself how privileged his life is, compared to the poor men who work in the furnace room. Just thinking about it makes him want to cry. Then he suddenly has an idea. He once heard someone talking about convicts and how some of them were sent far away to a penal colony. Perhaps this was one of those places? But Andrews says no, the men who work in the furnace room do so because they choose to.

'Do they get a lot of money for doing that job?' asks Lolo.

'Not a lot,' replies Andrews.

So why do such horrible work? Oh dear, thinks Lolo, not really understanding anything.

Next they go to the watertight compartments for which the *Titanic* is famous. Andrews explains how they function, which is quite simple. If one of the compartments is opened the water goes into it and stays trapped there. There are five compartments in the bulkheads at both the front and back of the ship but in the sixth ones, the walls end a metre from the ceiling. With this Lolo lifts his head and looks very serious.

'But when the water comes high up in the compartment, the water overflows!'

'That's right, my clever little friend. It flows into the next one, which in turn fills up and overflows and so on until all the compartments are full. Only we'll never get to that situation because there are a lot of pumps ready to start working at a moment's notice, to pump any incoming water back into the sea. So in fact the compartments won't have time to fill up. Anyway, the hull is double thickness at the front and the back, so there's no risk of water getting into the ship.'

'Yes, I know, Daddy told me.'

'Good,' says Andrews, 'and now, if you like, we could go to the bridge and have a look at the map room.'

'Yes please!' exclaims Lolo and holding Andrews's hand, they take the lift to the bridge. There are several officers there, including the second-in-command, Henry Wilde. At thirty-eight he's a well built, broad-shouldered man who has long experience of working alongside Captain Smith. William Murdoch, the first officer is also there. He's an old sea dog, who has survived several disasters at sea, especially on the *Arabic*. He's standing next to Charles Lightoller, the second officer, a hard man, ambitious, and efficient at his job. It's midday and the officers are getting ready to plot the position of the sun against the horizon. Andrews hands Lolo over to Murdoch and goes off.

'You see, my little one,' he says to Lolo. 'When we know the exact position of the sun we can calculate where we are on the ocean and then we mark it on a map. We do this every day so we go in the right direction. Come with me and I'll show you.'

They go into the map room where Captain Smith is drawing the position of the ship on a huge map of the Atlantic Ocean. The map is covered in vertical and horizontal lines. Lolo is breathless with delight. He has always dreamed of meeting an important ship's captain and here he is, standing next to the one in charge of the fastest ship in the world. Murdoch leads him to the big wheel on the bridge and lets him not only hold it but also steer. What a fantastic thrill for a little boy!

'Now you can tell your parents you have driven the *Titanic*,' he says, smiling at Lolo.

Just at that moment two of the crew arrive on the bridge and ask to speak to the Captain.

'Who are you?' asks the Captain in a brusque tone of voice.

The men, who are standing to attention, reply they are lookouts, Frederick Fleet and Reginald Lee.

'At ease, what do you want?'

'We can't find our binoculars. We told the second officer they had disappeared just after we left Southampton, but he hasn't given us any replacements.'

'What on earth is all this about? Why are you bothering me? Go and see Lightoller about it, it's his business not mine!' roars the Captain.

The lookouts salute the Captain and go off looking very angry. They had asked the second officer for replacement binoculars several times but had not been given any. Surprisingly enough, there is a shortage of binoculars on the ship and Lightoller isn't able to produce any for his lookouts. He has a pair of his own but wants to keep them for himself.

'D'you know what a risk we're taking, Bob?' says Fleet despairingly. 'There's no problem for tonight but in a couple of days it'll be another matter.'

Lolo watches them go and suddenly feels terribly disappointed. He hadn't understood what was going on but he had seen the Captain telling off the two sailors. His image of this great and important Captain has been tarnished. His idol is a mere human being.

Murdoch asks Lolo if he wants to ask any more questions. He says he is rather puzzled about one thing.

'How do you drive a ship at night? Do they have headlights like a car?' he asks.

Murdoch smiles at his question. He replies there are no lights powerful enough to use on such a big ship. So there are lookouts, like the men who came to speak to the captain. They sit in the crow's nest high up above the water. There are six men who take it in turn, every four hours, two at a time, to keep a lookout for anything that might be in the way. He says they have excellent eyesight and can see anything up to five hundred metres away in fine weather. In bad weather the ship has to go more slowly than usual. If a lookout spots something that might be dangerous for the ship, he sends a message to the bridge and whoever is steering then changes course. Murdoch explains how officers and sailors who are on night duty have to be at their post at least fifteen minutes before they begin their work, so their eyes can get used to the darkness. Only people with very good eyesight can be in the navy!

Lolo goes back to the cabin accompanied by a sailor, only half satisfied by Murdoch's answers to his questions. He's thinking about the little fishing boats he saw in Queenstown harbour. During the day they can easily be seen but what would happen to them if they were in the path of a *Titanic* at night when it was very, very dark?

CHAPTER 7

FIRST CLASS

LOLO IS VERY DISAPPOINTED not to be able to tell his daddy about his adventures in the belly of the ship and on the bridge.

'You can tell me all about it later,' Michel says.

He had had an invitation from Charles Bedford to have lunch in the first-class dining room and didn't want to be late. Isidor and Ida Straus would be there but Charles had warned them not to say anything about Michel's real identity. He had told them he was travelling under a false name, just like Lady Duff Gordon.

Because he is impatient to talk to someone about his adventures, Lolo begins to describe what he has seen to Momon as they follow Michel up the grand staircase. Momon is a captive audience but once they reach the first-class dining room, Lolo has to keep quiet.

The headwaiter is expecting them and they are led to a large table where several people are sitting. Charles Bedford gets up to welcome them.

'Hello Michel! Welcome!'

Charles lifts up both the children and whispers in Lolo's ear, 'Look who's sitting at our table! Andrews, Mr and Mrs Straus, and Mr Stead!'

Lolo smiles with delight.

This dining room seems to be more luxurious than the second-class one mainly because there is much more space between the tables. The walls are panelled in the same oak as the staircase and there are Jacobean-style armchairs upholstered in hand-embroidered material.

Michel is a little bothered that he is late. He has an excuse ready but before he can open his mouth, Andrews gets up and shakes his hand.

'I'm very pleased to meet you, Mr Hoffmann. Your big boy is a wonderful companion. (Lolo is pleased at this, though he's a bit embarrassed and blushes.) I've told everyone about our tour of the ship; since I left your son on the bridge at midday, I assumed you might be a little late and you are excused by all of us. Lolo's maturity astonished me. Tell me, how old is he?'

'He's three years and ten months.'

'I can hardly believe it. He asked such pertinent questions and he has an incredible sense of observation and direction.'

Ida and Isidor Straus look at the children with great interest.

'My dear Mr Hoffmann, you have such beautiful children! In twenty years you will have ready-made business partners!'

Michel relaxes in his chair. They're playing the game!

'I must say, we haven't yet recovered from the surprise of seeing you here,' whispers Ida who is sitting on his left. 'You're certainly very courageous to abandon your flourishing business without knowing what the future holds for you. We're very happy to have crossed your path at such an important time in your life. I want you to know we'll do everything we can to help you start your new life.'

'I'm very grateful to you,' Michel replies. 'The idea of emigrating to America came to me several times over the past few months. The attraction of the unknown perhaps, and the need to prove my talent as well as the challenge of confronting life in a new country. One needs considerable courage but also a lot of recklessness.'

'Don't underestimate yourself, Mr Hoffmann,' interrupts Isidor Straus. 'I believe you to be a very competent man. You are right to want to live in the United States. Nice has become too small for you. I like a young man to have initiative and spirit. Remember you can always count on us to help you. You know very well I never say anything I don't mean. And I always keep my promises.'

Michel feels very grateful to be offered so much support and encouragement by this wonderful couple. But at the same time, he wonders what they would say if they knew the whole truth about what he has done. He doesn't dare look at Charles who knows everything about his flight from Nice and the stolen passport.

Lolo, overjoyed to find himself sitting with his heroes, can't take his eyes off Andrews. He smiles at Lolo before telling the others more about their tour of the engine rooms and how the little boy steered the ship.

Naturally conversation at the lunch table centres round the *Titanic*. Andrews is keen to hear comments about the ship because he wants to make improvements in various ways. Far from being satisfied with his creation, he spends much of his time looking for faults not yet apparent. The ladies' lounge, for example, rather concerns him at the moment. He is perturbed because it is used so little.

'My dear Mr Andrews,' says Ida Straus. 'Don't let it bother you! There's nothing wrong with your lounge; it's simply a matter of the changing times! More and more women smoke and fewer and fewer want to be confined to a place where they can only talk with other women. I'm not speaking about suffragettes but someone like me.[1] I don't go to this lounge because I prefer to be in my husband's company.'

'That's why you rarely see me in the smoking lounge,' laughs Isidor. 'I enjoy my wife's company but she can't stand the smell of smoke; at home I only smoke in my study. I'll be frank with you, Mr Andrews, as regards the ladies' lounge, I'm afraid you're behind the times. I can't see any point in creating this kind of ghetto where the fair sex is meant to be kept out of the way. You're living in the last century. Keeping women at home while the men go out and enjoy themselves is no longer the rule of thumb. *Kinder, Kirche, Kuche*, the three Ks as we say in German: children, church, and kitchen used to be the way things were. But nowadays habits in society are changing as quickly as science and industry are developing. Women are becoming emancipated and I don't blame them.'

Stead and Bedford agree with this wholeheartedly but Andrews doesn't seem to be very convinced. As for Michel, he knows only too well the implications of such social change and keeps quiet about the subject.

After the main course the children are bored and are allowed to leave the table. Unlike some children in first class who have to sit quietly under the strict eyes of their nursemaids, Lolo and Momon run around the tables. Suddenly Lolo comes to a halt in front of a beautiful young woman. Madeline Astor is chatting with her husband, the famous millionaire, John Astor, who is in his fifties. It's the beautiful lady in the train and she's nearly as beautiful as his mummy.[2]

'Madeline,' says John Astor, 'I asked our steward, Simpson, to place my bet for today on the distance the *Titanic* will cover. I've bet she'll do over five hundred miles. We lost some time yesterday because of calling in at Queenstown, but today the ship's going at twenty-one knots. Guggenheim opted for four hundred and fifty, Widener for four hundred and eighty and Archibald Gracie, always the optimist, for five hundred and ten. We should win three thousand dollars.'

'You never grow tired of making money, my dear John!'

At that moment Madeline catches sight of Lolo.

'Hey! It's the little boy I met in the train. How are you doing, my darling?'

She lifts him onto her knee and hugs him. Suddenly she feels a small hand pulling on her arm.

'It's my little brother, Momon!'

The young woman knows enough French to understand what Lolo says and makes room on her knee for Momon too. Her perfume evokes a kind of magic for the children and they sit, smiling under its spell. She whispers something in their ears and puts them down. She rummages in her silk handbag and gives them each a silver coin.

Michel and the others watch the scene and he blushes with embarrassment. He doesn't like the idea of the children accepting money from a stranger.

'That young woman is very rich and famous,' whispers Charles in his ear. 'You have to let her do it.'

Michel goes off to fetch the children and says a brief hello to the young woman. Both she and John Astor nod their head in reply and Michel returns to the table.

Stead doesn't really join in any conversation at the lunch table. He observes the people at nearby tables and doesn't much like the carefree atmosphere surrounding him. The bets people are making on the speed of the ship irritate him immensely. He finds human folly unfathomable. He is, however, quite intrigued by Michel and the children. They are different to other people here. For example Bedford is obviously a close friend of Michel's but yet he would never have thought so at first. Lolo's independence and way of guessing lots of things is remarkable. What a funny little boy he is. Stead finds himself becoming quite fond of him.

'So it isn't true that the ship can't sink,' whispered a quiet voice close to his ear.

Stead is astonished by what seems to be telepathy. He is just at that moment thinking about the possibilities of something happening to the *Titanic*.

'No Lolo, it isn't true,' he replies. 'A ship that cannot sink exists only in fairy stories.'

'Yes that's what I thought. So why does everyone believe it? Even grownups.'

'Most of all grownups, Lolo. Often when people grow up they think they know everything better than other people do. Talk to Andrews about his ship. I think you'll find he knows very well the *Titanic* can sink. The only difference between his ship and others is simply one of size and strength.'

'Yes he told me that.'

Stead is enjoying this intimate conversation with Lolo. He decides it's preferable to wasting his time talking with the adults here.

After the dessert Mr and Mrs Straus leave to return to their cabin. Michel would like to do the same but Bedford takes him by the arm.

'I think Stead wants to take the children to the puppet theatre so why don't you come and have one of my excellent Havanas?' he says.

Stead and the children go off hand in hand as if they had been friends for years and Michel follows Bedford to the smoking lounge. In the middle of a small group, Madame Lucile (Lady Duff Gordon) alias Madame Morgan, is smoking a long cigar, and is deep in conversation with Mr Andrews.

'Mr Andrews, I have heard you're a little worried about the ladies' lounge. There's no reason to blame yourself. It's a very nice place, but what do you expect? Women can be very annoying. If I were you I'd transform it into a nursery where young women can leave their children with some competent nursemaids while they go off and have some fun. It would be very popular.'

Before Andrews has time to reply, Captain Smith walks into the room along with some of the richest industrialists in America:

Benjamin Guggenheim, Colonel Archibald Gracie, Major Archibald Butt, Francis Millet and Henry Burkhardt. Seeing Captain Smith, Madame Lucile leaves Andrews and goes to greet him.

'Ah, Captain, I'm so happy to see you. We're having a little fashion show this afternoon in the main lounge and we would be most honoured if you would join us.'

Smiling sweetly at the industrialists she exclaims, 'and of course, you too gentlemen!'

Madame Lucile, who is married to Lord Duff Gordon, is a well-known figure in the gossip columns. She is the first person to have opened a fashion house in London using live models. This had outraged high society in London who took a very dim view of this sort of frivolous Frenchwoman who had so quickly become queen of French fashion in London. She had the knack of presenting people with a *fait accompli* and in this way, without asking permission, she had gone ahead and arranged her fashion show in the main lounge. Michel can't stand the woman and he hides behind Bedford so she won't see him.

Stead and the children have a wonderful time at the puppet theatre. The medieval story of Genevieve of Brabant is being shown and different theatrical devices are used. The combination of marionettes, shadow puppets, and magic lantern slides is very exciting. The children are thrilled with being plunged into the fairy-like atmosphere. Although some of the scenes, with dark sinister shadows around the poor Genevieve, and dark, menacing clouds in the sky might have scared them, there were plenty of sunny visions of forests and gothic castles to compensate for the scary parts. When the curtains close Momon jumps up but Lolo stays in his seat, still completely wrapped up in the story.

'Come on Lolo!' orders Momon. 'It's finished.'

Lolo, reluctant to leave the little theatre, follows Stead and Momon to meet up with Michel. Charles had been rather embarrassed when Michel had hidden behind him to avoid being seen by Madame Lucile, but Michel reassures Charles.

'Obviously I don't want Madame Lucile to see me, but don't worry, Charles, I have no intention of hiding behind a false name all my life. As soon as I get to New York I'll revert to my real name. All my documents are in order.'

As soon as the children see Michel they run into his arms and start telling him about the puppet theatre and how wonderful it was. He's pleased to have them back and, leaving Bedford and Stead, he and the children walk off hand in hand.

'What a mess he's made of things,' Bedford confides to Stead. 'As if life isn't difficult enough. Why does he have to complicate it?'

'I agree,' mutters Stead. 'And what a crazy idea to choose a voyage on the *Titanic* with the children.'

Watching the Navratils disappear along the corridor, they both shrug their shoulders and with a sigh, light their cigars.

CHAPTER 8

A WICKED DECEPTION

LOLO AND MOMON wake up at about seven o'clock on the morning of 13 April and jump onto Michel's bed. He has slept well so he doesn't mind being persuaded to get up. An hour later the three of them are on their way to the Turkish bath again. They walk along the corridor of level F, the most direct way of getting to the stern of the ship. The officers call it 'Park Lane' while the crew call it 'Scotland Road'. The crew's quarters are here and it is always bustling with activity. It is about a hundred metres long, just like a road. Arriving at the Turkish bath, Lolo hesitates for a moment, then taking a deep breath, he starts to play hide-and-seek in the steam with Momon. The steam doesn't frighten him any longer and Michel praises him for overcoming his fears.

While the children play, Michel sits in the hot steam thinking of nothing in particular apart from the relaxing sensation enveloping his body. He lifts his head and notices the ceiling. Images evoking Queen Victoria and the silent film star Rudolph Valentino are encased in sculptured gold. The vulgar ceiling makes him smile. On the *Titanic* everything is indulged, even bad taste.

After the Turkish bath they go to the swimming pool where the children have another swimming lesson. Then, as yesterday, they go to the third-class dining room for breakfast.

Walking back along 'Scotland Road' Michel finds himself having contradictory feelings once again. The steam bath and the swim has made him feel very relaxed and yet he can't help dwelling on the subject of the letter he had given to the chambermaid in London to post to Marcelle. He is dying to get to New York to send off some news to her.

By contrast, the children have never felt happier since they left Nice. Lolo's wonderful experiences on the ship seem to have wiped out all his sad feelings about missing his mother. Momon, despite his young age, has also been stimulated by his experiences so far on the ship. He is talking more and more and can run almost as fast as Lolo. He now insists on washing and dressing himself. Michel is amused by this and lets him more or less do it without interfering too much. They find Mirella in the dining room and Lolo runs up to her.

'You don't come and see us any more, Mirella. Are you ill?'

She blushes, and lifting the children onto her knee, gives them both a big kiss. Olaus comes to help her. He doesn't understand French but he's very good at imitating the children, repeating what they say.

'Mirella,' he says in English, 'we could take them to the fancy dress party this evening! Ask them if they'd like to go.'

Lolo thinks it's a fantastic idea.

'A fancy dress party? Like the ones in Nice for the flower festival and the carnival? Oh yes! Will you make me a Roman Emperor's costume Mirella? It's very easy, all you need is a sheet off a bed.'

Michel chats to the group of people he had talked to yesterday. The attractive young man called Daniel Buckley joins the group. He boasts a great deal and is a huge success with the young ladies.

While Michel is chatting, Lolo's curiosity gets the better of him and, despite knowing he shouldn't, he sets off to explore the kitchens. He watches as the chefs, wearing tall white hats, shake frying pans on the stoves. Then he notices a big room with a wood-burning oven in it. A big man, with flour on his face, is using a large wooden paddle to shovel all kinds of bread into the glowing oven. The smell of hot bread is irresistible and Lolo goes towards the oven.

'Good morning, sir!' he says to the baker who immediately recognises his southern French accent.

'Well, well, a little laddie! What are you doing here? You must be lost!'

Lolo is amazed. The baker is French and speaks with a southern accent. Before Lolo has time to say anything, Charles Joughin, the baker from Marseilles, lifts him up and shows him the rows of buns on flour-covered shelves. They have just come out of the oven.

'Aren't they lovely? You can have as many as you want. Here, fill up that paper bag! A little fellow citizen deserves something special.'

Lolo goes off a few minutes later with his arms full and bumps into Andrews, who is rather surprised to see him. Hoping he hasn't been missed, Lolo creeps back into the dining room.

Michel, still talking to some of the group, has been looking over his shoulder wondering where he had gone.

'Where have you been, Lolo? I was worried about you. I've told you not to go off alone like that. You're too small and it's dangerous. Remember when you went off to the Palm Garden? Something might have happened to you.'

Lolo says nothing and lowers his head. Soon great big tears fall on to the paper bag he's holding. Michel cannot bear to see either of his children unhappy so he starts to joke with him.

'What are you hiding in your paper bag, little magician?'

Lolo looks at his daddy and then his face brightens up. Michel laughs and calls Momon.

'Momon, look what Lolo's got!'

Back in their cabin Lolo tells his daddy about everything he saw in the kitchen and especially about the jolly baker from

Marseilles. A knock at the door interrupts his flow. It is the chief second-class steward, John Hardy. He says he has to collect some papers, left by mistake in a car in the garage on F deck. He asks if the children would like to go with him and have a look at all the amazing cars there. It's a rare opportunity for the children to see such a fine collection of Daimlers, Rolls Royces, and Bugattis.

Michel is very touched he should find the time to be so thoughtful because he's a very busy man. He thanks Hardy and the children go off with him. Lolo is crazy about cars. He's really excited to be able to see all the cars in the garage belonging to the wealthy passengers on the ship. Most of the millionaires on the *Titanic* never move without their cars and drivers. The garage is behind the engine room. The most up-to-date luxury cars, representing the best the car industry has to offer, are parked on several levels in the garage.

Lolo is wide-eyed at the sight of these cars with their luxurious interiors of leather, mirrors, and cocktail cabinets. Their bodywork shines brightly thanks to the drivers who polish them every day. They look as if they have just emerged from a showroom. In the end, however, Lolo decides the smallest car there, a little French Panhard, is his favourite. He says the others are too big.

The day passes far too quickly for Michel and the children. They spend the afternoon on deck with Beesley, Pritchard, Mirella and Olaus who play the kind of deck games typical of all transatlantic crossings. First of all there is a sack race for the adults. They then go on to play deck hockey, badminton and even have a pillow fighting competition. Lolo and Momon have never seen grownups playing around like children before. They laugh till they cry with the other children who are watching their parents make fools of themselves. One of the other children, called Louise Laroche,[1] a little French girl of sixteen months, charms Lolo. Her face is covered in chocolate. Smiling at her, he tickles her under the chin.

That evening after dinner, at about nine o'clock, the chief steward, Hardy, is walking along the corridor past cabin twenty-six when he sees three mysterious figures coming out. There is a very small Roman Emperor crowned with a laurel wreath, an even smaller Pierrot, and a tall Columbine. Three characters straight out of the *Little Nemo* stories. The fancy dress party is a great success. A room has been specially decorated for the twenty-four children from second class. It has a dance floor and there is a big buffet. Lolo makes a new friend at the party. Her name is Lorraine Allison. She's a pretty little five-year-old from Montreal, the land of caribou and snow according to Lolo. She speaks French with a strange accent. They talk about all sorts of mysterious things together and dance a waltz several times. In-between dances, Lolo hears someone speaking with a Nice accent and discovers it is one of the musicians, Roger Bricoux, who comes from Monte Carlo. There are eight musicians in the band and Roger is very proud to have been offered a job on the *Titanic*. There had been a lot of applicants, much more experienced than he.

Knowing the children are in Mirella's good hands, Michel goes to the library hoping to find some peace and quiet. He wants, most of all, to avoid the fashion show arranged by Madame Lucile. She is supposed to be travelling incognito, under the name of Morgan. It is a pretty silly thing for someone, as well known as she is, to do. He buries his head in the latest edition of *Atlantic Daily* and finds out there is an eclipse of the sun tomorrow. It can be seen as a full eclipse in Saint Germain en Laye, a town just outside Paris and as a partial eclipse in Nice. Before he has time to finish the article he hears a familiar voice and Stead appears.

'Ah you're keeping out of the way too,' he says. 'That woman is fearsome. She's managed to get Bedford to go to her fashion show and you know as well as I how much he detests these things. Just imagine, because there are no professional models to hand she's persuaded all the women from first class to show her clothes. Of course now they're all competing to be the best model of the day; all, that is except Madeline Astor, who's been forbidden by John to join in, and our dear Ida who's with Isidor in their cabin. Even the middle-aged women are taking part in this ridiculous exhibitionism. I got out quick after a few minutes.'

He gets a newspaper and sits next to Michel reading it. A couple of hours later the two men are sitting in the Parisian Café with two large whiskeys. Stead starts pouring his heart out to Michel.

'You know, I'm extremely worried about what's going to happen to the *Titanic*.'

'But you must be joking!' exclaims Michel.

'Unfortunately no, I'm not joking. Look here, for a long time now, ever since their ships have got bigger and bigger, our captains have got into the annoying habit of neglecting the safety of passengers for the sake of speed. The game is all about this little Blue Ribbon. Rival companies take great pride in trying to snatch it from each other. The Cunard line has had it for several years and now the White Star Line is trying to get it off them. If the *Titanic* doesn't manage to break the speed record for an Atlantic crossing, Ismay has got another ship up his sleeve. Andrews has already designed a longer and faster one called the *Gigantic*. The company has sound financial backing so they they're not going to be beaten by anyone.'

'I beg to differ, Stead. If the *Titanic* sinks, she will obviously never be able to sail again, so the White Star Line will be completely compromised.'

'Maybe you're right,' Stead admitted. 'In any case this is the danger that hangs over us. There's a special term, "The angle", marking a point in the North Atlantic where ships going to New York change course so as to avoid floating ice. As a result of a meeting fourteen years ago, which Ismay attended, representatives of all the major transatlantic shipping companies agreed to move the famous "angle" further to the east. Instead of sailing due west and changing course at the last minute towards the south, near Newfoundland, it was decided ships should take a southern course much earlier. The voyage to New York is therefore lengthened. Needless to say, many ship's captains do not follow this rule. You'll see the *Titanic* also breaking the rule, probably with the White Star Line's blessing. They want to show other companies they are the best, rather than thinking about the safety of their passengers. But that's not all. Do you know how many lookouts are used for a quarter of the night? Two, perched fifty or so metres above the water in the crow's nest. What's more, the poor men don't even have any binoculars! They disappeared somewhere between Belfast and Cherbourg. An agent from the Cunard line or from Lloyds, went on board and spirited them away. How on earth can you see an iceberg from far away, even in daylight, without binoculars?'

'But,' cuts in Michel, 'I've heard icebergs shine brightly at night. They can be seen from a long way off.'

'That depends on how old the iceberg is, or, more correctly, how long it has been in the open air. If it's just left an ice floe, the ice is shiny and translucent and almost invisible at night so it can't be seen until the last moment. Which by then is too late. If it's been floating for a long time it becomes white and so it can be seen from a long way off. Another way of spotting an iceberg is by the foamy fringe that swirls round the base of it. Unless the sea is as calm as a millpond, in which case it disappears. We've got a sea like that at the moment. If this fine weather continues tomorrow, we'll have the worst possible conditions for going through this dangerous area.'

'Well then,' Michel laughs. 'It would be a good idea to write a will before tomorrow evening.'

Despite his laughter, Michel is concerned about the worried look on Stead's face.

'There's no doubt about it. The *Titanic* has only got sixteen lifeboats and four Engelhardt canvas boats. With so few boats, how on earth are more than half the passengers going to be saved? I heard Andrews saying each of the sixteen davits could hold two lifeboats, which would make enough to take off everyone if necessary, but the White Star Line decided to put only one in each. No doubt in the name of this wicked deception about the *Titanic* being unsinkable. So there we are, even in 1912 no one is safe from being shipwrecked…'

Michel is silent while Stead puffs at his pipe. The smell of Virginia tobacco hangs heavy in the air. Michel is stunned to see him able to envisage a catastrophe in such a calm frame of mind. But if what he says is true then he'll have to think hard about how to save himself and the children. He can just imagine the scene with crowds of people fighting to get into too few lifeboats. And the ensuing panic… No! Why think in this way! The possibility of an accident are minute. Nobody is going to put two thousand, two hundred and twenty two people at risk for the sake of a Blue Ribbon.

'Not facing up to the facts,' Stead goes on, 'is the most common thing in the world. Our multimillionaires on the *Titanic* are as blind to the possibility of her sinking, as the most ignorant immigrants in third class. For different reasons to be sure. The former have complete confidence in science, technology, and the industries they own, while the latter believe in miracles – one of which is the *Titanic*. It is a real miracle for everyone except us, my dear Hoffmann.'

If Stead stresses the gravity of the situation even though he knows it makes Michel nervous, it is only because he thinks he is helping him come to terms with the possibility of an accident. He is preparing him to be able to cope with the children. But it's more than Michel can take this evening. He gets up and politely says goodnight to the old man for whom he has a lot of respect, despite his gruff manner and a tendency to over-dramatise everything.

Lying on his bed later, Michel gazes at the sleeping children. Has he really exposed them to danger on the *Titanic*? Stead was so convincing about the possibilities of an accident. Michel felt unnerved by his words and that is why he suddenly got up and left. Now he is back in his quiet cabin he is able to brush aside the spectre of danger Stead had so bleakly outlined. How could he have such a lack of confidence in Captain Smith, a man of sixty and very experienced in his profession? This post on the *Titanic* is his last one. He's retiring next year so why should he compromise his reputation by taking foolish decisions, risking tragic consequences?

Although Michel has carefully tried to push his anxieties to the back of his mind, Stead's words have opened up a breech in the wall behind which they lie. He looks at his watch, another reminder of Marcelle. How on earth can he sleep with so many doubts and such remorse going round and round in his head? He gets up, puts some clothes on and goes down to the third class.

Every night in third class immigrants from all over Europe dance and drink till the early hours of the morning. The tables are overflowing with glasses and bottles of all kinds of drinks: Hungarian sweet wine, German wine, Yugoslavian slivovitz, Scandinavian vodka, Italian Chianti, and English beer. A Frenchman plays the accordion accompanied by Irish fiddlers and a man playing the spoons. People are dancing and shouting and enjoying themselves. Michel feels sleepy with the effect of alcohol and collapses into an armchair. Through his drunken stupor he thinks he can hear a violin coming towards him, creaking and groaning a mournful dirge.

Some time later Michel is awakened by a young Russian singing a sentimental song from his village and playing a balalaika. Michel feels his eyes flooding with tears. Images of his childhood in Slovakia float into his mind. It's a lost world. His family is all scattered because of immigration. He drinks glass after glass of vodka until he passes out. For the first and last time in his life, he has been drinking to forget. Eventually someone carries him back to his cabin and leaves him lying on his bed, fully dressed.

CHAPTER 9

IN THE ICE FLOES

LOLO HAS A STRANGE DREAM that night. He is drifting in darkness on one of the little paper boats he often used to make with his mummy. The sea is so calm, it seems almost solid. After a while the boat stops. He gets out and starts walking on the sea. It is freezing cold but he continues to walk until a huge transparent mountain, shining like a diamond, blocks his path. He is looking at the amazing landscape when he suddenly hears voices shouting for help. When he turns round, his boat has disappeared. Then he feels some big hands grab his ankles and try to pull him down into the depths of the sea.

He wakes up feeling terrified. He bursts into tears and runs to his daddy who is fast asleep on his bed, fully dressed. Lolo doesn't manage to wake Michel but does manage to wake Momon who immediately starts to cry. This commotion still doesn't bring Michel out of his heavy sleep. It is eight o'clock on the morning of 14 April 1912.

After a few minutes, the children, who are cuddling up to each other, stop crying and start to giggle. Because their daddy doesn't wake up, they dress themselves. Leaving the door open behind them, they run off to the second-class dining room where Trevor and Lawrence Beesley are having breakfast together. When they ask the boys where their daddy is, Lolo says he is still asleep.

Michel is splashing his head with cold water when the children get back to the cabin. A steward, concerned to find the cabin door open and no sign of the children, has awakened him.

Michel has taken some pills to alleviate a migraine and his black thoughts have disappeared. He feels full of energy and instead of being cross with Lolo for having gone off to the dining room unaccompanied; he congratulates his son on having used his initiative.

Half an hour later they are strolling on the upper deck and Michel's hangover has almost disappeared. It's a beautiful day with a very calm ocean reflecting the clear sky. The smooth surface of the water is like a baby's skin. There are neither waves nor the least bit of foam on the horizon. Deckchairs are full of sun worshippers but the deck is strangely silent. It was as if beasts, humans, wind and water were all observing the Lord's day of rest.

Michel is hoping to walk on deck until the morning service, at eleven, in the first-class dining room. In fact before then, at ten, if one can believe in the White Star Line's rules, there is a lifeboat drill. He thinks it is very important for them to join in the lifeboat drill. Ten o'clock passes and nothing happens. Perhaps Captain Smith is going to wait until everyone is gathered together for the service. In fact the lifeboat drill never materialises.

At that very moment, a meeting is taking place in the map room. Lord Ismay, officers Wilde, Murdoch and Lightoller together with the engineer, Andrews, are examining the map of the North Atlantic. They are looking at the area just south of Newfoundland where the *Titanic* will be sailing this evening. They're discussing the 'angle', the point where the ship changes course to avoid ice floes. The *Titanic*'s destiny lies in the hands of three men: Captain Smith whose career is at stake; Ismay, whose company is at stake; and Andrews, who has both his reputation and his largest ship at stake.

'Captain,' says Andrews pointing to an 'angle' that Ismay thinks is rather too cautious. 'It would be best to change course south here, before seven o'clock this evening. We will already be above the fortieth parallel and you know the hull of the *Titanic* isn't designed to withstand the force of ice floes.'

Ismay thinks the ship should continue its course due west and not change direction until tomorrow. Captain Smith, Murdoch and Lightoller seem to agree with him.

Suddenly the door opens and Bride comes in, puffing and panting, with a telegram in his hand. Captain Smith takes it and without looking at it puts it in his pocket. It is a message from the *Caronia* saying there are ice floes much further south than the usual 'angle'.

'I suggest,' continues Ismay, 'that we go on as far as 41 degrees north and about 49 degrees west. I'm sure your ship will withstand a few little pieces of ice, Mr Andrews. We're doing twenty-one knots this morning. Yesterday we covered more than five hundred miles. At this rate we will easily do more than six hundred miles today.'

Andrews protests at his suggestion but nobody listens to him. He can't make a decision by himself; the others have to agree. He decides to keep quiet, and hope frventlythat everything will be fine.

The Captain was going to be late for the service in the first-class dining room; it is already ten fifty-five. He leaves the service early, forgetting about the lifeboat drill. The Navratils have waited in vain.

The special Sunday lunch finishes at about three o'clock. Afterwards, Mirella and Olaus suggest a game of bridge in the lounge but Trevor declines. He's going to the radio room and Lolo, whom he invites to go with him, is overjoyed with the idea. They find turmoil when they get there. The transmitter is not working properly and Phillips thinks the condensers have burned out. He has taken the machine to pieces. The pile of private messages on the table, waiting to be sent, is growing bigger and bigger. What a lot of work there will be that night. Knowing quite a bit about such things, Trevor helps Phillips with the transmitter while Lolo stands by Bride who is in the process of receiving messages. The day before a message had come from the *Rappabannock* warning about a large ice floe. It had damaged the ship and was now travelling in the direction of the *Titanic*. Bride had taken the message sent from the *Caronia*, to Captain Smith. Since then, there had been more ice warnings from below the forty-second parallel. One from the *Noordam* at 11.40am, a second from the *Baltic* at 1.42pm, and a third from the *Amerika* at 1.45pm. Bride had delivered them all to Captain Smith but he had simply stuffed them into his pocket unopened. It wasn't a radio officer's job to worry about the captain's reaction to messages. His job was simply to pass messages on.

Because nobody comes to collect Lolo, Trevor takes him back to the cabin where Michel and Momon are resting. He then returns to the radio room.

Michel is awakened at 7.30am by the children arguing. The cabin is unusually cold and when he opens the porthole, an icy draught blows in. Noticing small icicles on the outside frame of the porthole, he quickly closes it and takes some fur coats, specially made for this trip, out of the trunk. Lolo and Momon can't believe their eyes. They had always thought fur coats were only for grownups. Putting them on, they both admire themselves in the mirror before going to the boat deck. While they had been taking a nap, the air temperature had dropped by 9 degrees to zero. The sea had started to freeze over at minus 2 degrees.

'Why is it so cold, Daddy? It was very nice this afternoon. The sun was like the sun in our garden.'

Michel and the boys wander up and down the deck. The sun is low on the horizon and the ocean, smooth and flat, is like a trough of molten silver. The vast sky is a strange transparent blue, shining like an ice cave.

The *Titanic* is now travelling faster than it ever has since they left Southampton. As the bow ploughs through the deep water it leaves soft lines in its wake. This strangely lit universe fascinates the Navratils, including Momon. They lean on the rail watching the distant horizon running away from them. It is a voyage through time rather than space, surrounded by a silence both physical and magical.

Despite nagging worries, Michel calmly explains they are approaching a very cold part of the ocean. He says icebergs will soon surround them.

'Under the ocean there's a kind of cold river called the Labrador Current. It carries huge blocks of ice from ice fields in the north as well as pieces of glaciers that fall into the fjords in Greenland. These séracs[1] fill the ocean over areas of hundreds of metres. They are like floating mountains and can be as high as a hundred metres. They're called icebergs. Beneath the surface they are eight or nine times bigger. Sometimes they can over turn so it's not a good idea to be too near one!'

Lolo loves listening to his daddy explaining things, even if he doesn't always understand everything. Fjords, ice fields and icebergs are such mysterious words to him. The strange sound of them fills him with pleasure. He imagines an incredible landscape where the sky itself is frozen; soft-eyed reindeer pull Father Christmas in a sleigh full of toys with little Lorraine sitting on a fur-covered throne.

Michel thinks about Ida and Isidor Straus and shivers. This evening he is unable to throw off Stead's depressing predictions. They seem to be less of a fantasy than they did the previous evening. Perhaps danger is now more real because they are approaching the ice floes. But he can't believe and doesn't want to believe what Stead told him. He can't imagine himself getting the children ready for a possible shipwreck. It seems crazy. Better to be like everyone else and believe the *Titanic* is unsinkable.

The weather is getting colder and colder so he suggests they go to the gym to warm up a bit. Lolo and Momon have turns on the bicycles and then Lolo shows his little brother how to row. The instructor, MacCawley, noticing how determined Lolo is, shows him how to push the oars without letting them go too far down into the water.

As the Navratils are leaving the gym, Trevor hurries past without noticing them. It's seven fifty five and he's on his way back from the radio room where Bride has been showing him the ice warnings. In addition to those received from the *Caronia*, the *Noordam*, the *Baltic* and the *Amerika*, there have also been two messages one after the other from the *Californian*. Together with the *Caronia*, her captain has decided to drop anchor for a day in order to miss the ice floe. The warnings all confirm there is an ice floe of a hundred and fifty kilometres long, blocking the *Titanic*'s path.

When Bride had delivered the ice warning messages to the bridge, he had overheard orders being given for all lights on the ship to be kept on, as a security measure. He had also been there when Boxhall, who was relieving Pitman on a new shift, was told the exact position of the *Titanic*.

For the second-last dinner of the voyage, the Navratils are invited to join Lord Bedford in the French restaurant. Lolo is thrilled at the idea of seeing Andrews again as well as, perhaps, the Captain. They arrive early. While waiting for Charles, they take a short stroll on the neighbouring promenade deck. Lolo spots Bedford. He is accompanied by a French friend, Pierre Maréchal, the famous pilot, who has also been invited to dinner. Even if Michel hadn't known he was French, he would have guessed he was because of the way he looks. He is a very small man with a huge moustache and shiny black hair combed flat, with a side parting. On his long nose there's a pair of tiny round spectacles. A pilot. What a stroke of luck for Lolo! He already has a lot of questions on the tip of his tongue but, although it's very difficult, he has to be patient. Pierre Maréchal doesn't waste any time telling aviation anecdotes.

'A month never passes without a well-known pilot disappearing,'[2] he says.

Lolo asks if pilots could avoid accidents by jumping out of their planes with an umbrella. The suggestion makes Pierre Maréchal laugh.

'What are you going to do with this child,' he says to Michel. 'It seems to me you've got a ready-made engineer here. Listen, little fellow, an Austrian called François Reichelt invented a sort of umbrella, he called a parachute, for jumping out of a plane when it's flying. By using it the pilot can land safely on the ground. Unfortunately for him, he hadn't quite got it right. Last February he jumped off the Eiffel Tower to test it and was killed because it didn't work. However I still think it's an excellent idea!'

Lolo takes in everything that Maréchal is saying. He is very impressed to hear how a woman called Harriet Quimbey had just crossed the Channel on a solo flight, less than three years after Louis Blériot. It had paved the way for other women to achieve successes in the twentieth century in what had, up to then, been exclusively a masculine domain.

'The world of aviation,' he goes on, 'is fast making remarkable progress. For example, there is also Salmet who has recently flown London to Paris non-stop, not to mention hydroplanes that the navy is soon going to be using.'

This evening the children have their own special menu suggested by Mr Gatti, the restaurant manager. It includes guinea fowl legs with mashed chestnuts and strawberry tart with ice-cream. They have real crystal wine glasses just like the grownups and a waiter regularly tops up them up with their special 'wine' which is cold raspberry syrup.

Lolo, exchanging knowing looks from time to time with his daddy and Charles, doesn't miss a word Maréchal is saying. Momon goes to sleep between the cheese and the dessert course, his curly head resting on the table. Glass globes decorated with flowers, are scattered on the tables, giving out a warm glow. The room is filled with the chinking of silver cutlery on porcelain, the clinking of glasses and the musical voices of women. This evening there is an air of happiness, harmony, and serenity in the dining room. Warmed by this feeling of security, Michel looks for Stead, but cannot see him.

It's 10pm before the meal comes to an end and it's time to put Lolo and Momon to bed. As Michel gets up to take them to the cabin, the Captain leaves Widener's table and goes to the map room to find out the exact position of the *Titanic*. Arriving on the bridge where Murdoch is about to take over from Lightoller, the Captain notices the thermometer is registering a half-degree below zero. He looks at a message that Bride has just brought,[3] asks Murdoch to reduce the speed of the ship and to wake him up if it gets foggy. Then, without further ado, he goes off to his cabin.

Murdoch starts his watch on the bridge while Frederick Fleet and Reginald Lee, who have just relieved their predecessors in the crow's nest, scour the dimly lit horizon. The floating ice has increased but they haven't yet seen any sign of an iceberg. The *Titanic* is going at twenty-one knots.

Momon doesn't wake up when Michel puts him to bed and Lolo, after an exhausting day, goes to sleep immediately.

Michel isn't at all sleepy so he goes for a walk around the ship. First, he goes down to F deck and into the third-class dining room where, as usual, there's a noisy party atmosphere. Otto Schmidt is playing the piano, banging out chords with his left hand while his right hand runs up and down the keys. Michel watches him for a moment. The young people he had been with the previous evening ask him to join them. Olaus and Mirella are waltzing, getting dizzier and dizzier, but Michel has no urge to dance with a stranger. He slips away leaving behind the strains of the waltz.

Taking the stairs, he goes along the white corridor leading to his cabin. He listens outside the door for a moment. The children are sound asleep so he goes off to the second-class dining room. He finds about a hundred people gathered together, with RP Carter, for evening prayers. People are singing hymns accompanied by a young man on a piano. Michel quietly closes the door and goes to the library. It is almost empty. He bumps into Beesley, who is just going back to his cabin after having spent the evening reading, and has a chat with him. Beesley is carrying several books and intends to read in his cabin. Michel thinks he should do the same. Finally, he decides he really feels like having some company. He goes up to the first-class smoking room, hoping to find either Charles Bedford or Stead.

CHAPTER 10

ICEBERG STRAIGHT AHEAD

WITH THE EXCEPTION OF the smoking room, where groups of people are playing bridge or sitting around chatting, the first-class lounges are deserted that evening. Most passengers are feeling tired because of the icy north wind, and have gone to bed earlier than usual.

Charles is engaged in a lively discussion with Harry Widener, Clarence Moore, a keen hunter, and Major Archibald Butt. The major's very short hair is hidden under a peaked cap and his thick neck is tightly encased in a stiff military collar. Charles acknowledges Michel with a nod of his head but Stead is not there. Michel is overcome with gnawing apprehension, and he can't seem to throw it off.

The ship is nearing the ice area. But she has obviously not changed course in order to avoid the ice floe mentioned in the messages received during the day. The unsinkable *Titanic* is going to be tested by icebergs. So be it. Michel will help in the confrontation between the iron giant and the ice monsters. A much better idea than shutting himself in the cabin and hiding his head in his pillow. It means he will be one of the first to get the children out of danger if there is an accident. He goes to the upper deck where his eyes take about five minutes to adjust to the darkness. He walks to the front of the ship, not far from the crow's nest where the two lookouts are scouring the horizon. The Captain has given orders for the lights on the front upper deck to be turned off so the lookouts won't be distracted. Michel is amazed to discover the *Titanic* is travelling completely in the dark without a single light to illuminate the way ahead. What's more, the crow's nest is about twenty metres from the prow of the ship. It doesn't exactly make the lookouts' job very easy, especially since they don't have any binoculars. There's no moon but it's a beautiful starlit night. Although it's about minus two degrees and freezing cold, Michel is snug and warm in his silver-fox-lined coat, identical to the ones he had made for Ida and Isidor Straus. Leaning on the rail he looks at the stars and dreams about space, wondering if one day perhaps man might conquer it. He notices the halos of light around the lamps at the back of the boat where thousands of little ice needles are hanging, dancing in the air.

He stares at the ocean. It is so immobile it seems to be paralysed. Then he suddenly realises, what he is seeing is not water, but ice. A thin film of it has started to cover the surface, making the ocean look totally immobile. Here and there he can see large areas of ice forming greyish bundles. They float on the surface and beyond them, in the distance, he can just make out a tall dark shape, probably several hundreds of metres long. Suddenly a familiar voice beside him warms his heart. It is Stead.

'There we are! Wasn't I right? Look how we're charging through an ice field! D'you think Murdoch has taken the initiative of slowing down the ship? Certainly not, because he doesn't want to risk losing his job. He's already been demoted in favour of Wilde,[1] provisionally of course, he doesn't believe it's permanent. And our dear Captain is soundly asleep.'

In reality Stead was wrong because on Captain Smith's orders, Murdoch had reduced speed, from twenty-two knots to twenty-one, but the difference was hardly noticeable.

Stead continues after a long silence.

'You know as well as I, we have no chance of avoiding a

collision. Even if we avoid one, two, or even three, icebergs we'll hit the fourth one. What d'you think those poor lookouts can do without binoculars? They can't possibly see any icebergs till the last moment. By then it'll be too late to avoid hitting them. So when will the catastrophe be? D'you want to bet on it? I give us less than an hour before we have a collision.'

Lost in thought Michel doesn't say anything, in fact he hasn't heard a word Stead has been saying because the whole situation is completely unreal. This huge vessel, symbol of progress and the victory of man over nature is heading for a point of no return into the dark obscurity of an invincible frozen monster. More than ever he has the sensation of travelling in time and he feels a thousand years old.

It is 11.30pm and at this moment Mirella and Olaus are dancing in the third-class dining room. Suddenly Mirella sees something flash by. Turning her head, she sees a huge rat running panic stricken across the room. She screams hysterically and feels faint. While Olaus takes care of her, Daniel Buckley, Martin Callagher and Carl Johnson chase the rat, followed by the rest of the young people. Unfortunately, someone comes into the room just as the rat reaches the door and it disappears.

Mirella recovers from the shock of seeing the rat but she is convinced it is a sign of bad luck. She clings to Olaus who tries to comfort her. Finally, they leave and go to Olaus's cabin. They have to take Scotland Road, alias Park Lane to get to it because it is at the front of the ship, a few metres from the waterline. The area is for men only and, in theory, Mirella is not supposed to be there but they reach cabin E 10 without bumping into anyone.

In the radio room Phillips is working flat out and Trevor is helping him. Bride, exhausted with his comings and goings to the bridge, has gone off to his cabin to get some sleep. He's supposed to relieve Phillips at midnight rather than at two o'clock because poor Phillips is at the end of his tether. After managing to repair the transmitter at seven o'clock that evening he had found hundreds of personal messages waiting to be sent all over the world. Among them were numerous bets about the speed of the ship.

At 10.30pm the *Rappahannock* had signaled for the second time about the presence of icebergs in the area and Trevor had sent the message to the bridge. For the past half-hour Phillips has been trying to send a betting message to Cap Race. Just as he finally manages to get through, Evans, the radio officer from the *Californian*, interrupts him to warn she is completely at a standstill in the ice, not far from the *Titanic*. Phillips is exhausted and, unable to cope with two jobs at once, shouts without listening to what he is saying.

'Silence, silence! I'm on the line with Cap Race!'

Evans doesn't push the matter and, closing the transmission room on the *Californian*, goes off to bed. The *Californian* is only fifteen miles away but no one on board the *Titanic* is aware of how close she is. The message that Evans sent from the *Californian* never reached the Bridge.

High up in the crow's nest, Frederick Fleet and Reginald Lee are very tense watching the immense darkness. Their eyes are very tired. They've already seen the outlines of large dark shapes on the horizon several times. They sense danger and are worried because, despite icebergs being in the area, the ship hasn't changed course.

That morning, when they had been in the map room, hadn't Andrews, the engineer, spoken about going south at about 7.00pm? It's now 11.35pm and yet nothing has happened. The ship is still going due west. They are especially worried by the clear translucent night. There is neither the trace of mist nor the slightest sound. It is like sliding on a mirror. It's too simple, too easy. Will they suddenly be taken by surprise by something that doesn't first loom up?

Aware of their heavy responsibilities they scrutinise the horizon, one beyond the portside and the other beyond the starboard. Suddenly Fleet shouts, 'Lee, Look!'

Taking one look at the dark outline five hundred metres in front of them he grabs the telephone and calls the bridge.

'Iceberg straight ahead!'

'Thank you,' replies Murdoch phlegmatically, before shouting to the helmsman, 'Starboard hard down!'

Having given this order he runs to the speaking tube and shouts an order for the engines to be shut off then put into reverse. This automatically activates the doors closing the watertight compartments. The helmsman pulls the wheel over with all his weight so the ship will turn away from the iceberg. But because of her size, the giant responds slowly. She needs about twenty seconds to obey the order. She starts to turn at the same moment as she hits the iceberg, thirty-seven seconds after the lookout has shouted. The gigantic block of treacherous ice, only five or six metres from the waterline, scratches the starboard side of the *Titanic*. The steel plates are very fragile because of the icy water, and burst open in six places underneath the waterline.[2] The rivets shatter and despite being small, the breaches in the side of the ship let in a lot of water.

While this is happening, Michel and Stead, leaning on the rail side by side on the portside, are interrupted in their silent thoughts by an unexpected movement of the ship. The *Titanic* is turning sideways!

Stead automatically puts his hand in a pocket and takes out his watch. It's exactly 11.40pm. They look at each other. Suddenly they see a huge dark shape passing about six metres below them, close to B deck. It seems to brush against the *Titanic* but they don't feel the slightest impact. Michel bursts into laughter.

'That's the first one! I should take off my hat to you, Stead, you're right!'

Stead signals for him to be quiet, and listens. Thirty seconds pass and suddenly the ship stops. A heavy silence fills the deck; there's no longer any vibration. It is as if they are suspended in mid-air. It's all so strange. Michel feels the need to touch Stead to make sure he's still there. Suddenly the sound of footsteps makes them jump. Captain Smith, Murdoch and Boxhall, one of the officers, lean over the rail.

'Yes, it's certainly an iceberg!' exclaims the Captain. 'Boxhall, go down to the engine room and find out if there's any sign of water!'

The Captain, who sleeps lightly when he is on board, had felt a quiver and had immediately woken up. Since he had taken the precaution of sleeping in his clothes, all he had to do was to put on his jacket before dashing to the nearby bridge. He congratulates Murdoch on his presence of mind and waits quietly for Boxhall's report.

As for everyone else, nobody on the ship thought the *Titanic* had been touched. The majority of people had heard nothing more than a slight noise, like a piece of fabric being torn or, lower down, like the sound of a knife being sharpened. Crockery had chinked in the first-class dining room where several stewards and waiters were sat around resting after their work. Charles Joughin, the French baker, was kneading some dough when a saucepan, balanced on the corner of a shelf, rolled on to the floor. Lawrence Beesley who was reading in his cabin noticed the light vibration, usually making the curtains move a little, had stopped. By contrast, Mirella and Olaus in their little cabin on level E on starboard, just above the collision, were covered in pieces of ice tumbling through the half open porthole. They heard a sound like tearing steel.

The Captain and officers return to the bridge where

everything seems to be in order. Michel and Stead slowly go towards the stairs. The old journalist has recovered from the uneasiness that took him to the deck and feels tired.

People are now rushing on to the upper deck. They are curious. They want to know why the ship has come to a stop. Andrews walks by looking preoccupied. He has had an urgent call to go to the bridge. Ismay follows him, a short way behind. Then the Captain appears, asking people to return to their cabins or the lounges. Nothing serious has happened.

Michel feels as if a heavy weight has been lifted off his shoulders. Even if Stead was right to think the worst, he presumes the possibility of a collision is much less now. After this incident, the officers will be extremely cautious and vigilant. As soon as the *Titanic* gets underway, every precaution will be taken to avoid an accident. Without giving 'the incident' any further thought, and letting Stead get on with his own observations on the subject, he goes and joins Charles and his friends in the smoking lounge.

There is less optimism on the bridge. Boxhall has reported there is no sign of damage and everything is in order. But Smith is not very happy with such a superficial inspection. He orders him to go down again and contact the crew in charge of the engine room and the stokeholds. He's to inspect the hold and the watertight compartments to see if there is any sign of damage.

Boxhall isn't keen on going so far. Almost immediately he comes across Charles Henrickon, the chief stoker, who runs towards him.

'Stokeholds five and six are flooded! He shouts, gasping breathlessly. 'I was in the middle of working in five when there was a terrible noise. Water came pouring in and we saw a tear in the hull about sixty centimetres long. I ran to six where it was even worse because the hull was open in several places! Two stokers were having a chat in-between shovelling when the alarm went off. The red light went on, as it did in number five, above the watertight compartment, and the door immediately closed. The water rushed in and the stokers barely had time to leap on to the emergency ladder to avoid being drowned!'

Boxhall is just about to go off and report all this to the Captain when someone shouts to him. It's one of the postal workers, and he's very agitated.

'Mr Boxhall! The post rooms are under water and its nearly reached G deck in five minutes! We're having to move the mail sacks into steerage!'

So, despite appearances, the situation is serious. Boxhall gets back to the bridge at the same time as the second-in-command, Wilde. They have a meeting. Murdoch cannot be blamed any more than the lookouts.

Smith thinks about their request this morning. If he had ordered one of his officers to give his binoculars to Fleet or Lee, this catastrophe might never have happened. He feels very guilty about it. Suddenly he remembers another error he has made. One with equally serious consequences: he forgot to order the lifeboat drill. It is unforgivable.

The door opens and Andrews, wearing evening dress, rushes in. He's just been to have a quick look at the damage. He is beside himself with anger. Two seconds later, Ismay looking equally out of place, opens the door. He's wearing slippers and pyjamas with a coat hurriedly thrown over his shoulders to cover his nightclothes. There is a brief silence. Nobody dares speak. Andrews in despair, thinks what a terrible mistake he made that morning by not insisting his advice about the 'angle' be taken seriously. Finally, he joins Wilde, Murdoch and Ismay who are standing by Captain Smith. The Captain's looking anxiously at the clinometer. The ship is listing five degrees towards starboard and it is only ten minutes after the collision. They all look at each other, their faces deathly pale under the brightly shining electric lights.

'Captain, do you think it is serious?' asks Ismay in a trembling voice.

'I don't just think it is. I'm certain it is! Come with me Wilde, and you too, Andrews, we're going down to see the damage for ourselves.'

Lightoller and Pitman, asleep in their cabin, were woken up by a shuddering noise when the ship collided with the iceberg. Lightoller went on to the deck in his pyjamas, looked both at the starboard and the portside and not being able to see anything unusual, was on his way back to the cabin when he bumped into Boxhall. Hearing there had been a collision, he immediately got dressed and went to the bridge. Pitman too, was trying to find out what had happened when he ran into a gang of stokers carrying their bags to the upper deck.

'What's happening?'

'Water's got into the stokeholds! Our dormitory's already under a foot of water. It's at the front, near the portside and it'll be completely flooded in less than an hour. We're moving our things upstairs.'

Smith and Andrews, back from their inspection, are briefing all the officers, apart from Lowe, who is still sleeping.

'Gentlemen,' says Smith, 'I regret to inform you that the *Titanic* has not got long to live. You know as well as I, the carina is only twice the height of a man. Unfortunately the collision has happened just under the waterline, approximately at level H, in a place where the carina is not reinforced. Six compartments have been hit. The iceberg scraped against the ship making six small holes in the riveted area.'

'But,' protests Ismay, 'we can mange for a long time with six compartments flooded.'

'No, Mr Ismay,' cuts in Andrews, despondently, 'the ship can handle three flooded watertight compartments but no more.

You seem to forget, only the bulkheads of compartments one to five, joining D deck, are completely watertight. The others stop at F deck. The progression of the flooding is fatal: sooner or later the water from number six will flow over into seven and so on. The rivets in the hull have burst open over an area of about a square metre, which means seven hundred tonnes of water a second is flowing into the ship. In an hour, even taking into consideration the pumps, there will be nineteen thousand cubic metres in the front hold and twice that volume in two hours. The first six compartments, as well as the post room and the squash court are already flooded. The *Titanic* will sink in about two and a quarter hours!' Oh! What insight that little boy has! He says to himself. No, my design is not perfect, no, the *Titanic* is not unsinkable…

'So, gentlemen, you know what has to be done.' says Captain Smith.

'Lightoller,' he orders, 'take charge of embarking the odd numbers on starboard and you, Murdoch, the even numbers! Boxhall, go and find the passenger allocation list. Most of the mechanics and stokers should stay where they are right up to the end so they can keep the pumps and the electricity generators going for as long as possible. Send the coal trimmers and stokers who aren't busy, to help the crew. As for you, gentlemen,' he says, turning to the rest of the officers, 'go and wake up the passengers and tell them to put on their life-jackets. Ask them to wait for the embarkation signal. When the signal is given, make sure the passengers from each class go the embarkation area allotted to them. Don't make any exceptions to this rule or else we'll have total panic.'

Meanwhile, Phillips is still sending private messages. He is so absorbed in his work, he doesn't immediately realise the ship has stopped.

Quarter of an hour has passed since the accident: it is 11.55pm when the alarm clock rings in the next door cabin. Bride who is relieving Phillips at midnight, is finding it very difficult to wake up. He is sitting on the edge of his bunk when a terrible din breaks out above them, making it impossible to hear the transmitter. Phillips jumps up and opens the door to see what the noise is all about.

'What's going on, Jack? It's like a thousand train engines whistling all at once!' he shouts.

Down below in the engine room the crew is making a superhuman effort to stop the engines. Steam is coming out of all the safety valves, the joints, and any possible hole that it can escape through. The noise is so unbearable that Bride puts a jacket on over his pyjamas and goes on to the deck. The three funnels are sending out jets of steam so powerful, it is like a volcanic explosion. He immediately goes back into the cabin and carefully closes the door. This terrible din will continue for nearly two hours, gradually getting softer but bothering everyone on board. The noise level eventually increases passengers' worries and anxieties.

Bride exchanges some small talk with Phillips who then goes to his little cubby-hole of a cabin, and starts to gather together some clothes. It is exactly midnight.

CHAPTER 11

A Child Disappears!

'COME ALONG, get up Lolo!'

The child takes a minute to surface from sleep. Trevor is already reconsidering whether he should have come to disturb his little friend. He is just about to leave when a sleepy little voice mumbles, 'What? What is it?'

He rubs his eyes. Trevor finds some warm clothes and talks to Lolo while hurriedly dressing him.

'We've bumped into an iceberg. There's a huge piece of ice on the third-class promenade, on D deck, near the prow. You've never seen ice before have you? It's not something to be missed!'

Lolo gradually wakes up properly. Ice? Like in the *Little Nemo* stories? He can't wait to see it. Trevor carefully closes the cabin door, leaving Momon sleeping peacefully, and they set off for D deck. But they lose their way because there are so many twists and turns. In the maze of corridors and doors, they end up where they started off and decide to go down to Scotland Road. At least they won't get lost there.

Ten minutes later they reach D deck. It's covered in chunks of ice; a piece of iceberg, weighing several tonnes, broke up when it fell near the mizzenmast. It looked as if the mast along with the crow's nest had almost been knocked over. Fleet and Lee had managed to escape just in time.

On the upper deck, four storeys above Lolo and Trevor, some first-class passengers are standing in the exact place where, twenty minutes earlier Stead and Navratil had seen the iceberg. It's an excellent position from which the millionaires can watch the emigrants having snowball fights. Some of the young people like Jack Thayer and Harry Widener are green with envy and are eager to join in.

In the middle of the noisy crowd of laughing third-class passengers, Lolo picks up pieces of ice and watches as they melt in his hand. How mysterious it is, so beautiful, so shiny, and turning so quickly into little drops of water!

Near him, Trevor cranes his neck looking for Mirella who he hasn't seen since the evening before; even though Olaus is now looking after her, he still feels a certain responsibility for the beautiful young woman.

He suddenly notices a distinguished looking grey-haired man, dressed in navy uniform, with braid on his sleeves, doing something really strange. He could be taken for an officer. He is bending down filling a silver ice bucket with pieces of ice. He is Ben Guggenheim's valet and on his master's request, he's picking up pieces of the iceberg for his whiskey!

'You know what, Lolo,' says Trevor, 'this ice isn't salty. Taste some if you like!'

Lolo tastes some. The ice melts in his mouth and he would like to pour some raspberry syrup into it. He thinks he will never find such delicious barley sugar again. But where does this ice come from?

Lolo looks overboard. Not far away he can see dark, still, menacing, large black shapes coming out of the water. Dark giants with bad intentions. But Trevor reassures him. These are icebergs but they're not dangerous because the *Titanic* is unsinkable. Lolo remembers the watertight compartments that aren't watertight. He associates these large dark shapes with death, coming to take away all the passengers on the *Titanic*. He thinks he's going to die. It doesn't scare him. On the contrary,

God had said: 'Let the little children come unto me!' It would be funny to get to know another world!

Quarter of an hour passes. Little by little, people on deck go back to their cabins to escape from the cold. Most of them, not wanting to miss this amazing sight, had run to the deck in their nightclothes. Nobody feels there is any danger and they happily go back to their cabins.

Trevor and Lolo don't feel the cold. But Trevor is a little worried when he thinks about the messages Harold received during the afternoon. Despite all the warnings, the *Titanic* had not changed course. Influenced by Bride and Phillips, he too had not thought the warnings to be important. But now, he feels concerned by them. He thinks about Mirella and he misses her. He stops Daniel Buckley just as he's going back to the dining room where people dance every evening. Yes, he saw Mirella dancing with Olaus.

'Are you coming Lolo? We'll go and find her. I'll take you back to your cabin a little later.'

They go back down to Scotland Road via a service staircase. Much to their surprise, on reaching the beginning of the corridor that runs the length of the ship, they see it is covered in a shallow film of water, stretching out of sight along the immense sloping corridor. There's a bustle of activity. Crew, stokers, coal trimmers, electricians, and mechanics are all gradually being chased from their places of work or their dormitories by the water. They're running away from the flooding. Some of them are grabbing precious odds and ends from their cabins and running to the upper deck. The lifeboats have started to be prepared. Ordered to help with this manoeuvre, they are carrying their bags with them. Everyone is shouting because of the noisy whistling from the funnels. Trevor thinks he's dreaming. The sight of what is going on in Scotland Road, empty twenty minutes earlier, is now really worrying him.

Lolo, watching the strange things taking place, bombards Trevor with questions.

'What's happening? Why is there water in the corridor? Are the watertight compartments full too?'

Trevor is so overcome he cannot answer. He is beginning to understand the seriousness of the situation. It's an indisputable fact: the ship's taking in water! He can hardly think straight. Lolo isn't frightened; on the contrary he's excited. Trying to take in this bizarre scene, they both stand still for a few moments, their feet in water.

The hustle and bustle above them is on the increase. More and more people are rushing to go upstairs and Trevor thinks he can see familiar faces. He automatically rubs his eyes. Recovering from his momentary surprise, he finally thinks about the danger Lolo is in. He grabs him by the hand and sets off, with the majority of the others who are running as fast as they can, to the back of the ship. Suddenly he hears a voice behind him.

'Hello old boy! D'you know we're being chased from our cabins by water? This damn iceberg has collided with us. It's made a hole in the hull!'

It's Martin Callagher speaking. His cabin is at the back of F deck, below Olaus's cabin. That evening he had decided to read rather than join the others and had heard the same noise of tearing steel that Mirella and Olaus had heard, only louder because of the proximity of the impact. He had jumped out of bed to go and find out what had happened and when he got back, there was two feet of water in his cabin.

Carried along by the anxious crowd, Trevor and Lolo reach a small service staircase where they stop to catch their breath. Trevor lets go of Lolo's hand and sits him on a nearby step. Lolo looks at the crowd below. A thought flashes through his mind: if the ship is taking in water, Momon, all alone in the cabin, is in danger. What's more, his daddy is going to be very worried that his big boy isn't there. Without thinking, he joins the crowd.

Carl Johnson had joined them. He was talking to Trevor.

'Have you seen Mirella?'

'I saw her dancing with Olaus before the collision. But seeing a rat terrified her. They left the dining room together and I haven't seen her since.'

Trevor suddenly feels panicky. He curses his stupidity. Why on earth did he bring Lolo here at such a dangerous time? Michel would be looking for Lolo to make sure he was safe. If the *Titanic* is taking in water she could easily sink. My God! A shipwreck! There's not a minute to lose. He puts out his hand and looks down. Lolo has disappeared...

Up above in the first-class smoking lounge all the doors have been closed because of the loud whistling noise. Conversation continues relentlessly. There is a total lack of understanding about the peril the ship is in. Bedford is busy talking politics. He is calculating the chances of the German socialists after their last success in the Reichstag elections. He's stressing the danger of pan-Germanism and the imperialistic politics of Kaiser Wilhelm II, to a German called Alfred Nourney[1] They're having a fierce argument. Not far away, Michel, feeling completely at ease, is listening with great interest as some millionaires recall the early days of the railway in the United States. They're saying what a great step forward it was when the east was joined to the west by the transcontinental railway in 1869.

Navratil was asked about his projects in New York. He has taken Isidor Straus's proposition very seriously. He's thinking about introducing a line of luxury ready-to-wear fashion in Macy's department stores. This idea of this young man starting anew seduces his listeners who talk movingly about their history. They recall the heroic past when their families emigrated from old Europe to the United States. Nearly everyone else here is second-generation born American.

'European immigrants are a real godsend for shipping companies,' laughs Charles Hays, 'like the settlers in the Far West for American railways! The White Star Line understands the former and you'll see rival companies following suit. It's in their interest.'

Bedford, looking worried, joins the group.

'Excuse me for interrupting the conversation, gentlemen, but haven't any of you noticed the strange tilt of the liquid in our glasses?'

At first no one understands what he is saying. Then they take a look. It's true. The whiskey and the brandy in their glasses is at an angle of about twelve degrees. The men look at each other dumbfounded. Nobody dares make a remark about the situation. Then Harry Widener says mockingly, 'This is just collective hysterics, my friends! Open your eyes! Take a grip of yourselves!'

Michel hasn't the heart to reply. So the iceberg has damaged the *Titanic*. Is the situation therefore serious? Could old Stead be right?

Widener, Thayer, and Major Archie Butt are just going towards the door when Captain Smith walks in. He is frowning and his lips seem thinner than usual.

'Gentlemen, I regret to inform you the situation is worrying. Go to your cabins, dress warmly, take the minimum amount of things, and proceed to the upper deck. The stewards have already alerted your families. Fasten your life-jackets and wait for the call to board the lifeboats.'

Smith walks off. Major Butt follows him and says in a low voice, 'Board the lifeboats? You're joking Captain! For a little list of ten degrees? But the *Titanic* is unsinkable!'

'So unsinkable she only has two hours to live! G, F and E decks are under water at the front. The situation is catastrophic. Keep it to yourself or else there will be panic on board. But persuade your friends, as best you can, to hurry up and to follow my instructions.'

Butt slowly returns to the smokers who are waiting in silence for him.

'Gentlemen, make no mistake, the situation is serious. Don't waste any time! Go and find your loved ones and do as the Captain ordered!'

There was an outcry at his words. Everyone was convinced from the beginning that even God could not sink this ship and she was going to sink? It's a joke! The ship will at least stay afloat until help arrives.

Bedford, remembering Lolo's answers to his questions about the water tightness of the ship, starts to speak.

'Unfortunately gentlemen, only the compartments in the bow and the stern are really watertight. The rest are joined to each other. In these conditions, the flow of the water is mathematical, we're going to sink…'

This statement is unquestionable. Everyone goes silently in the direction of his or her cabin. Bedford looks for Michel but he has disappeared. Captain Smith's warning had been enough for him. So, the iceberg had mortally wounded the iron steam-ship and neither Stead nor Michel had believed it. The light touch of the Ice Mountain had seemed like a caress in the darkness, but it had mercilessly torn the hull.

So much time lost talking and listening to these wealthy men with their fat investments. Suddenly in the face of danger it all seems so pathetic. And the children are alone. What if the steward has already led them away? What if he doesn't manage to find them? The idea of it makes his hair stand on end. He thinks about the sixteen lifeboats up there. They can't save more than half the passengers. And the icy ocean is three or four kilometres deep. Gathering all his strength he has only one objective: to save the children and to save himself with them. He runs off, battling with the dense crowd. A strange crowd, coming and going, intertwining like phantoms on staircases and corridors. An atmosphere like the Venice carnival! People are dressed in the most incredible ways: pyjamas, diaphanous, revealing nightgowns over which has been thrown a sable cape, or a Siberian wolf coat, bath robes, evening gowns, evening dress with black bow ties, starched collars, tweed suits, rolled neck sweaters, wide brimmed hats with flowers or feathers, fur boots, mules on bare feet, patent leather shoes, a complete jumble of clothing half covered with large light-coloured life-jackets.

Michel seems to be the only one panicking. He stumbles into people and is told off for his rudeness. These civilized human beings around him are going up to the boat deck as if they're off to a gala ball. Despite having been warned about the situation, most of the first-class passengers refuse to believe in the seriousness of the danger they are in.

As for Bedford, he doesn't hesitate. He goes off in pursuit of his young friend. Michel needs help because there will be a fight to get on to the last lifeboats. He must move quickly if the children are to be saved.

During this time Phillips has been sending the first CQD[2] alert without giving any thought to any other messages. On Captains orders, all private messages have been cancelled. Not in the least bit worried, the chief radio officer jokes with Harold Bride while sending details of the ship's position as calculated by Boxhall. The first replies soon arrive. The transatlantic ships that picked up the distress calls are all extremely sceptical. Most of his radio colleagues think it's a practical joke. Messages came first from the *Frankfurt*, at eighteen minutes past midnight, followed by the *Mount Temple*, the *Virginian*, and the *Birmingham*. Bride hasn't had time to get dressed and is continually running between the radio room and the bridge.

Far from the impact, the first-class lounges empty slowly.

People leave reluctantly. They can't admit there is any danger.

Meanwhile, down below, Lolo has been absorbed by the crowd moving towards the end of the corridor, where the water hasn't yet reached. Carried along by the flow of people, he has finally reached the staircase leading to second class. Pushing his way through, he finds the door guarded by a sailor holding a pistol. He is not letting anyone pass! The crowd gathers together. It is hopeless to try to get through the door. He would be suffocated. Panic-stricken, Lolo goes in the opposite direction in search of Trevor.

Trevor has gone off to find Lolo. He has noticed a very steep staircase on the right of the corridor, leading to a gaping hole. Leaning over he sees water lapping in a sinister way, six metres below on F deck. Floating on the water are hundreds of sacks of post, which the postal workers must have been forced to abandon. Through some narrow cracks he can see the lower levels, fully lit by electric lights. What if Lolo has fallen into this hole? He makes a close inspection and then joins the crowd. He goes towards the far end of Scotland Road and passes Lolo without seeing him. Lolo, crying his eyes out, is going in the opposite direction. Once at the end of the corridor, the thought that Lolo might have fallen into the hole he has seen, makes Trevor turn back. He's walking against the crowd now and keeps bumping into faceless people. Finally, after battling his way through, he reaches the post office staircase and leans over to look into the water again. It's hopeless. There are even more sacks of post floating on the water.[3] The water level has risen and it's difficult to see much because the sacks hide the lights. Not knowing what to do next, Trevor stays there. He is haunted by the possibility of Lolo being drowned because of him. At that moment he hears the familiar voices of Mirella and Olaus. They're about three metres away and have just abandoned their flooded cabin. Suddenly, a great rush of water sweeps Trevor head first down into the hole and he disappears.

CHAPTER 12

CAUGHT IN A TRAP

MICHEL ALMOST COLLIDES with Andrews, the engineer, as he arrives at the corridor going towards his cabin. Andrews is running nervously all over the ship urging people to put on their life-jackets and to leave their cabins. He's talking to Mrs Hoghes who now realises that her daughter Rosalind was right about her premonition.

'Come along, Madame, put your life-jacket on like everyone else!'

'I didn't want to alarm the passengers.'

'Put it on immediately if you value your life. It's your duty to set a good example.'

Then, turning towards Navratil, 'Ah! Mr Hoffmann! Don't hang about any longer. You must get to the embarkation deck quickly. But what about the children?'

'Exactly, I'm going to find them.'

'You've already wasted too much time! Go quickly! Your life and theirs is at stake.'

Michel gets to his cabin. He opens the door with a crash, puts on the light and calls out to wake the children. To his horror he discovers only Momon replies.

'Lolo! Where's Lolo?' he shouts at little Momon.

'Dunno! Not see him!' he stammers.

Michel is in such a panic; he can't manage to dress the little boy. He's thrown all his clothes on the floor and doesn't know which to choose. Just then someone knocks at the door. It's the chief steward, John Hardy, who has taken it upon himself to supervise passengers putting on their life-jackets.

'My son! I've lost my son!' shouts Michel.

Momon starts to cry. Hardy puts his comforting hands on Michel's shoulders.

'Come along, sir! Keep calm! This isn't the time to lose your head. Here, I'll help you dress the little one and then we'll see. Look after yourself too. Wrap up as warmly as possible and put on your life-jacket! It's at the bottom of the cupboard by your bed, the children's ones are there too.'

At that moment the door is thrown open and Trevor appears. He's deathly pale and is holding his life-jacket.

The sacks cushioned his fall and he hadn't even touched the water. He had called Lolo as loudly as he could but there had been no reply. Torn between hope and despair he had looked for a way out, climbed over a heap of post sacks and spotted a ladder. He was hardly wet. He had found Mirella and Olaus who thought they'd never see him again. He told them how Lolo had disappeared.

'He's surely not fallen in the water. The crowd must have carried him along. We'll find him!' Olaus had said. 'Go and tell Michel quickly. We'll see to Lolo. Meet in the third-class dining room in fifteen minutes. We'll have Lolo with us!' Trevor looked at his watch that had stopped when he had fallen: half past midnight. He looked up and saw a ladder going to the upper floors. Without hesitating, he climbed up and reached second class, not far from the Hoffmann's cabin.

'Michel, it's terrible! I came to get Lolo half an hour ago to show him the pieces of iceberg on D deck. But on the way back here I lost him in the crowd. Mirella and Olaus are looking for him, come quickly!'

'Since Mr Pritchard is here to help you,' interrupts the steward, 'please excuse me. I need to go and help your neighbours. If I see your son, don't worry, I'll take him straight over to the lifeboats.'

The steward, who had to see to a dozen or more families, quickly disappears. Trevor piles as many clothes as he can on Momon while Michel puts on a thick sweater, a jacket, and his fur coat, and tries to fasten his life-jacket. Within less than two minutes the door opens again and Bedford appears.

'I've come to help you, Navratil. But where's Lolo?

'Lost! We're going off to find him.'

In two words, Charles knows what's going on.

'Navratil?' asks Trevor as they leave the cabin.

'Yes, Navratil! Hoffmann is a pseudonym. That doesn't matter now. We must save the children. Quick! Run! It's a quarter to one. Time to meet Mirella.'

They're swept up in the crowd once again, in the corridors and on the stairs, going against a tidal wave of people. Momon's wearing two pairs of socks, two sweaters, a waterproof jacket, long underpants, flannel trousers and his fur coat, made so he could grow into it; the large life-jacket over all his clothes makes him look like a big turtle. Bedford has put him on his shoulders. Trevor is carrying Lolo's clothes and life-jacket. Michel runs in front of them. Momon, soaked in sweat and terrified, most of all by his daddy's panic opens his mouth to shout but nothing comes out.

It is becoming more and more difficult to move. Each class has its own embarkation area but there's complete chaos. According to White Star Line rules, third-class passengers are supposed to go to the embarkation area on D deck. The Captain has sent two groups of sailors to the third class to be in charge of putting women and children on to lifeboats. But on the portside, because of the list of the ship, the lifeboats are too far from the deck to get into them. The unfortunate people gathered there are powerless to do anything about it. They see lifeboats descending one after another, only a third or half full. They are unable to stop them.[1]

None of the lifeboats from starboard stop at D deck either. This is probably because no one is able to handle the tricky manoeuvre. The lifeboats are out of reach, but scraping the hull – it is a real Tantalus torment. Ironically, the sailors sent to save the women and children are preventing them from embarking by using force!

The passageways assigned to second-class passengers have not been opened but they are allowed to go to the upper deck.

It seems as if the Captain had ordered first- and second-class passengers to be saved first. But this is not so.

During all this, Michel, still charging ahead, reaches the door connecting second and third class on D deck. He comes up against an armed sailor.

'Open the door! My four-year-old son is waiting in third class. We're going to find him.'

'Impossible! I've got orders not to let anyone through. There are about a hundred people back there, waiting to come out. I can't make an exception for you. There'd be a human tide blocking your way.'

Navratil and Bedford look at each other with dismay. But Trevor is already guiding them to the miraculous ladder that comes out in a third-class corridor. Five minutes later they're in the third-class dining room. In contrast to the turmoil in the corridors with the terrible noise from the funnels, it's relatively quiet in here. Otto Schmidt is playing the piano and a group of people are singing 'Nearer my God to thee'. Their faces are contemplative and serious. Each one of them knows the water will soon reach the room because when a ship sinks the rear tends to go up while the front goes down. Then they will be on level F where the water won't take long to completely flood in. There's something deeply tragic about this group of believers, gathered together in serene acceptance of their death. Michel finds it very distressing. Families are grouped together hand-in-hand, according to size, the mothers and fathers holding their smallest children in their arms. Then on the third row he spies Mirella and Lolo. She's on her knees. He's standing there looking serious and praying with all his heart, his little hand on his best friend's shoulder. He suddenly sees his daddy and his brother. His face lights up and, oblivious of the solemnity of the service, runs towards them through the congregation. Michel is too distressed to speak. Charles puts Momon down and Michel passionately hugs his two sons.

Mirella joins them, followed by Olaus. After quietly closing the door behind them, the little group quickly sets off to the steep ladder that leads to second class. There is no time to lose. But when they get to the ladder, they are shocked and horrified to find there's no way out. Someone has locked the trap door from above.

The crowd in front of the door leading into second class is getting very impatient. There's an atmosphere of revolt in the air. The sailor, cornered, is shouting. He's only following his orders. It will soon be the third-class passenger's turn to board the lifeboats. All that's needed is a little patience. Bedford and Michel followed by Trevor and Mirella, who are carrying the children, push their way up to the sailor.

'Let us through! We are second-class passengers!'

'And what proof do I have? Have you got your second-class tickets on you?'

Of course, no one has. Bedford argues with him and gives their cabin numbers. Nothing happens. The door stays closed. Understandably, this fuels growing hostility from the people around them. So this is democracy! How dare this man mention privilege so he and his friends can be saved when all around them women and children are waiting in vain to be called to the lifeboats?

Michel kisses the children in an effort to calm them; Charles, Mirella, Olaus and Trevor feel very small. And the hands of the big clock on the luxurious staircase move, unyielding, under the fixed gaze of Glory and Honour.

~ ~ ~

In Nice, Marcelle, who has had no news of her husband and children for a week, is sleeping fitfully. She has woken up several times drenched in cold sweat. She senses something terrible is about to happen. She gets up at about eleven o'clock, opens the window and stares at the moonless starry sky. Perhaps Michel and the children are looking at the sky too? What wonderful warm air! And they, are they cold? Are they thinking about her? About her despair? If only she had said no to Rey de Villarey, Michel would never have run away with the children. Marcelle closes the window quietly and gets back into bed. She's tormented by guilt and can hardly sleep.

At precisely one o'clock her dream returns: Michel appears. She doesn't recognise him at first. She can see only a long white corridor with strangely angled walls. In the distance, a dark silhouette staggers along holding the side of the walls. Little by little the shape takes form and she can make out her husband's features and the colour of his face. It is white and wax-like. With great difficulty, Michel tries to articulate some words in a barely audible voice. But the corridor tilts more and more. Michel sways stretches out his hands to hold on to the walls and the vision disappears. Marcelle wakes up in a state of high anxiety. She is sitting on the bed, a hand stretched out.

Ten minutes later she is lying on the bed with her eyes wide open. Her mind is clearer than ever. She's convinced she's experienced second sight. A strange feeling. Still even stranger is this total lack of emotion that comes over her after the anxiety. It's as though she is a neutral zone where a major event is taking place. As if someone is writing on her with newly made wax. She feels totally receptive. There's nothing to do but wait. She closes her eyes and falls into a trance that is like a very deep sleep.

~ ~ ~

On the *Californian*, cadet officer Gibson and the second officer, Herbert Stone, more and more curious about the strange events on the mysterious ship, eight miles away, feel drama in the air. When the third officer, Victor Groves, had informed Captain Lord about a large liner, its lights dimmed, seemingly stuck not far from them, he had ordered the crew to signal them by semaphore. There had been no reply. Evans had gone to his cabin at midnight after having shut down the radio receiver.

At ten minutes after midnight Gibson sees white flares in the sky. Then more appear at four-minute intervals. He goes and tells Captain Lord who simply says to him, 'They are signals arranged by the company!' And he tells him not to disturb him any more.

Nobody dares to wake up Captain Lord again.

Around 12.15, Groves tries to contact the ship by radio. But he doesn't know he is supposed to activate the magnetic part of the machine first, and the transmitter is silent.

Now Gibson and Stone can see another series of white flares being set off with the same rhythm.

'It's very odd, all the same,' remarks Stone thoughtfully. 'A ship doesn't send up flares in the middle of the night without good reason. Something must be wrong. Gibson, try semaphoring this ghost ship with lights again!'

But it is in vain. The *Titanic*, shining with hundreds of lights is deaf and dumb. Captain Lord and Evans, the radio officer, the only people who could change the course of history, are fast asleep.

In the radio room of the *Titanic* no one is idle. Bride has spent his time running from the radio room to the Captain's bridge and still hasn't finished getting dressed. Neither he nor Phillips has the heart to joke any more. Since sending the first CQD they have come to understand the reality of the situation. Andrews, running like the wind, comes to tell his young friend Bride that the big, beautiful steamship, his child, his miraculous creation, has been mortally wounded and only has an hour to live. Bride is deeply upset, as much by the despair he sees in Andrews's eyes as by the appalling news.

He jumps up and spontaneously hugs him. Andrews embraces him in return.

'I'm responsible for this catastrophe. Half the so-called water-tight compartments are linked. It's an unforgivable mistake. Everyone here still really believes in the myth of her being unsinkable. Imagine, there are scores of women who don't want to get into the lifeboats because they think they're not safe enough. I had no wish to destroy this myth when there was still time, but now the first lifeboats are being lowered and they're half-empty. Each empty place means one more death!'

For a moment Bride thinks Andrews is going to collapse. He is shaking, his head in his hands. Then he pulls himself together and, giving his friend another hug, runs off.

The radio waves are sizzling across the North Atlantic. News of the terrible disaster is being broadcast. The *Titanic* has already reached the continent, powerlessly following the events of the catastrophe. For the first time in naval history, people are taking part at a distance in the agony of a ship. But even if technological progress makes it possible to follow the tragedy minute by minute, nobody can do anything about it. This night, the whole world is aware of the absurd blind confidence that humankind has in the name of progress…

The first SOS signal is heard at a quarter to one. It is the *Carpathia* that receives it: 'CQD—CQD—SOS—SOS—

CQD—SOS. Come immediately. We have hit an iceberg. CQD—OM (old man). Position 41° 46'N, 50° 14'W.'

The idea comes from Bride. It's the new international distress signal and he jokingly says to Phillips, 'Send an SOS, it might be your last chance!'

Now he is in no doubt it is their last chance. Unfortunately, apart from the *Californian* who should, with some careful navigation, be able to arrive in less than an hour at the scene of the catastrophe, all the other ships are too far away from the *Titanic* to be of any help. The *Mount Temple*, the *Birma*, the *Virginian*, the *Baltic*, the *Frankfurt*, the *Amerika*, the *Prinz Friedrich Wilhelm*, the *Parisian*, the *Provence* and the *Olympic* reply, but none of them have any hope of arriving in time to rescue anyone.

No one on the *Olympic*, the twin ship cruising several hundreds of kilometres from there, imagines the extent of the disaster. Just before the *Titanic* sinks, a message comes from the *Olympic* at about one twenty-five saying 'Are you going south in our direction?'

The only concrete hope comes from the *Carpathia*. At the time of the first SOS she is fifty-eight miles from the *Titanic*. The radio room sends a message: '*Carpathia* at fifty-eight miles, arriving soon!'

She immediately changes course in the direction of the ship in distress. She is sailing at about fourteen knots and will take at best, four hours to reach the *Titanic*.

'By which time, old man, we're all going to be dead!' says Phillips bitterly, furiously getting back to work, while Bride finally manages to get dressed.

A number of passengers are now asking about some mysterious flashing lights. They can easily be seen by the naked eye but no one identifies the *Californian*. If it's a ship then why isn't she moving? Why isn't she coming to the rescue? The theory of a collective hallucination starts to circulate.

In front of the closed door, almost crushed to death by the crowds who are getting more hysterical by the minute, Michel feels like stone. People are aggressive, they feel claustrophobic, and their survival is at stake. He has a vision of his letter being blown away by the wind just as the young English chambermaid takes it out of her pocket to put it into the post box. He is certain this is what happened to it. He weighs up the horrifying consequences of his recklessness. Everyone is probably going to die in this rat-trap. Even if he manages to save the children from dying, they won't be identified because they're listed under the name of Hoffmann. What will happen to them? How will their mother find them?

Marcelle must be contacted at all cost. He's thinking about her a lot. The shouting and pushing around him distracts him but through sheer force, he manages to concentrate and has a picture of her in his mind. She's in her nightclothes sitting on her bed and she's looking straight at him, wild-eyed. Tears shine on her cheeks. She stretches an arm out towards him and opens her hand. The image immediately disappears. It is one o'clock precisely. Feeling deeply upset, he whispers in Lolo's ear, 'Listen very carefully, Lolo, your name isn't Hoffmann, it's Navratil, Michel Navratil, like me. Remember this, it is very important so you will be able to find Mummy!'

But Lolo isn't listening to what he says. He hasn't been able to get rid of this horrible fear, churning his stomach over for the last few minutes. This is not how Lolo imagines being at death's door: there should be a great bright light there and not a long wait like this, trapped in front of all these desperate people. Sobbing and shaking, he clutches his daddy. Charles, Trevor, Olaus and Mirella, going through the same agony, smile weakly. Slowly, Navratil pulls himself together. But the door stays closed.

CHAPTER 13

NOBLESSE OBLIGE!

WHILE THIRD-CLASS PASSENGERS are crowding in front of closed doors in the belly of the ship, up above, the most ludicrous, banal, and pathetic things are happening. Groups of people are coming and going in bizarre get-ups. Some look as if they're going motoring or skiing, others as if they're going to a ball. Not to mention the crowds of dreamers and sleepwalkers dressed in nightclothes. God knows why they haven't dressed warmly. It's too late to go back to the cabins. The water at the front of the ship is higher than D deck.

To complete this strange parade, the orchestra in full evening dress, is playing on A deck and will continue playing until the ship sinks. Their apparent self-sacrifice is very moving but they are not simply playing to soften the end for hundreds of passengers who are inevitably going to die. The musicians, some of whom are very young people, undoubtedly find courage through their love of music, to face death. They have not, however, volunteered to play. The Captain has asked them. He wants a distraction from the sound of the whistling funnels, the noise of pulleys lowering the lifeboats, not to mention the screams of women being dragged from their husband's arms before getting into the lifeboats. Strauss waltzes, selections of operettas and operas are all part and parcel of an effort to draw attention away from the tragic reality of what is happening to the *Titanic*. Thanks to the music, panic on the upper deck is avoided. People feel secure and no one is losing their head.

After he left Michel, Stead had gone off to bed without being aware of the seriousness of the situation. He is awakened around half past midnight by loud banging on his door. The steward, Etches, after warning Ben Guggenheim, helping him to get dressed and putting on his life-jacket, has come to help Stead. For a moment Stead is angry about the idea of the ship having been fatally damaged without him having questioned it. How did it happen? He had predicted a disaster, he had written his will before embarking on the *Titanic*, and he had scoffed at the blind confidence passengers, the officers and Andrews had in the ship. But he hadn't been capable of realising the seriousness of the situation even when the collision had taken place under his nose. That he had been on the scene when the accident happened makes it seem all the more ridiculous. He feels impotent.

One way or another, it is of little importance now the end is near. Stead feels he has made a good contribution to the world. The only thing annoying him a little is realising he won't have the opportunity to write about the sinking of the *Titanic*. All the same, it is infuriating. He had made a prediction to Michel saying something would happen in less than an hour and then not damn well recognised what was going on. Stead isn't very polite to the steward who is doing his best to help him. He's very pig-headed, for example, about wanting to put his overcoat on top of his life-jacket.

'No, sir! It will get in the way when you're swimming,' Etches says patiently. His distinguished passenger's rudeness doesn't much worry him. Shouting from the neighbouring cabin tells Stead the poor steward has to face even more wrath and he regrets having been so rude to him.

Twenty minutes later Stead is watching the unbelievable farce on the upper deck.

High up on the bridge Captain Smith and Ismay, the

president of the White Star Line, who's ambition of being awarded the Blue Ribbon has been thwarted by fate, are leaning over the rail looking at the deck. The first officer, Murdoch, stands behind them in silence. He has come to report the lack of success with the embarkation manoeuvres: passengers are refusing to obey orders.

Murdoch feels responsible for the catastrophe even though, in the Captain's words, 'The ship is but an instrument in God's hands.' He now knows the order he gave during the crucial thirty-seven seconds between Fleet's phone call and the collision with the iceberg, is going to be fatal for the majority of passengers. He blames himself for not having given an order for the ship to increase speed while turning rather than to go into reverse. The Captain has tried to reassure him several times. But just like Andrews, he refuses to listen. By his side, Ismay mutters between his teeth, 'Look at those crazy fools dancing on a volcano!'

Some couples have, in fact, started dancing including old Isidor and Ida!

Just then, Lightoller comes up shouting hysterically, 'Captain we'll never get anywhere while this music is playing. It's bewitching these first-class women! They don't want to board the lifeboats! They're saying it's too cold and the lifeboats aren't safe. They'd prefer to stay and listen to Hartley's damned music.'

'I agree with Lightoller,' Murdoch butts in, 'it would be better to give the passengers wine rather than waltzes. This music is giving them a false sense of security and no one will want to get into the lifeboats.'

'Worst of all,' adds Lightoller, 'are these rumours, going round like wildfire. People are saying the *Olympic* will be here in two hours to tow the *Titanic* to Halifax. They're also saying we're lowering the lifeboats filled with women and children to relieve the weight on the ship, to stop her sinking. And other foolish things. It would be better to call each person to take his or her place in the lifeboats using a loudspeaker.'

'Oh really?' says Captain Smith white with anger, 'and what will all those who are not called say? Do you want to create total panic? If so, then it's the best way of doing it. If you use loud speakers, within less than fifteen minutes you'll have people killing each other.'

He turns to the officers.

'Go back to your positions at once! Persuade the women to get into the lifeboats or put them in by force. And get the rope ladders ready!'

'Aye aye Captain!'

The first lifeboat to be put into the water is number seven, from starboard. Dorothy Gibson, the beautiful woman who had asked Michel, near the big clock, when 'this place' would arrive in New York, is in it, along with her mother and several admirers. There are also some sailors and a junior officer with her. She's wearing the same Paul Poiret[1] dress she'd been wearing the other evening, a sable coat is casually draped around her shoulders. The boat is lowered on Murdoch's orders but he has not managed to fill it. Without stopping, it goes past D deck right under the noses of women and children from third class who are queuing up to get off the ship. At this moment an order is being given to lock all doors from third class. Only women and children, escorted in convoys to the upper deck from where they can be put on to lifeboats, are being allowed through.

Lifeboat number four should have been lowered first. It stops at A deck, the embarkation area for first-class passengers. Here there are the biggest fortunes in America: the Astors, the Carters, the Smiths, the Ryersons, the Wideners and the Harpers with their Pekinese, Sun Yat Sen along with their Egyptian guide, Hamad Hassah. In total there are about forty people gathered together in the area. But it's closed. Lightoller is giving orders for everyone to wait with their families until they are given the signal to move. Because of the cold, people have gone into the gymnasium and are calmly chatting amongst themselves.

A little later on the upper deck, Stead sees Lightoller and Murdoch running towards the davits. He follows them. The manoeuvre is going well. Some lifeboats are already in the water; others are ready to be lowered. The two first officers, Lightoller at portside and Murdoch at starboard, are explaining to all the men how women and children are being put into the lifeboats first and they will follow.

Standing at portside, Stead looks around him. He can't help admiring the spirit with which most men are making way for the women and children. They don't even attempt to claim a place for themselves. There is a kind of consensus, a predominantly chivalrous attitude. John Astor tries hard to be allowed to go with his wife, Madeline, into lifeboat number four. He explains she is 'in a special condition'[2] and she needs him to be with her, but he accepts Lightoller's refusal without any fuss, 'Fair play,' he says, bowing. He turns to Madeline. 'Don't worry, my darling. I'll take a later boat.'

All the husbands say the same thing to their wives. But for the most part the women have a terrible choice. They can either survive with their children or die with their husbands.

Stead hears a nearby conversation between Jacques Estrelle, an American originally from France, and his wife May. An officer has already escorted May twice, as far as a lifeboat on the point of leaving. On both occasions she has gone back to her husband. Jacques is now insisting she should get in a lifeboat.

'Remember our children need you. This time I'm going to the lifeboat with you to make sure you get into it.'

May is unable to hide her tears. Jacques shows no emotion.

Stead watches as they go to lifeboat number sixteen. After having made sure May is safe, Jacques joins Astor who has just been separated from his wife. He offers him a cigarette as if nothing unusual has happened.

Stead thinks he is in an easier position as a bachelor. He notices how some women allow themselves to be persuaded to leave their husbands. Some on the other hand cling to their husbands' neck, refusing to leave the ship. They have to be carried shouting and screaming into the lifeboats.

The terrible noise from the steam in the funnels has died down considerably. But it is still loud enough not to be able to speak without shouting.

All of a sudden the noise stops. An unnatural silence fills the decks and the rest of the ship. A prelude to the silent ocean and, for most of the passengers, to the silence of death.

Up until now the atmosphere amongst the passengers, patiently waiting to get into the lifeboats or to die, has been fairly lively and sociable. Hartley, the conductor, is lifting his baton ready to start up some ragtime jazz when silence falls like a stone. The movement of his arm stops, the musicians seem to be paralysed, the passengers on the deck are transfixed. Conversations cease and terror-stricken children, burst out crying. The danger takes on an undeniable reality and people stop pretending.

When the orchestra strikes up ragtime music, the first- and second-class passengers go back to what they were doing when they were interrupted. But from now on, however, they look serious. People are hiding their anxieties from their loved ones, women and children. The conversations apparently continue as playfully as before.

It is at this moment that Lowe, who Murdoch and Boxhall had forgotten to wake up, arrives on the bridge asking to be given up-to-date details about what is going on. His arrival coincides with a phone call from the quartermaster, Rowe, from the front deck. He has just seen one of the lifeboats in the water. No one had thought of telling him about the fatal collision with the iceberg and he didn't know anything about it. Boxhall tells him to come to the bridge with a supply of white flares. As soon has he gets there he starts setting them off. He sends them for over an hour without getting any response.

A group of sailors are assigned to each lifeboat. They lift off the canvas covers, and put in some supplies: bread, biscuits, spirits, and some lanterns. They then put the cranks on the davits and move the boat out. Their next job is to help passengers into the boat, following them to make sure they are safely on the ocean.

But confusion reigns among the junior officers in charge of the manoeuvres. The passenger lists have not yet arrived. They are improvising. Women and children, closest to the boats ready to leave, are put into them straight away. But a few men have slipped into some of them before women and children have had chance to get in. Amongst them are some agile bachelors from third class. They have managed to break out of their prison and climb up the ropes of luggage derricks and get on to the upper deck.

Murdoch, on starboard, is allowing men to occupy places that are empty without automatically picking on queue jumpers whereas Lightoller, on portside, is mercilessly chasing them away. He would rather let the boats go off a quarter, a third or half empty than let any man on board apart from the accompanying crew.

It is easy to imagine the feelings of injustice and revolt taking hold of women, torn from husbands who now face inescapable death, when they discover unknown men sitting next to them.

Time is getting short and the lifeboats continue to be lowered only half full. There are only twelve people in boat number one. The occupants introduce each other. Among them are Lord and Lady Duff Gordon accompanied by Miss Francatelli, their companion. She's lamenting on the loss of a new night-dress left in her cabin. Abraham Saloman who later becomes president of the committee of *Titanic* survivors, and Mr and Mrs Henry Stengel, wealthy American industrialists, are also in the boat. The five other passengers are stokers and a junior officer, George Symons, who is in charge of the lifeboat.

Stead looks at them with bitterness. He suddenly thinks about the hundreds of women and children in the third-class embarkation areas, still hoping for a lifeboat to stop and pick them up. To crown this horror, the convoys organised by the Captain haven't yet arrived. The hysterical dense crowd massing at the closed doors, down below on D deck, won't let them through. The sailors in charge manage to take only two people to the lifeboats!

Why is help available to only half the passengers on the *Titanic*? The davits are big enough to hold thirty-two lifeboats rather than sixteen.[3] Why are the lives of women and children in third class being sacrificed?

Stead feels overcome by a feeling of revulsion. *Noblesse oblige?* All right! But this is nothing more than a grotesque farce. There are, without doubt, a number of people such as Guggenheim, behaving like gentlemen, but Stead can't help judging others as behaving in a vile, disgusting way. Guggenheim has just appeared on deck with his personal secretary. They're both wearing evening dress complete with top hats and tails, hard collars and cuffs, and bow ties. They have decided to die like gentlemen. By contrast, some men are on the lookout on starboard, and as soon as there are no women in sight, they leap into a lifeboat and then start complaining because things are moving slowly. When the lifeboats are not full they receive orders to stay close to the *Titanic* before moving away, so people who have been left behind, can go down the rope ladders attached along the side of the ship. But no one follows these orders. It's every man for himself. Stead thinks about this disaster without managing to find a sane philosophy of life other than the one he always applies, even in the direst circumstances, of keeping his distance.

With half the lifeboats already in the ocean, Bedford, Michel, Trevor, Mirella, and the children are as powerless as the other poor souls standing in front of the firmly closed door. Stead, pre-occupied with watching what is going on, hasn't given a thought to his little friends, Lolo and Momon. Suddenly he realises neither Bedford, nor Michel, nor Lolo and his baby brother are on the deck. It has now become a matter of urgency to get the children on a lifeboat. Having been slow to leave at first, the lifeboats are suddenly being lowered very quickly. In half an hour there won't be any lifeboats left. Rrushing off to find them, he comes across Isidor and Ida Straus strolling arm in arm up and down the deck.

'Ida! Why are you still here? Don't you know there won't be any places left in the boats soon? My dear Isidor, what are you thinking about? Get your Ida to safety quickly!'

But Ida turns towards Stead and replies with a smile, 'My dear Stead, you forget we have been together, in peace and happiness, for forty years without ever being separated. We will die as we have lived: together and united forever!'

Stead looks at them and feels very emotional. Isidor has put his arm around her shoulders and is kissing her as if they have just fallen in love. He is speechless in the presence of such a simple, natural, heroic expression of marital bliss and discreetly moves away.

Further on, the Allison family is refusing to be separated. There is Mr and Mrs Allison, their daughter Lorraine, who waltzed with Lolo, and their baby, Travers, who is in his nurse's arms. Mrs Allison refuses to leave her husband and Lorraine is hanging on to her mother's skirt. Stead views this with a critical eye. Lorraine and Lolo should leave on the same boat if possible; it will help them to cope with the situation. Stead goes all over first and second class without seeing his friends. The Navratils are nowhere to be found.

CHAPTER 14

THE SEPARATION

THE SOUNDS MADE by the crowd at the door accessing third class reaches the circular lounge at the foot of the large staircase going up to first class. Rumour has it there is rioting. The crowd can be heard shouting and pushing and there are deafening banging noises.

Stead has to face it: third-class passengers are being denied access to the promenade and upper decks from where first- and second-class passengers are getting into the lifeboats. The majority of passengers are penned in like cattle. They are doomed to a horrifying death. It's unbearable, odious! He has to do something. What if the Navratils are in the crowd? It would explain their disappearance.

As Stead reaches the closed door on D deck he finds the second convoy coming through. John Hart, the chief steward in third class, is accompanying about thirty women and children. Stead, who has already passed the first convoy, looks anxiously at this second one. Lolo and Momon are not in it.

The shouting crowd is a harsh reality. As Stead sees a hand slipping into the gap in the door, a gun goes off. The junior officer in charge of guarding the door is suddenly submerged by a tide of passengers escaping from their prison.

How come the people here are being fired on?

Wilde, the second-in-command has given guns to all the officers and junior officers. In case of panic, they have orders to fire into the air. This is what has just happened at the third-class door. The crowd is outraged by this act of intimidation.

They surge through the now open door. Heading the crowd, Daniel Buckley leads them to the first-class staircase under the impassive gaze of Glory and Honour, soon to have only fish for company.

Behind Daniel Buckley are Lolo and Michel with Bedford carrying Momon, and behind them are Trevor, Olaus, and Mirella... Stead, leaping forward to greet them just avoids being knocked over by the crowd. Pushed from one side to the other he finds himself face to face with Bedford.

'Quickly! Go to the promenade deck!' Stead shouts. 'Most of the lifeboats have gone. There's no time to lose!'

Daniel Buckley is the first to get to the lifeboats. He arrives just as boat number four, with millionaires' wives, is being lowered. Lightoller has just angered everyone by not allowing Jack Thayer, who is only sixteen, to join them. John Astor, as calm as ever, takes a hat decorated with flowers from a woman near him and puts it on young Jack's head. He looks Lightoller straight in the eye.

'There, he can go! He's a girl now!' and he pushes him into the boat.

But Lightoller has no mercy. He orders Jack to get out and the boat begins its descent into the water. Taking advantage of Lightoller's attention being distracted, Buckley leans over the side of the ship. The boat is still within reach. It's now or never! He jumps and Lightoller is ready to shoot. Through a combination of pity, bravado, and the revulsion at what has happened to young Jack, the passengers wrap Buckley in a blanket and deliberately look the other way. This kindness saves the young Irishman's life.

Michel runs ahead of his little group, with Lolo. He's obsessed with only one thing: his impulsiveness is going to cost them their lives, all three of them. Quick, quick, get the children to safety! God help, protect, and save my children! Charles is still carrying Momon who is wide-awake but very alarmed. Mirella, Olaus and Trevor are following close behind.

When they reach the first davits on portside, they can't believe their eyes. There's not a lifeboat in sight; the davits are completely empty. Then Trevor sees a boat still hanging above davit number four.

'Quick! Over there! There's one left!'

'One what?' asks Lolo, very confused and still hanging on to his daddy for dear life.

Michel is too distracted to reply. They all rush off to davit number four on portside but stop about two metres from it. A circle of sailors is surrounding it.

'Sorry, this boat is full.'

Bedford, Stead, and Michel stand still with the children, waiting for the next boat while Olaus drags Mirella over to starboard. He hopes to get his loved one to safety. They arrive to find boat number thirteen being lowered into the water. They hang over the side of the ship trying to see if anyone they know is in it. It's only about three metres below them. A young man standing at the back lifts his head.

'Lawrence!' she shouts.

'Mirella!'

The descending boat speeds up; the voice is already far away. Here at the front of the ship the ocean is only twelve or thirteen metres below the upper deck. But the shouts of the crew muffle sounds coming from below.

Beesely is desperate. A minute before, Murdoch had called, 'Are there any women still waiting?'

Lawrence had looked but hadn't seen any. There were some but they were hidden behind men from third class, hoping to get places for their family.

'Then jump in!' Murdoch had shouted and ordered the

boat to be lowered.

Lawrence had jumped in good faith but now, looking up, he can see Mirella.

'Go back up! Go back up!' He shouts. 'I want to give my place to someone else!'

But the situation is hopeless. The lifeboat has already landed in the water.

The last lifeboat on starboard, number fifteen, is now ready to go. It has just been filled by some of the crowd from third class who have rushed over from number thirteen. The junior officers had to fire into the air to get some men out of the boat. They had forced their way into it and the officers wanted their places for women and children. In no time at all, the lifeboat like three or four previous ones is overloaded. There are seventy-two to seventy-five people in it instead of the sixty-five it is supposed to hold.

The lifeboat disappears very quickly. Suddenly there are the most terrible shouts and screams. Because the ship is listing, lifeboat number fifteen is coming down on top of number thirteen. The two men in charge of the manoeuvre frenetically try to cut the ropes still holding it on to the *Titanic*. Beesley looks with horror as the other boat comes hurtling down towards them. In a second they will be crushed to death. Happily the ropes break. With the help of arms pushing as hard as they can against the side of the ship, the lifeboat is clear of the *Titanic* and safely in the ocean. There is a huge splash nearby and number fifteen is in the water too.

Mirella and Olaus, without thinking about what they are doing, lean right over the side of the ship, almost falling in the water. They give a sigh of relief. Lawrence is saved! They look at each other. There is no hope for them. Olaus holds out his arms and they embrace. They go off slowly, accepting their fate. They await death together, like old Isidor and Ida Straus.

Despite of the orchestra's heroic efforts to continue playing, an air of gloom hangs over the deck. It is as if they are playing a death-watch. Lost! We are lost! There will be no more lifeboats leaving. The davits are empty on both the portside and starboard.

For several minutes Michel thinks he will go mad with the horror of it all. Not only has he kidnapped his own children but he has condemned them to death. If only he hadn't allowed himself to be lulled into a false sense of security. If only he hadn't been seduced into listening to Guggenheim, Charles Hay and Wickner holding forth in the smoking lounge, he and his sons would have been first on the embarkation deck. All three of them would have escaped in one of the first lifeboats! Instead of thinking about his children, he had foolishly fanta-sised about getting well in with these millionaires.

He is suddenly overcome with dizziness. He staggers and falls on to a coil of ropes. He lies trembling, his head in his hands. His dizziness is made even worse by the 39-degree list of the ship.

Lolo is deeply upset at the sight of his father lying prostrate at his feet, his head hidden and so silent. He waits for a while not knowing what to do. Then, very slowly, he stretches out and touches his daddy's hand.

Michel lifts his head in surprise, grabs Lolo and hugs him very tightly. The bear hug makes Lolo feel safe and secure and he begins to speak very quietly. Meanwhile, Bedford has put the sleeping Edmond close to them. He has wedged him between an air vent and some coils of rope to stop him from sliding overboard. He is now trying to see what is happening on the deck.

Nobody witnesses the last moments Lolo Navratil spends with his daddy.

'D'you know who I've just seen? The baker who gave me some buns. You remember how you told me off? He brought some bread for the lifeboats and he had a great big bag of buns left. He gave it to me! He's a very funny man! He sings very loudly and he can't walk properly, he wobbles. I think he smells like a bottle of wine. Would you like a bun?'

Navratil pulls himself together a little and hugs his son even more tightly. How come this four-year-old can be so perceptive at a time like this and so much braver than he?

They eat some of Joughin's buns together and it is comforting for them both. Michel feels a sudden pang of guilt about having been so cross with Lolo the other day. He wishes he could take it all back.

'Our dining room is under water now. The one down below I mean. Isn't that funny? The lights are still shining in the water. I saw them through a hole in the crew's quarters when I lost Trevor.'

Michel puts his arm around his son again, but in a different way this time. There's deep tenderness in his embrace as they whisper together. Lolo is so strong and he is so weak!

Lolo's strength gives him courage and he begins to think optimistically that all is not lost. Stead and Bedford have gone off to find a way of saving the children. Yes, Michel thinks, they will find a way somehow.

Michel looks up and catches a glimpse of Pritchard pacing up and down. His head is bowed and his hands are behind his back. Michel feels his blood boil at the sight of Trevor. Anger wells up inside him. He's responsible for this situation. He dragged Lolo into the third-class trap. The children are going to die because of him. Then, as if Trevor can read his thoughts, he looks at Michel. There is terrible despair in his face. Michel feels ashamed of his anger. He doesn't really have the heart to bear Trevor any ill will. After all, he has faithfully looked after Lolo throughout the trip. Fate has intervened, that is all.

He starts to think of the children's mother, Marcelle. What

will her feelings of loss be when she finds out the three of them are dead? Will she be able to cope with the dreadful pain she will inevitably feel?

'Trevor, I beg of you, run to the radio cabin and if there's still time, send a telegram to my wife. She had custody of the children and I deserted her. Send it to Marcelle Navratil, 26 rue de France, Nice. Tell her I beg her forgiveness. Say our last thoughts are with her and the children are very courageous. Go quickly! God be with you.'

Climbing the steeply angled deck now sloping towards the ocean, Trevor disappears into the night. Michel feels a rush of cold air round his shoulders and shivers. Momon starts to wake up. Tightly huddled together, the three Navratils talk about Marcelle in a whisper.

Meanwhile, Stead and Bedford are looking for Captain Smith. The boat deck, deserted five minutes earlier, is now filled with a still crowd, their voices muffled. People are hanging on to the steeply angled deck as best they can. When it was obvious the davits were empty, the third-class passengers moved slowly. The last ones to appear, still thinking they will be saved, lean over the side of the ship. They hope to find a lifeboat not yet lowered into the icy ocean. The shiny black paint of the new ship is barely dry but now it is pierced with the trembling halos of hundreds of little lights, most of which are a long way under the water. The smooth side of the ship is clearly lit but they have to face the facts: all the lifeboats have gone. The passengers hanging over the side of the *Titanic* are wild eyed as they watch the small boats floating on the shimmering, glassy, half-frozen ocean.

The lifeboats are so near and yet, so far.

Some are overcrowded while others are almost empty. Third-class passengers on D deck had watched women in their fancy fur coats filling up the lifeboats. They had felt outraged and helpless. Now, in their heart of hearts, they hope for a miracle. It is this that enables them to deal with the shock of the catastrophe without going crazy. Other passengers realised from the beginning; they were going to die. They are the ones who now stand quiet and hopeless, staring vacantly into the darkness. There are many children amongst them but even they[1] are silent.

There are no officers in sight. Stead and Bedford go to the bridge. It is deserted. Suddenly they hear voices. Some of the crew are on the super structure above the officers' quarters, a few metres away and are feverishly doing God knows what. Stead beckons to Bedford and they climb after them.

Two minutes later Stead leans towards Charles, his face beaming: 'It's not too late for the little ones. They're unfastening the canvas boats – four Engelhardts, I think. Each one can hold up to forty-nine people!'

He disappears then returns, less sure of himself. 'The boats are so damned well fixed down, it seems to be impossible to unfasten them!'

Bedford hesitates. Should he go and let Michel know? But he shouldn't be given false hopes. It would be better to wait until the first boat has been unfastened. The minutes tick by. Bedford can see, not far away from him, a ladder three quarters submerged in water. It leads down into the ship. Leaning over he can see several floors. He doesn't want to count how many there are. Why torture himself for no reason?

Finally Stead's head re-appears. He's beaming again.

'There we are! Boat C is unfastened and D is almost done. Run and tell Michel. And little Mirella if you see her!'

Trevor arrives at the radio room too late. The transmitter has just stopped working. The battery is down. Now only very weak messages are heard. All the lights on the Titan in distress are showing signs of being tired. Just as the two radio officers feel cut off from the outside world, a warm message comes from Cottam, the radio officer on the *Carpathia*. It gives them hope. There could still be a dramatic turn of events. As for the *Titanic*, its messages are increasingly panic-stricken. At 1.06am: 'Prepare your lifeboats. The front is sinking!' At 1.10am: 'The front is rapidly sinking!' At 1.35am: 'The engine rooms are under water!' Phillips sends his last message at 1.50am: 'Come as quickly as you can! Boilers are almost completely under water!'

Now it is the end. The telegram for Marcelle Navtratil is not sent, the children and Mirella are going to perish…. Suddenly Trevor notices something happening on the boat deck. Yes! There is an attempt to hang another boat on davit number four. So, Lolo and Momon have still got a chance.

Holding on to the rail, Trevor waits for his friends, Phillips and Bride, who are preparing to confront the last part of their voyage. From the radio room there is an overall view of the sinking *Titanic*. A good third of the front is totally immersed, doing a nosedive into the ocean. At this point it is 3,862 metres deep. The rear of the *Titanic* rises up, high above the surface. Just like the steamship in Rosalind's dream. The water is rising insidiously and in less than ten minutes, it will flood the radio room. The sight of the deck leaning towards the still ocean where reflections of white flares are mixed with thousands of the shining stars falling from them, is totally surrealistic.

Trevor looks up and sees, to his amazement, great streaks in the sky: showers of stars bursting forth one after the other as if the galaxy is crying because the *Titanic* is sinking. He watches the show for a few moments with a lump in his throat, then goes into the cabin.

Trevor joins Bride who is giving his boots to Phillips, still in shirtsleeves. Then Bride takes over from his heroic colleague at the receiver, trying to hear far-off voices attempting to communicate with the *Titanic*. Trevor takes their life-jackets from a trunk. Phillips quickly collects a few papers, puts on a thick sweater and a coat, and takes over from Bride. Trevor is helping Bride fasten his life-jacket when the door opens wide and the outline of Captain Smith appears. It throws a Chinese shadow through the doorway, as in a nightmare.

'My children, you've done your work. Now think of yourselves. It's everyone for himself!'

He disappears into the shadows from where he came. But Phillips refuses to leave the receiver while there is an echo of the world outside, even if it is hardly audible. Trevor and Bride feel heavy-hearted listening to the dying sounds. Finally there is complete silence. Nostalgic strains of the 'Tales of Hoffman' take over. Defeated, the two friends leave the radio deck and go, or rather slide, towards the rail.

All of a sudden Phillips, in his cabin, shouts out. A coal trimmer hiding behind a wall is attacking him and trying to drag his life-jacket off him. Trevor and Bride go back and quickly overwhelm the thief.

The list on the deck is getting worse. They have to separate and say goodbye to the little room where they had been able to keep in contact with so many friends across the ocean and which will have saved many lives once the *Carpathia* arrives. Lying on the floor, with his arms strangely stretched out, is the still body of the unknown thief who attacked Phillips. The room is already plunged into mourning. Phillips and Bride embrace each other and go off. The first goes to the stern which continues to rise upwards to the sky. The second, along with Trevor, joins the officers who are still trying to unfasten boats A and B, on the roof of their quarters. They will never see each other again.

When Bedford comes to tell Navratil the good news he has difficulty in finding him because there is a large crowd around. Then he spots him, still sitting on the coil of ropes, holding the children in his arms, whispering to them. It was as if nothing else was important. They are completely indifferent to the jostling crowd. However, time is passing.

'The children are saved! Other lifeboats are being got ready. Lolo and Momon can go in the second one, D. It's going to be lowered in a few minutes.'

Michel doesn't immediately latch on to what he's saying. He can't believe there is still hope. But Lolo clearly understands his daddy won't be following them.

'Charles, Daddy has to come with us! I don't want to leave without him!'

'Don't worry, little captain,' Michel cuts in, 'I'll meet you later. I'll go in the next boat.'

This is a lie he is not ashamed of. His heart is bursting with joy. Saved! They are saved!

He jumps up and goes to davit number four where the canvas boat D is being hung. As for Stead, he's watching the preparations get underway for boat C. Out of the corner of his eye he's also watching Ismay whose patience is stretched to the limit. After Lowe has somewhat brutally pushed him aside when he disapproved of the way the manoeuvre was proceeding, he now stands in silence, watching these later boats leaving. It looks as if he is determined to get on the next one. He doesn't want to miss his turn. As boat C is hung on davit number one from where it will be lowered into the water, a crowd of people rush towards it. The man in charge, McElroy, has to fire into the air several times and the crew drag off the men who've got into it. Just as the boat is being lowered, Ismay jumps into it, like Buckley had earlier. Murdoch lets him go.

Martin Callagher, who has led a convoy of women and children from third class, helps them get into the boat. But one of the women has not judged the distance between the boat and the side of the ship properly and falls headfirst into the boat. The woman immediately behind her, no doubt terrified by the sight of this accident, does something even worse. She trips up and disappears between the boat and the ship. She screams in horror. Martin, with an extraordinary fast reflex, catches one of her feet and with the help of one of the sailors, pulls her up to safety.

Lightoller tries to hurry up the preparations of the other Engelhardts but A and B are impossible to unfasten. He watches the water rising. The *Titanic* has at the most, only thirty-five minutes to live. Boat D is almost ready and will be lowered in five minutes.

Captain Smith's voice suddenly comes booming from a huge loudspeaker. 'Do not fill these boats! Draw alongside the bottom of the rope ladders!'

The orders are repeated several times. People hear the orders and start to climb down the rope ladders towards the water expecting to be picked up, but no boats appear.

Suddenly the *Titanic* keels over towards starboard. People are thrown to the ground and roll to the edge of the ship. Passengers on the rope ladders are forced to let go and they fall into the ocean. Wilde's voice rings out, 'Everyone to portside to balance the ship! Everyone to portside!'

The crowd gets up with great difficulty and makes for portside. There are so many people that the large ship does redress her list a little.

The Engelhardt D is full. Mirella, despite Olaus's pleadings, has just given her place to a woman with two children. Lying in each other's arms, the young couple wait for the end.

It's time to separate. Michel says bye bye to Momon who kisses him. He is handed, like a parcel, to a young girl. He starts to cry only when he finds himself amongst strangers, without his daddy and his brother.

Lolo loses his courage at this terrible time. He refuses to leave Michel and clings to his neck. But then, Stead rushes up carrying little Travers Allison. He is crying his eyes out. Stead did not manage to drag Lorraine from her mother's arms. Their nurse-maid, however, followed him. It wasn't possible to persuade Mrs Allison to either leave her husband behind or for her to be separated from Lorraine[2] who clung desperately to her. Lightoller puts the nursemaid and baby on the boat. It is hugely overloaded.

Michel puts Lolo on a coil of ropes and kneels in front of him. 'Lolo, I'm going to give you a message for mummy and you must never forget it. Tell her I love her and I ask her forgiveness for all the hurtful things I have done to her. Now go, my little Lolo, and don't forget, you have to look after your little brother! You are the oldest; you have to be the daddy! Above all, remember your name: Michel Navratil, like me. And don't worry, we'll see each other on the *Carpathia*. I'll take the next boat!'

Lolo's face lights up: daddy's taking the next boat! In the meantime he's the head of the family and Momon needs him. He now accepts the separation from his daddy without too much trouble. Michel, deeply upset, tries to hold back his tears. He feels as if he has a mountain on his stomach, that his heart is going to burst. When he at last decides to put Lolo on the boat his eyes fill with horror: it is starting to be lowered and is already two metres down. Michel lifts his son into his arms and puts him on the rail. He hesitates through panic. Safe hands, down below, stretch out ready to catch him. He is literally thrown down into the boat. Strange but safe hands carefully grasp him and the canvas boat reaches the end of its descent into the glacial ocean.

CHAPTER 15

THE LAST MINUTES OF THE *TITANIC*

THE *TITANIC*, the unsinkable floating town that 'even God cannot sink,' is dying. Her prow and more than a third of the front of the transatlantic steamer is in the ocean. The stern, and part of the rear, is out of the water. The list on portside is quickly getting worse. There is no longer any class distinction on board. Crew and passengers alike are awaiting imminent death. Stokers, stewards, cooks, coal trimmers, passengers rich and poor, men, women, and children hold on to the ship's rail desperately fighting against the implacable weight, pushing them towards the brink. An angle of about 40 degrees means those who haven't the strength to hold on are thrown into the water. Some people sense the rising danger but hesitate to jump into the hostile ocean. Fear, fear of a horrible death in dark, frozen water. And even more terrible, being swallowed up in the abyss.

A huge ship reputed to be unsinkable, on its inaugural voyage, sinking beneath their feet is an apocalypse. Grief has come to everyone at a time when they are most happy. All hopes of a new life in the New World are suddenly obliterated. Everyone sees his or her life flash before them like a fast back-tracking film. And for many there is mixed remorse. Do they deserve or have they provoked this fate by choosing to travel on board the finest ship in the world? Who cannot have doubts? How can they not believe, even if they think it absurd, they are not part of a catastrophe brought about as a punishment for past sins?

Rosalind's mother, Mrs Hoghes, weeps bitterly. Her little girl was right! Why on earth did she not listen to her?

'Now it's every man for himself,' Captain Smith says to his crew. Happily no one hears him. If they had, there would have been a battle for the remaining life-jackets and access to the last two canvas boats still obstinately fastened down.

There is certainly panic among some of the passengers. Some have gone crazy through being locked up in third class. Some, understandably, lost their heads when they discovered the dramatic shortage of lifeboats. But the crew has done their best to calm them down. The majority, however, are accepting their fate and facing death calmly. The mechanics and the stokers are amongst the bravest. Some of them have worked until the last moment, until the engines and furnaces were flooded. They kept on working so as to keep the pumps and electric generators going. These men are familiar with the terrible deaths that can take place in ship's engine rooms: drowning and fires when boilers explode. The anonymous heroes on the *Titanic* are those who stayed down below until the bitter end, knowing there would be no lifeboats left.

Michel, holding on to the rail, watches as the boat the children are on rapidly disappears towards the dark ocean. The little overloaded contraption bravely descends to the surface of the water without a hitch. The water is now very near. So little distance separates him and his sons. He has never cherished them as much as at this tragic moment! He can see Lolo and Momon waving and calling to him. They are very distressed. Despite his courage, Lolo cannot cope with such a dreadful reality. The weight of this tragedy is too much for a little boy, not yet four. The baby too must know something terrible is happening. Watching them makes Michel weep. He doesn't feel self-pity, just sadness for the children. His eyes are consumed with them, knowing it is the last time he will see them. He can still see their desperate little faces clearly, but soon his tears get in the way.

'Daddy! Daddy! Come here! Jump, Daddy! Don't leave us alone!' shouts Lolo.

Momon's trembling voice joins in too.

No! It's unbearable! Lolo and Momon can't leave me!

Without thinking, Michel climbs over the rail and stands on the edge, ready to jump. Then he feels something holding him back. Four strong hands pull him on to the deck.

'We've arrived just in time!'

Stead and Bedford stand in front of him. Michel makes another desperate dash to the rail but they grab him and hold him by his arms.

'Have you thought about what you're doing Michel?' asks Bedford. 'You know their boat is already overloaded! There's no room for you! Do you want to die in the ice right in front of your children?'

Michel, hardly more than a boy himself, is shaken. He can scarcely breathe. All the experiences of the previous six years flash in front of his eyes: the emigration to Nice from Presbourg, his two years as a tailor's apprentice, meeting Marcelle and their marriage in London, their total happiness, the purchase of the fashion house in rue de France, the birth of the children, the success of his business among the wealthy clients in Nice, Marcelle's affair with Momon's godfather, the hurt pride, the heartbreak of love, the resulting lack of interest in the business and bankruptcy, and finally, the flight to America to protect the children and start life anew. Did he deserve such a cruel end?

Michel is overcome with feelings of outrage. No, he does not deserve to die. And all his plans for a bright future for the children, taken away from their mother for their own good? If Marcelle gets them back what a terrible education they will have. Everything Michel wanted to prevent will now inevitably happen. And what if Marcelle doesn't find them? What will become of them?

For a brief moment, out of weakness, his whole being is outraged at the idea of death. Michel wants to live. He wants to be with the children again. He faints and falls, rolling over and over down the sloping deck. The world keels over around him. The water is closer, so what? He will be able to swim to boat D. But at the last minute, his friends grab hold of him. His torment is prolonged.

Michel gets up and, holding on to the rail again, peers at the nearby ocean. The little lights on the boats are further and further away. Little boat D is lost among all the other boats. The young man climbs the slope towards the stern to find his friends. Bedford, understanding his despair, embraces him. Michel is grateful for his feelings of affection. It gives him the strength to pull himself together. Furious about this lack of faith in himself, he stands up straight and thanks his friend.

Charles has no family to leave behind. The grandeur and beauty of the agony between the shiny blocks of ice, as white as the Milky Way and the infinity of the celestial arch, stun him. He would feel almost euphoric if it wasn't for the unjustness of the death of all these innocent people, victims of pride and the importance of big business, particularly the White Star Line and its president, Ismay. Where is Ismay now? Did he manage to get off the *Titanic?*

At 2.10am the last of the crew are on the deck. Most of them do not have any life-jackets. Like the one Mr Astor had ripped open to show Madeline what it was made of, many life-jackets have been left in the flooded cabins.

The crew is grouped together with their workmates because they neither had the time nor the occasion to get to know anyone else. Some of the stokers and mechanics haven't had time to put on warm clothes. They have come from temperatures of 45 degrees by the furnaces to minus 2 degrees on the deck. They are dressed in only trousers and vests, still soaked in sweat. Despite everything, they manage to joke amongst themselves about the irony of the situation.

The crew from the dining rooms, mainly French, share cigarettes and bottles of vintage wine rescued from the kitchens. Their white jackets and aprons can be seen underneath blankets or overcoats thrown on at the last minute. Rosalind's mother, standing with a group of chambermaids and stewards, thinks about the steamship in her daughter's dream. Will the *Titanic* also break in two before it completely sinks?

Some members of the crew decide to jump into the ocean and swim to the lifeboats. Samuel Hemming, a maintenance man who helped launch some of the lifeboats, manages to reach lifeboat number four and is dragged on board. Frédéric Hoyt, one of the passengers from second class, whose wife is on the same boat as Lolo and Momon, also jumps overboard. He swims to the boat and is pulled into it. He takes the oars and starts to row so as not to freeze to death. What bad luck for Michel who had been stopped from doing this very thing by his two well-meaning friends.

Stead joins Michel and hangs on to the rail alongside his young friend. They had been standing together like this a few hours earlier, watching for icebergs while waiting for the fatal collision. They were quiet. Stead asks himself what made him get on the *Titanic* when he knew it would sink. He was not pushed by some suicidal need. On the contrary, he had never had the wish to die. His journalistic instinct had simply overridden everything. Stead had predicted there would be a disaster. He would be able help with it, that is all. He would quietly accept the consequences of this decision. If the possibility of saving his life without taking a woman's or a child's place, had come up, he would have jumped at the chance.

He is completely resigned to own death now, but not to the death of most of those around him. He looks round with bitterness. There are entire families with three, five, or even eight children gathered around their parents. Clusters of poor human beings, hanging on to the side of the ship, are simply waiting to die. Mothers and fathers clutch the smallest children in one arm, holding on with the other so as not to slide along the fatal slope. The older children, are clinging on to rails, sometimes so high, they are almost out of reach. Some of them weep silently, nearly choking with terror. Others seem to be amazingly calm and serene.

Stead nudges Michel and points out these innumerable silent scenes. There is a magic silence in the darkness. Myriad stars wink at all those who are getting ready for a peaceful death and seem to say, 'Have courage, you will soon be delivered. Your parents and friends who are already dead are waiting to welcome you into a better, fairer world.'

But for those who, by contrast, show their silent fear of death, no one, oh, but no one can say anything…

Michel is thinking that if divine justice exists, he has been punished for his sins. No matter how good the reasons were for taking the children from their mother, he is now paying the price for their abduction. But if he is suffering, physically, because of what he has done, his soul is happy and peaceful knowing the children are safe. The ocean is very still and they won't be cold with the layers of clothes they have on. The women will look after them and the *Carpathia*, coming to rescue everyone in the lifeboats, will be here by dawn.

Michel is surprised to discover he is finally coming to terms with his own death. He turns round wanting to talk about it. Stead has disappeared while Charles is looking avidly in the direction of the bridge where people are desperately battling with the canvas boats, A and B. Michel turns his back to the ocean. He is forcing himself not to think any longer about the little canvas boat D. It is now too far out of sight to be able to make out any faces. He can no longer see either the children's dejected faces or their solitude. He follows Charles in the direction of the smoking lounge.

Only seven minutes have passed since boat D touched the water. At moments like this, time passes quickly. However, real time takes its course. The list on the ship has increased and to reach the smoking lounge Bedford and Navratil slide on the sloping deck as if on a toboggan. The water has almost reached the smoking lounge.

Michel muses about not having given Lolo his passport (the one with Navratil rather than Hoffmann written in it) so his son can be identified. He fleetingly imagines a new drama, conforming to his deepest wishes: the children are believed to be orphans and will be adopted by an American family. The plans he has for them come to fruition…. But Marcelle's despair if she never finds out what has happened to them? And the trauma for the children becoming doubly orphaned! Michel immediately stops thinking about this. He's sure Marcelle has received his message. She will find the children and it will be all the better for them.

Two minutes later the list on the ship increases even more. The rudder and the propellers are now out of the water. The band is still playing by the smoking lounge. They are holding on as best they can but Fred Clarke, who is playing the double bass, has the greatest difficulty in holding on to his instrument. It keeps slipping along the deck. He ends up clutching it to him, with the metal point stuck into the floor. The instrument is not supposed to be restricted in this way and he can't play properly. Michel sees Roger Bricoux and Georges Krins; both young men are around the age of twenty. They're laughing and joking as if they are in the casino in Monte Carlo. Bricoux makes a questioning movement with his head. Michel signals back, yes, the children have been saved.

The smoking lounge is still dry and Michel finds the group he'd been with two hours earlier. Stead is sitting lopsidedly in a large armchair wedged against a wall. He's smoking a big Havana. Charles Hay and Ben Guggenheim are swigging back a bottle of champagne. Other bottles are lined up waiting to be opened. Harry Widener has gone off to look for more but comes back empty handed. The stock room is now flooded.

The conversation lasts five minutes. Michel notices Stead and most of the other men have given their life-jackets to the staff. He was just asking himself why he shouldn't do the same when the *Titanic* tilts violently. Everyone slides down the sloping room and rolls on to the heaped up armchairs below, near Stead. Andrews, sitting on a table fixed to the floor, is the only one not to fall. The men all get up and reach the door with great difficulty. Bedford stays behind and asks Andrews, who is not wearing a life-jacket, if he's coming with them. He doesn't reply. He just stares at the little walnut tables with their pink lampshades, and the green gaming tables. Then his gaze rests on a painting representing the arrival in the New World. Andrews is going to die swallowed up in his unsinkable ship. His decision is irreversible.

Michel is waiting outside for his friends and Charles joins him. Stead follows but suddenly turns round without saying anything. He goes back into the smoking lounge, opens a bottle of champagne and wedges himself in a corner waiting for the end. He swigs mouthfuls of champagne not far from where Andrews is sitting.

The dining room on C deck is under water. Charles and Michel see a hotch potch of floating armchairs, tables, trays, and chairs; they can hear crockery clinking together in cupboards. They stop for a moment. It's a very strange sight. Then they start going up the deck to the veranda where they join a small group of passengers who are lodged together, watching an unexpected show.

Joughin, the jovial baker, is throwing basketwork chairs and deckchairs through a window. He's drunkenly singing at the top of his voice. Songs like, 'Cherry Time' and 'Sweet White Wine' are interspersed with the sound of yet another chair going splash into the water. After all his 'work' he roars with laughter until the next chair comes floating by. It is 2.15am. The lights on the *Titanic* are now getting weaker and weaker, giving out a bronze glow.

The band stops playing for a moment, then the hymn 'Autumn' rings out. Solemnly superb, a prelude to the sinking ship like a prayer to the firmament.

After that events speed up. The front of the ship plunges into the water and three minutes later the rear is lifted up into the air. Michel feels as if all hope is not lost. He will fight to survive until the end, even though he is not afraid of death. He sees the canvas boats A and B falling into the water. Charles climbs with him up to the top of the stern at the moment when the *Titanic* is at 65 degrees or 70 degrees. They find Otto Schmidt, the pilot Pierre Maréchal, and Joughin there, wedged against the parapet. Joughin is holding a bottle of whiskey in each hand, singing loudly in between swigs. Passengers taking refuge at the stern find themselves lifted seventy-five metres above the water level. Most of them fall in clusters into the water and are immediately killed. More agile passengers climb on ropes or hang on to the rail for dear life. Michel and Charles are among the latter.

The officers and sailors in charge of unfastening the remaining Englehardt canvas boats finally manage to do so. Boat B, still empty, falls just at the moment the *Titanic* starts to move and lands on the side of the ship, which is in the air. Some of the crew has the bright idea of getting into boat A, waiting for the water level to rise as the ship sinks.

At 2.18am, there is a tremendous cracking noise. As in Rosalind's dream, the ship breaks in two, vomiting thousands of objects and scattering them on the ocean before they sink. The basket-work chairs and deckchairs float off. Joughin could have saved himself the trouble of throwing some of them overboard. To crown the horror of it all, there is a shower of sparks as the second funnel falls, crushing about thirty people who are attempting to swim away from the ship. The two canvas boats are thrown about thirty metres from the ship, stopping them from sinking with the ship but half filling boat A with water. Ida and Isidor Straus clutching one another just below the funnel and, praying together, are killed instantly. With the break-up of the ship, the boilers in the middle are thrust into the water where they explode, sending out enormous jets of steam. This immediately kills all those who have been thrown into the water nearby.

Some of the passengers, like the ones who gathered together in prayer in the third-class dining room, choose to die inside the ship and do so when the front went down.

Seconds earlier, Bride, Phillips, Trevor, Mirella, Abelseth, Lightoller, Callagher, Archibald Grace, Jack Thayer (who John Astor had tried to put on a lifeboat), his friend Milton Long and hundreds of others, had jumped into the water, when it was only a few metres from them. Archibald Gracie is struck by an oar and sinks quite deeply in the ocean. He swims and when he resurfaces he sees boat B upturned. He pulls himself on to it and sees Jack Thayer a few metres away. He helps him up. The falling funnel has missed Jack by only a few metres. The suction caused by it sent him down into the water and it has taken extraordinary energy to resurface near the upturned boat. His friend, Milton Long, who had jumped with him, has not been so lucky and has disappeared.

Lightoller was caught in one of the huge in-draughts of air, and sucked into one of the *Titanic*'s air vents. Happily for him there was a grill on it and he was stuck against it for a minute before the reverse happened; a violent rush of air threw him into the water and he landed by boat B. He was hanging on to the upturned boat when Milton Long had been thrown fifty metres away. Bride was thrown into the water and, when he surfaced, he found himself trapped underneath the boat. With a tremendous effort he managed to get out from under it.

Mirella and Olaus jumped hand in hand. The brutal contact with the water caught them unawares and they let go of each other. Olaus feels some hands grasping him round the neck, nearly strangling him. He roughly pushes the hands off, but the poor creature who had caught hold of him isn't wearing a life-jacket and is drowning. He tries to hold her head up out of the water but she grabs his neck again. He has to abandon her to avoid being dragged down with her. He swims with all his might to boat B where Phillips and Callagher have managed to reach Gracie and Thayer. He is pulled on board where he finds Trevor in the middle of pulling Mirella on too. She has just seen Otto Schmidt drowning. The exhausted girl lies in the bottom of the boat like a wet rag. Unfortunately, the boat, after it had been righted by a wave, is half full of water. Mirella, incapable of moving, is lying with her back in the icy water. Trevor dies, overcome by the cold before Olaus could manage to pull him from the water. Olaus faints and collapses in a heap by Mirella.

Only the rear of the ship is on the waves. It rises majestically, transforming the outside deck into a vertical side. One after another, the survivors, including Astor, Guggenheim, his valet in dress coat and tails, and Widener, are thrown into the freezing ocean.

At precisely 2.20am, without causing the least wave or any

sort of turbulence, the rear of the majestic giant goes into the waves vertically, gently setting down those who are hanging on to ropes and rails. Michel and Charles find themselves a few metres from each other in the water.

~ ~ ~

In her bedroom in Nice Marcelle is still sitting on her bed, wide-awake at 2.20am, New York time. She can see the figure in the corridor that had appeared earlier. The slope has increased so it looks like a passageway in a mine. At the back, climbing with great difficulty on the angle made by the floor and the wall, slipping, pulling himself up and pressing with both hands on the right hand wall, is a man trying to get up the slope. There is something very strange about the shape of him and Marcelle cannot identify what it is. Finally Michel manages to get right up on high and holds out a letter to her. His hair is bizarrely white and his clothes are stiff. She takes his hand and shivers because it is ice cold. Feeling terrified, she takes the letter. It is a bereavement letter, trimmed in black. It instantly loses its colour and is replaced by a strange landscape, frozen, neither blue, nor black, nor white, nor liquid, nor solid, nor dark, nor light. Then the image disappears as quickly as it came. Marcelle screams without being able to stop. Her stepfather, Antonio, wakes up with a start, runs from the adjoining bedroom and takes her in his arms.

'Marcelle, for the love of God, wake up! You're dreaming!'

The terrible screams stop. Marcelle looks at Antonio and says in a flat voice, 'Michel is dying.'

Marcelle's mother, Angelina, comes into the bedroom. Marcelle looks straight through her. It is as if she can't feel anything anymore, as if she is anaesthetised. A few minutes pass. Angelina and Antonio don't dare move. Finally in a flat neutral voice Marcelle says, 'Open the window!'

Angelina does so. With the time difference between France and America, it is 7.30am in Nice. The spring sun streams through the window, lighting up the bedroom where Marcelle and Michel had been so happy together.

CHAPTER 16

IN THE LIFEBOATS

AFTER LOLO WAS DROPPED from the rail of the *Titanic* he landed in the arms of a young girl that he recognised. He had seen her on the ferryboat crossing from Calais to Dover, and had noticed her on several occasions on board the *Titanic*. Her blonde hair is pulled up into a high chignon, with wisps forming a halo round her freckled face. She has eyes as green as the English Channel and a wide smiling mouth. Her name is Margaret Hays but she is not related to Charles Hays who has stayed on the *Titanic* with Guggenheim, Astor and Widener.

If she had delayed getting on the lifeboats it was because she wanted to make room for women with children. She is only twenty-five years old and is very fond of children. She has used part of an inheritance to open an orphanage in New York and she is the director of it. The two little French boys are under her wing from the moment they get into boat D.

Margaret had already noticed the Navratil children and thought it was strange for them to be travelling without a mother. And here they are, the last to get off the *Titanic*. She knows their father has stayed on the sinking ship. The most important thing at the moment is to make sure the children do not witness the final terrible event. But despite her attempts to distract them, the children won't sit down. They are staring at their father waving to them from the *Titanic* not far away. With the distance between them increasing and the upsetting image of the mortally wounded ship, Lolo and Momon start shouting, desperately, 'Daddy! Daddy! Jump! Come with us! Daddy! Daddy!'

Their shouts go on and on, setting off a round of wailing and weeping amongst the other children in boat D as well as in nearby boats.

'Quickly! Quickly! Move away!' say the women in the boat.

The men row with all their might and the boat moves away a little. When Lolo sees Frédéric Hoyt swimming in their direction he is filled with hope. He watches intently as he makes a desperate effort to swim to their boat.

It's daddy, it must be him, he thinks to himself. But it is Frédéric who is pulled on board and Lolo realises he has made a mistake. He is terribly disappointed and slumps into a silent heap. Neither Momon nor Margaret can shake him out of it.

All of a sudden the men stop rowing and the lifeboat slows down. The *Titanic* is breaking in two. There is a terrible din as the boilers explode on contact with the ocean. A shock wave reaches the lifeboat and icy water comes rushing in before the boat is turned round by the force of the surging waves. The survivors find themselves confronted by a dying *Titanic*.

Margaret hugs Momon tightly in her arms to stop him from seeing the final moments of the sinking ship. She draws Lolo close to her but is unable to stop him from watching what is happening. The front of the ship starts to go down slowly. The belly of the ship, as if her heart has been bared, stares out. Lolo watches as a thousand and one lights disappear little by little into the dull water, leaving behind luminous, rippling, streaks that are soon lost in the dark abyss.

Lolo, transfixed, watches the sinking ship long after the hostile ocean, smooth as polished marble, has swallowed up the front. His body feels weak and he is sleepy. He looks around him for a familiar face among the adults and children, desperately in need of tenderness and reassurance. He feels himself being torn apart by grief, as if he could die. He is trying not to think that his daddy may be dead. Nearby, a little girl with her face in her hands is weeping. A young woman holding a sleeping baby tries to cheer her up. Exhausted by emotion and tiredness, Lolo drops off to sleep for a short while. The unnatural silence seems to go on forever. The survivors in the lifeboats, believers and non-believers, join together in prayer and Lolo wakes up with a start.

The passengers in the lifeboats look in disbelief upon the incredible sight they are now witnessing, as if it were the end of the world. The rear of the gigantic ship is standing vertical, majestically pointing towards the sky. Just before she sinks into the waves, the quivering porthole lights go out in unison. The giant sinks silently towards the dark abyss and rapidly disappears into the ice fields, covered in newly formed crystals. It is a sight of unforgettable beauty, on a huge scale. People are dumbstruck. On boat D, mothers have hidden their children's heads in their skirts. Babies like Edmond are sleeping, the adults and little Lolo are quiet, overburdened with the ghastly beauty of the shipwreck.

The moans and groans of hundreds of victims suddenly break the silence hanging over the ocean, empty apart from icebergs. The air is filled with the most excruciating sounds. More than a thousand people have found themselves being plunged into icy water, less than two degrees.[1] Some of them cannot cope with the shock and die almost immediately through congestion of the lungs. The others, screaming, cling to each other, and fight over bits of floating wreckage, trying to haul themselves out of the water to escape the terrible stranglehold of the icy sea.

Lolo scrutinises the ocean around him. 'Daddy! Where is my Daddy? And Mirella? And Trevor? And Charles? And my friend, the old man? We must find them and get them out of the water immediately!'

Margaret pulls him close to her and strokes his cheek but does not reply. She feels a huge lump in her throat and is overcome with emotion. Tears stream down her cheeks, leaving them streaked with grime. Lolo lifts up his head and sees how sad she is. Her sorrow makes him feel brave and his hopes are raised. No, his daddy and his friends are floating in the water and we'll soon pick them up. Lassitude overtakes him and he closes his eyes, trying to forget the torture of the collective agony that the survivors are mostly powerless to do anything about.

The swimmers hope to be picked up by a lifeboat in vain. So as not to hear the terrible cries for help, so as not to see the poor children separated from their parents when they fall into the water, so as not to see old people, so as not to see men in their prime, young men and women, fighting for their lives in the ice, nearly all the lifeboats pull away as fast as they can, abandoning the poor souls to their horrific fate. The survivors dread the possibility of their lifeboats being overturned by those in the water trying to climb in. It is an absurd worry because it is impossible for anyone to reach up to the edge of a boat unless those on board help them.

Quarrelling breaks out on the lifeboats. Women, whose husbands or adult sons were left on the *Titanic*, and some of the other passengers, beg to allow as many people as possible to be pulled up out of the water. But the majority wants to get as far away as possible. The more spaces there are on the lifeboats, the more the survivors fear for their lives. Once the lifeboats have distanced themselves from the poor souls in the water, quarrels start again. The passengers on number six, for example, want to go back, but Hitchens, the quartermaster, refuses. Number four pulls eight people on board because they have managed to swim alongside. Boat B pulls up two people as well as a baby. Captain Smith handed the baby over and swam off. He was never seen again.

In boat D, already overloaded (55 instead of 49 people in it), nobody speaks about going back to help. The men row away as quickly as possible to avoid hearing the shouts and screams. Progress is slow and the sounds are carried a long way. Lolo, awake again, feels his hair stand on end at the sounds of those in distress. Perhaps his daddy is crying out for help. He must be saved! Trampling on those who are lying at the bottom of the boat covering their ears so as not to hear the terrible sounds from the icy sea, he goes to the man in charge of the lifeboat.

'Please sir, go back! My Daddy stayed on the ship and perhaps he's swimming in the ocean. Save him!'

Nobody hears him because they are all talking at the same time. Margaret suggests singing hymns to muffle the sound of those still struggling for life in the water. Psalms, sung with all the strength the survivors can muster, ring out across the ocean, interspersed with copious weeping. Other boats join in and the singing continues for an hour.

Lolo is now in the arms of one of the men he had seen with Charles and his daddy on the *Titanic*. He's called Björn Steffanson, a lieutenant, and Sweden's naval attaché in Washington. Along with his friend, Hugh Woolner, he had helped the officers ward off the would-be hijackers of boat C. He had then helped women and children get into boat D. While Michel was saying good bye to the children, Murdoch had asked for two men with some knowledge of boats, to be in charge of it. Steffanson and Woolner had volunteered and had jumped into the boat just before Lolo. Steffanson had taken the tiller while Woolner had taken the oars near Margaret.

Lolo is passed from hand to hand and back to Margaret's knees. He's fighting and crying with the anger and frustration of his lack of power over the situation. Why can't they save all these people who are shouting in the water? It's not fair. At a very tender age he is suddenly discovering the arbitrary nature of life, including unfairness, evil and the lack of solidarity amongst humankind.

It takes Margaret half an hour to calm him down. She whispers words of comfort in his ear, satisfying his demand for truth without hurting him too much: there isn't enough room on the lifeboat. We can't go back and give false hope to people. Lolo must remember he is the head of the family now and has to look after Momon. Perhaps his daddy has found a space on one of the two boats that were left. He has to wait for dawn to come and, with it, the rescue ship. Lolo goes back to sleep.

He wakes up at about three o'clock feeling hungry. He remembers the baker's buns. He takes them from his pocket and offers them round. All the other children are asleep. It is getting colder and colder. Everyone's hair is covered in frost. Frédéric Hoyt whose clothes are soaking wet, rows like a mad man, three times faster than usual. But the boat doesn't move very fast. In fact the canvas covering is not that watertight and it lets in water. It constantly needs bailing out. The water tends to run down into the flat bottom of the boat. The people lying there gradually get more and more numb with cold. In an effort to keep warm, passengers take it in turns to row. Lolo remembers what McCawley told him about rowing but nobody will let him have a turn.

Elsewhere the atmosphere is somewhat stormy. While Madeline in number four gives her shawl to a little girl from third class who is crying, while a sailor in number five offers his socks to Mrs Dodge who is wearing mules on bare feet, while in number six Mrs Brown, a nice energetic lady, wraps her fur stole round the feet of a sailor whose teeth are chattering, a woman in number eleven is annoying everyone by setting her alarm clock to ring at five minute intervals. Lord Duff Gordon and Henry Stengel in number one are arguing about who is in charge. Stokers in number three are refusing to put out their cigarettes even though the smoke is bothering other passengers. All the people in number five are quarrelling. Nothing like that on boat D. Woolner had filled his pockets with biscuits and oranges and he feeds Lolo and the other children until the *Carpathia* arrives.

The singing more or less dies down at the same time as the shouting from the people in the water stops. By three o'clock, cries for help are very faint and no longer reach the lifeboats. Lolo rocked to sleep by the movement of the boat dreams about his mummy. Margaret has said she would come to find them in New York, which confirmed what his daddy had said. His eyelids flicker but he is not deeply asleep because his feet are cold. At first it did not bother him but gradually it becomes very painful. It feels as if hundreds of tiny needles are pricking him. He looks down and sees his feet are in water.

Michel had done his best to prepare himself for contact with the icy water but what he actually experiences is impossible to describe: his whole body is paralysed by a devastating, aggressive onslaught, it attacks his heart, his intestines, and his nervous system to the extremity of his limbs. It takes several minutes to get accustomed to the icy water before he can move. He finally manages to overcome the paralysis and starts to swim. He sees Charles not far away. His body position looks strange. With great difficulty he swim over to him only to discover he is floating face down in the water. He died on impact with the ocean.

It is so painful in the icy water; Michel envies Charles his quick death. He feels as if a thousand red-hot pokers are stabbing him. Without waiting too long by his best friend and benefactor, he swims off, using as much energy as he can to withstand the freezing cold. He sees the upturned boat not far away with people trying to get on it and resolutely goes in another direction. Having swum about a hundred metres, he feels as though he has never moved faster, although the opposite has happened. Without noticing it, the cold has slowed him down. He reaches boat A. Once there he sees people trying to pull themselves into it and again decides to go in another direction. He ignores the fact that his friends Mirella, Trevor, Abelseth, Phillips, Schmidt and Callagher are there, just a few metres from him. He decides to swim straight-ahead as far as he can. If destiny is in his favour then he will find a lifeboat to rescue him.

Complete silence hangs over boat A. It has become ghostly. It is half full of water. About thirty bodies are heaped up in the bottom of it as well as on the gunwale. Their wet clothes are frozen and their hair is covered in frost. The boat looks as if it is slowly going to the island of the dead. From time to time one of the bodies on the gunwale falls heavily into the ocean and stays there, floating on the surface.[2] Finally, some of the survivors pull themselves together and start trying to bail out the water. Mirella, deathly pale, stares ahead, trembling. She hasn't the strength to move. Nobody has enough energy to row and after ten minutes, everyone becomes inert. The only thing keeping people alive is the rum found in the boat. They swig it straight from the bottle. Olaus puts Mirella in a dry place on the gunwale, and tries to keep her warm by massaging her limbs. He keeps this up for an hour. Nearby, Phillips is hardly breathing. Olaus looks at the ocean. Five metres away from the catastrophe, there's a huge amount of flotsam and jetsam, boxes, barrels, furniture, doors, planks, cupboards, and different kinds of things: toys, empty bottles, hats; he even sees a doll and a baby's bottle floating by.

Boat D is not faring very well. It is slowly but surely taking in water. Margaret has put Momon on her knee and Lolo is on a coil of rope. The adults are continually bailing out. The situation is just starting to get really bad when not far away, three boats, forming a line, are spotted. The people in boat D immediately shout to them and the rowers increase their speed, making the boat pitch and toss and waking Lolo up.

'What's happening, Mag?'

'We're calling the other boats so we won't be alone. Look over there, they're coming towards us!'

She never imagined this news could affect him so much. He gets up and shouts excitedly. 'I'm going to see Daddy again! I'm going to see Daddy again!'

'But no Lolo, that's impossible!' She butts in. 'These boats left before ours!'

Lolo doesn't listen to her and obstinately watches the approaching line of boats. At the head of them is number fourteen with Lowe, the fifth officer in charge. Following it are numbers ten, twelve and four. A rope about fifty metres long is keeping the boats together like a long umbilical cord. The poor people in boat D are very comforted by seeing them arrive. Once number fourteen is alongside them, Lowe examines the leaking boat with an expert eye.

'It's not very nice for you but this boat can stay afloat for another two hours! The *Carpathia* will be here in about an hour. Don't worry. We'll attach you to number four, so you will feel reassured.'

At this point Lolo, in a little voice anything but reassured, pipes up, 'And my Daddy? Is he with you?'

'What's your name?'

'Lolo, and my little brother who's asleep is called Momon!'

'And what's your surname?'

'My surname?'

Lolo, is hearing this word for the second time. Daddy did say to remember 'Your name is…' but he can't remember.

'I don't know!'

'Look – 'Lolo' *what*?'

'Lolo!'

Lowe loses patience. He has more important things to do than to listen to this little boy. He'll see to him later. He wants to distribute the 55 passengers in lifeboat fourteen among the other lifeboats so he can turn round and pick up survivors from the water. When the little flotilla is grouped together again, except for those who are sleeping, Lolo can see faces in the other boats. Steffanson watches him wriggling with excitement in the hope of seeing his daddy and feels very sorry for him. Cupping his hands he shouts in a loud voice.

'Have you picked up any survivors?'

'Number four have pulled up eight. D'you want their names?'

'Just ask if any of them put two little boys in boat D.'

Ten minutes pass while Lolo waits, breathless. Nearby there's great commotion. Boats are rocking while passengers from number fourteen are transferred to number ten then twelve and finally to number four where Daniel Buckley and Madeline are. Madeline sees Lolo and shouts in French: 'Oh! My little friend! How are you?'

Lolo bursts into tears, 'My Daddy, my Daddy, I want to see my Daddy!'

Steffanson at last gets a reply. None of the people picked up by number four have any little boys.

Lolo feels as if his heart is breaking. He's never going to see his daddy again, never again, never again. He can't even cry. Mag wants to hold him but he pushes her away. Momon, who has been sleeping all this time, wakes up with a start, gets up and seeing the icy water and all the strange people around him bursts out crying. Lolo turns to him and hugs him very tightly. Momon calms down and they sit passively side by side, cuddled up together with Lolo's chin resting on Momon's curly head.

Seeing them united in adversity like this, no adult could be anything but full of sympathy for them. The two little orphans feeling warmed by those around them settle down. Just then,

Mag gets up and points to the sky: over there is a shower of lights from some flares! It is 3.30am. The *Carpathia* is coming towards them, travelling at seventeen and a half knots, three more than its usual maximum!

The surrounding area becomes visible from the boats. The sun is rising on the horizon. After exchanging greetings and information with fellow survivors in neighbouring lifeboats, and the elation felt at seeing the flares, most of the men become listless. They're overcome with exhaustion and cannot move. The women had taken over the oars some time ago, keeping their spirits up by singing.

Meanwhile, Lowe has moved away in boat fourteen, empty except for two men from the crew. Lolo watches wide-eyed as day breaks. He is still holding Momon in his arms. Despite all the layers of warm clothes Trevor had put on him, he starts to shiver and his feet are so cold he cannot feel them anymore. Little by little, he forgets the horrors of the preceding hours and becomes absorbed in the dazzling polar landscape. Transported into the world of dreams, he's on the lookout for Father Christmas among the mountains of shining ice and the snowfields, stretching out of sight. Here and there, between the layers of ice, he can see deep blue lakes. He forgets the black and white death. An image of something that happened, only a couple of hours ago, but seeming much longer to Lolo, suddenly comes to him. Kneeling on the deck of the *Titanic*, his father waves goodbye, but this goodbye, Father Christmas tells him, simply means 'see you again soon.'

Time passes and Lolo, half-asleep, is deep in dreamland. The sky becomes pink, slowly turning rainbow-like in the east. In a short space of time a flaming emerald green appears and then the sun comes up. A huge blood-red ball slowly rises from the frozen ocean. Lolo is perhaps the only one on boat D to catch a glimpse of the aurora borealis. It vanishes and as he looks away he sees a shining dot crowned with white smoke, a long way off to the south. A ship is coming towards them. He falls asleep, overcome with exhaustion brought on by the horror-filled night.

A kilometre away, Lowe, looking for survivors, notices a white head on the water. A young man has frozen to death. His facial features are frozen but his eyes are still shining. Michel had swum haphazardly for an hour, going more and more slowly. The ghastly pain of the first few minutes had been overtaken by a bizarre sensation. It was as if his legs had gradually become pieces of wood.

By three o'clock, his body had become totally numb. He swam with only his arms even though his hands refused to do what he wanted. Then as the sky began to get light and he could see the triumphant morning star above him he finally stopped moving.

Nothing hurt anymore; his body ceased to exist. But he could still feel his heart beating and memories flooded his mind like a wonderful film. He relived his childhood in his village in Slovakia, on the banks of the proud Danube whose brown water tumbles like a rising torrent. Surging forward like the surrounding ocean, now covered in ice, he sees his grandfather appearing. He was also called Michel Navratil and has been dead for ten years. Now he's here with a big white beard, earrings, an immaculately groomed moustache and a big smile, lighting up his wrinkled face. Isn't it he who Lolo thinks is Father Christmas at the moment? The old man smiles at Michel and holds out his arms. Michel feels enveloped by a wonderful sense of well being. The aurora borealis shines with all its might for him and his son, another Michel Navratil. The line won't stop there. Little by little Michel sees a long farandole made up of all those who have preceded him. He hopes to join them for eternity. When Lowe reaches him, he has just stopped breathing.

On boat A, everyone has given up hope of being saved. Olaus

holds Mirella's frozen body in his arms. The water is up to his knees. Nearby, three bodies stare at the sky. No one has the courage to throw them into the ocean. Olaus blows on Mirella's face and whispers to her tenderly. She is smiling but Olaus knows there is no hope. She opens her eyes for the last time, and looks at him weakly. Then, like the lights on the *Titanic* as it sank, her eyes grow dim. Olaus holds her to him for a few minutes. He feels numb, anaesthetised, he can no longer think. The lifeboat will sink soon. The end is near.

Suddenly out of nowhere an empty boat comes alongside. An officer in uniform is standing up, waving his hands. Olaus finds the strength and the desire to live. He gets up with great difficulty and looks at Mirella. He remembers the marvellous hours they have spent together. He lifts up the little light body, now like a marble statue, cuts the life-jacket straps with his knife and slides her into the water. Mirella's body sinks gently down into the liquid abyss. He jumps into boat number fourteen and helps other survivors on board too. Only one of the women from third class, Rosa Abbot, has survived. A passenger from first class, Edward Brown, is dressed in a steward's uniform. No one has thought to ask him about this. For Phillips, the cold is as good a reason as any.

In the line of boats, people have decided they would prefer to separate because progress is very slow and everyone is in a hurry to get on board the *Carpathia* now not far away. Only the passengers on boat D want to stay strung together. While the umbilical ropes are being cut Margaret sees something very strange, and rubs her eyes. About a hundred metres away some men appear to be walking on the water! Soon, all those who are awake watch with astonishment as these strange beings call out for help. Boats four, ten and twelve go in the direction of the mysterious survivors of boat B.

Only a few people have died on boat B which is in a much

worse state than A. Jack Thayer has managed to withstand the cold but several passengers' feet, like Bride's, are frozen. The Englehardt is three quarters full of water. If it hadn't been for Lightoller's ingenuity, it would have sunk a long time ago. The wind gets up as dawn breaks and the icy breeze creates little waves that regularly lap over the side of the boat. Lightoller has regrouped the thirty survivors into two, standing on starboard and portside. He shouts orders and they all obey him: 'Lean to the right! To the left! Stand up straight!' Thanks to him, the boat is still afloat. One of the men in it, overcome with exhaustion, totters about. When the three lifeboats get close, boat B starts to pitch and toss. Is it going to sink just as help is here? To everyone's relief it becomes stable again and its occupants transfer to the three lifeboats. B conveniently waits until everyone is safe before sinking fast.

The little convoy of lifeboats sets off to the south. With the sunshine everyone's energy returns. The last biscuits are shared out and rum is given to the survivors from boat B. The outline of the *Carpathia* looms up imperceptibly.

Calmness returns. Nobody speaks. Then a voice coming from a long way away is heard singing God knows what. People look in the direction of the singing but the frozen ocean is empty. Small pieces of ice are being pushed to and fro by the breeze but has anyone heard of ice that sings? The voice gets nearer and nearer. A drunken voice, a very drunken voice. One of the icebergs turns round, blown by the wind, revealing a strange craft made of heaped up deckchairs. There's no helmsman in sight. However, on closer examination, a frost covered head and eyebrows appears from its midst. The head is singing. He's on the deckchairs with two bottles of whiskey for company, one empty, and the other half full. The head in question suddenly moves on seeing the lifeboats, gets off the deckchairs, and an arm emerges, firmly hanging on to the half full bottle of whiskey.

The man joyfully swims to the boats, splashing everyone. He looks as relaxed as someone in a hot spring pool! He is hauled on to boat number four but because his breath smells so foul, the passengers turn away from him. He falls into the bottom of the boat dead drunk and doesn't wake up until the passengers are taken on to the *Carpathia*.

After the *Titanic* went down, Joughin had happily made his way through the flotsam and jetsam drunkenly singing. From time to time he swigged a mouthful of whiskey from the bottle, his second that night, and it had given him courage. After an hour or so he was astonished to come across fewer and fewer swimmers. He had tried to have a conversation with people who were floating around but they were dead so he didn't get any replies. People didn't like his sentimental bawling so he wept a little and comforted himself with another swig of whiskey. This was how three and a half hours later, the passengers in boat B saw him coming towards them and hadn't been able to believe their eyes. Lightoller had called to him and a hoarse voice had replied in French. A stoker had recognised him and pulled him up out of the water. He kept on losing his balance and fell back into the water several times, always finding the energy to clamber back so as not to be separated from his bottles. Finally, he preferred to get back on his deckchairs and flounder in the water.

In the very overcrowded lifeboats everyone was worried. Would the lifeboats hold up? The vulnerable boats danced on the little waves caused by the icy morning breeze. Water splashed in. The situation was becoming alarming.

Mag put herself in a position where she could keep her eye on Lolo and Momon. While lifting up her head she sees a plume of grey smoke blown by the wind coming towards them. The *Carpathia* has come across the first lifeboats and has now come to a standstill a few hundred metres from them.

CHAPTER 17

ORPHANS OF THE ABYSS

ON MONDAY 15 APRIL, Marcelle runs out to buy some newspapers. She thinks her dream was a premonition and wants to see if any disasters have happened to explain it all. Marcelle is certain Michel is dead. Although she isn't suffering, she feels cut off from reality by an invisible blanket.

Rey de Villarey has offered to help but she has refused his offer. She needs to be alone. She is obsessed by only one thing: her children. The past week has been very difficult. There is still no news of them. Police investigations are at a virtual stand-still. Michel and the children have vanished into thin air. Michel Hoffmann, Navratil's head tailor, who bought his company when it went bankrupt, has written to her from Paris where he is on business. He told her how Michel and the children had lunched at his house, as they usually did on a Sunday, before they disappeared. Everything had seemed perfectly normal. The only thing to have slightly puzzled him was Michel borrowing his passport, but Hoffmann had forgotten to mention it.

Marcelle feels reassured by at least one thing: without doubt Michel has taken the children. The theory of them having been abducted by criminals and the subsequent horrors of such abduction is therefore dismissed. But where are Lolo and Momon? What has happened to them if Michel is indeed dead? Today's paper doesn't give any clues…

The following day, 16 April, the front page of the *Figaro* is practically all devoted to news about the eclipse of the sun, which will be seen at midday on the seventeenth. Exasperated, Marcelle is just about to turn over the page when she notices a short paragraph: 'Latest news: The *Titanic* has hit an iceberg. There is serious damage but there are no victims.' Marcelle doesn't want to waste time; the article doesn't interest her. She scours all the other newspapers, as she did the day before and then goes off to the police station to see about the lack of progress with the investigation.

On the morning of the seventeenth, Antonio brings her coffee and a pile of newspapers. One of the Nice daily papers is devoted to both the eclipse of the sun and the sinking of the *Titanic*. All the papers give contradictory news about the *Titanic*. It arouses her curiosity. The 16 April edition of the *Figaro* that arrives a day later in Nice has as a headline 'The Wreck of the *Titanic*'. There are differing accounts of the disaster and most of them are totally incoherent. First of all there is a write-up saying the *Titanic* has hit an iceberg but has stayed afloat. She is being towed to Halifax and will arrive the same day. Different ships have taken off passengers and no one has been injured. The following report says the opposite. The *Titanic* is sinking at the front and women and children have been put into lifeboats. Then a dispatch is received saying passengers have been taken off the ship and they are all safe and well. Other reports confirm the news: there are no victims of the disaster.

There is no concern amongst the specialists, because the *Titanic* is unsinkable. The blessings of the Marconi wireless system have been lauded. Thanks to Marconi, many people have been saved in record time. According to Welford, a ship owner, ice floes and icebergs have never been seen as far south as this. Convinced she is following a false trail by scrutinising these reports, Marcelle is just about to finish reading when her attention is drawn to a bold headline: 'The Last Hour: Havas Agency Report.'

'The White Star Line admits that many people have died in the shipwrecked *Titanic*.'

'The *Olympic* announces that the *Carpathia* arrived at the scene to find only pieces of wreckage amongst the ice.'

'According to their reports, the *Titanic* sank at about 2.20am, adding that about 675 people, passengers and crew, have been rescued.'

'Nearly all those rescued are women and children.'

'The *Californian* is staying in the area, continuing to search for survivors.'

As she reads this, Marcelle feels inexplicable mounting panic. The Nice newspapers report several hundred deaths. She feels weighed down by what she is reading. Slumping inertly in the chair, she drops the papers. Sheets of newsprint lie scattered on the floor around her. She is stunned. An image of the children crying for help fills her mind and she can't get rid of it. She makes a huge effort to pull herself together and gets up, shaking. Why isn't she weeping like everyone else? Why won't the pain go away? She has a cold shower and then walks round the garden for an hour. The crisis is over.

~ ~ ~

Contrary to Captain Lord, on the *Californian*, who had not known how to interpret the flares set off by the *Titanic*, Rostron, the Captain of the *Carpathia*, was extremely efficient as soon as he realised the *Titanic* had hit an iceberg. Even though he had not envisaged such a calamity, he had changed course as soon as the first message had been received. On learning the gravity of the situation, risking the lives of his 725 passengers amongst the icebergs, he did everything he could to get to the scene of the accident as quickly as possible.

So they would not hinder the rescue operations, Rostron ordered his passengers to stay in their cabins. Stewards were posted at the end of corridors to be on hand in case any of them felt nervous. At first no one wanted to believe it was really the *Titanic* sending distress signals. People thought up all kinds of crazy ideas of why the *Carpathia* had frantically changed course. They were even more astonished when the temperature gradually dropped to minus 2 degrees and the first icebergs came into view. Then some passengers started to realise the news was perhaps true.

Meanwhile, the crew and officers of the *Carpathia* were very busy on the bridge and in all the communal rooms. Lifeboats were uncovered and hung on the davits, lights were rigged up on the rails, gangways were prepared, slings and sacks for lifting up children, the sick and wounded were got ready, rope ladders were fixed to the side of the ship, and the derricks used for loading mail and luggage were prepared. The three doctors on board, Dr McGhee, an Englishman, a Hungarian and an Italian organised the first-, second- and third-class dining rooms into infirmaries and dormitories. The chief steward, Harry Hughes, had huge containers of soup, tea and coffee prepared, as well as hot grog, punch and whiskey. Everything, in fact, that might comfort those who had spent the night outside in a temperature of less than 2 degrees. Other stewards collected together piles of pillows, blankets and towels.

Towards morning when preparations for the rescue were finished, passengers on the *Carpathia* were allowed to go on the upper deck. Most people were sleeping and didn't want to be disturbed. But others were very helpful. They offered to let their cabins be used by women coming on board and were prepared to squash in with friends to make them available.

At 4.00am the engines stop. The *Carpathia* has arrived safely in the area of the alleged accident. Everyone on the upper deck stares at the ocean, radiant with the rising sun. Icebergs with their supernatural whiteness stretch as far as the eye can see and a layer of ice covers a large area of the ocean. It is a very strange sight for the passengers who had spent the previous afternoon wearing light clothes, enjoying the spring sunshine. Those who had just woken up could not believe their eyes! The horizon, however, is hopelessly empty. There's not a ship in sight. The terrible possibility of the complete loss of a large 'unsinkable' steam ship on her inaugural voyage is now on everyone's mind.

Suddenly someone shouts, 'I can see something over there, to the north, a black dot!'

'And there too, look! Lifeboats! They're not all dead!'

'Perhaps the *Titanic*'s adrift! Or she's hidden behind these icebergs!'

'Let's hope to God you're right!'

The *Carpathia* moves towards the black dots which get bigger and bigger. More and more can be seen. The passengers try to count them. Someone with binoculars shouts: 'Eighteen! I can see eighteen!'

'Impossible! There were about two thousand five hundred passengers on the *Titanic*!'

'So the others must have stayed on the ship….'

A heavy silence sets in. Totally strange after hours of the old tub's rumbling engines and vibrations.

Lifeboat number two has reached the foot of the *Carpathia*. Down below a woman, Mrs Douglas, screams hysterically, 'The *Titanic*'s sunk! They're all dead!'

But the sound of her voice doesn't reach the upper deck. Boxhall, the fourth officer,[1] quietens her down.

The rescue takes place very calmly. The purser, his assistant, and the chief steward stand at the top of the gangway ready to welcome the wretched survivors. Miss Evans, a very young girl is the first one on to the deck of the *Carpathia*. She falls weeping into the arms of the purser. 'The *Titanic* has sunk with more than a thousand people on board!'

The tragic news quickly spreads. The flag is lowered to half-mast. People silently weep at the sight of these women, pale as statues, coming on board. Boxhall, summoned by the Captain, confirms what the young girl had said. Yes, the *Titanic* has lost everyone and everything, except for those privileged enough to find room in the lifeboats.

Each survivor, on boarding the *Carpathia*, has to give their full name and say which class they were in on the *Titanic*. They are then taken to the corresponding infirmary to be looked after. A count of the survivors is quickly taken: about one thousand five hundred people have died in the catastrophe.

What most astonishes observers, as the lifeboats arrive, is how many of them are half-empty. The one carrying Lady Duff-Gordon for example, and Dorothy Gibson, the film star. And by strange coincidence, it is on these same lifeboats there is the highest percentage of men ...[2]

The first lifeboat draws alongside at 4.10am. Others follow until 7.00am with the exception of number twelve that doesn't arrive until 8.10am. It has great difficulty in drawing alongside because the wind has sprung up and threatens to capsize it. The rescue finishes at 8.45am.

Boat D with the two little boys in it arrives next but last. The other lifeboats in the convoy had to tow it. It would never have reached the *Carpathia* on its own because it was in as bad a state as A when Lowe had assisted it. It is easy to imagine the anxiety hanging over boat D. The occupants had seen boat B take in water and sink only a minute after its passengers had been transferred to other lifeboats. By now, boat D was taking in more water than could be bailed out and its condition was rapidly becoming critical.

Happily, number fourteen, still in the good hands of Lowe who had taken on board survivors from A, had passed close to D, tacking towards the *Carpathia*, and had taken it in tow. This had slowed down number fourteen considerably.

It is 7.00am when Lolo opens his eyes. He doesn't remember anything. First of all he doesn't notice the big black wall dancing in front of him. He's in Margaret's arms along with Momon who is just waking up, opening his eyes wide. The young girl has taken refuge on the gunwale because the water was up to her knees. Björn Steffanson and Hugh Woolner help the passengers out of the boat. The bravest men and women climb up the rope ladder hanging above Lolo. The others are hoisted up in rope cradles suspended from derricks.

For Lolo and Momon, the shipwreck, the terrifyingly icy night, and the agonising screams are already blurred. Luckily for them, the memories of that horrifying night in boat D are almost completely gone. But those memories from before the sinking of the *Titanic* remain intact. Lolo hopes more than ever, that his daddy has been saved.

Before the children have time to really notice, boat D empties little by little. Hugh Woolner's big hands suddenly grasp Momon and he is stuffed into a coal sack and hoisted up. The precious cargo rises into the air with a bewildered Momon shouting at the top of his voice. Lolo is very indignant. 'What are you doing! That's my brother! He must stay with me!'

'Don't worry little fellow, you're going to be reunited with him in a minute.'

The empty sack is already on its way back down. Lolo vividly remembers the incident on the quayside just before they boarded the *Titanic*, when the sack of potatoes he was sitting on was hoisted up into the air. He announces very forcefully, 'I do not want to go up in a sack of potatoes! I want to climb up the ladder!'

'Out of the question. It's too dangerous, you might fall!'

'No! I won't fall! I'm not a baby!' His big brown eyes shine angrily and fill with tears.

'Oh well, too bad, my boy. This is the only way you're going up there.'

He is lifted up, stuffed into the sack and quickly rises up the hull of the steamship. He feels very annoyed. But all the same, it's not bad to swing in the air like that. Is he going to laugh, or cry? While still trying to decide the pros and cons as he lands on the deck of the *Carpathia*, he finds himself in the arms of the purser, Brown. He is given a warm welcome on board the ship, asked how he feels and is given a biscuit. Brown then puts him down and asks him his name.

'Lolo,' replies the child.

'Lolo what?'

Lolo thinks about what his daddy had said, 'Remember that your name is….' A blank, he can't do anything about it. He can't remember. While the harassed purser adds Lolo to his list of children without parents, already the eighth, Lolo l oks around for his daddy. Why isn't he here to welcome them? Being welcomed by the captain is okay but Lolo wants his daddy. Gripped by fear and anguish, he forces his way into the crowd. He scrutinises the pitiful faces bending over to look at him, shoves people out of the way, and breathlessly runs from one man to another examining their faces. It is no use. His daddy isn't here.

In an instant, he understands. From now on, his life will never be the same as before. The world around him has lost its meaning. It has become empty. As empty as he feels inside. He is nothing more than a tiny body, an empty shell in a lonely world. He faints and loses consciousness.

'Where's Momon? I want Momon!' says Lolo in a shaky voice as he recovers consciousness in the arms of a steward.

He starts vomiting uncontrollably. At one fell swoop he is getting rid of the horrifying images stored in his mind since the evening before. When he recovers, he has forgotten all about the frantic race through the crowds to find his daddy. But he knows he is dead.

'Are you alone, sonny?'

'No, I'm with my brother, Momon.'

Noticing Lolo's fur coat, the steward takes him to the first-class dining room. There are a number of people there. Deathly pale, silent women and nervous men, feverish and exhausted, but not Momon. He is in fact, in the second-class dining room, crying and screaming loudly, calling Lolo with all his might. Women are congregating around him offering him hot milk, chocolate, croissants, and sweets. But nothing pacifies him. One of the stewards is very worried and goes to the upper deck asking if anyone has been separated from his or her little boy. At that moment, Margaret Hays climbs over the rail having just come up the rope ladder. 'Yes! Me! A baby aged two and a little four-year-old boy!'

'There's a baby, without parents, screaming in the second-class dining room, I'll go and get him.'

He returns carrying a struggling Momon.

At the sight of Margaret he calms down a little and his tears gradually subside. She takes him in her arms and replies very quickly to Brown's questions. Miss Margaret Hays, first class. And she has taken charge of the two children. She doesn't know their surname. Their father was travelling on his own with them and was left on the *Titanic*.

Brown writes all the information in his notebook and Margaret is at last allowed to follow the steward towards the reception area in first class. Lolo sees her coming in. He is in the arms of Madeline Astor who weeps when she thinks about her own child who will be born without a father. She pities the two orphans and wonders what will become of them. When she sees Margaret, who she knows well, she gets up and Lolo runs towards his brother. Margaret and Madeline hug and kiss each other and nothing can be heard except the four of them weeping. Emotions kept under control for such a long time are at last released. The four of them lie down together on mattresses in a corner of the dining room. They are comforted with all kinds of warm drinks with alcohol in some of them, plus a few drops of sedative.

The two children, lying side by side, talk quietly. Momon asks for their daddy and Lolo replies, 'Don't you understand, he is dead. Margaret told me!'

Surprised, Margaret refrains from interfering in the children's conversation because she has never ever said such a thing. But she immediately realises she must let Lolo say these things without contradicting him. He seems to be accepting the death of his daddy with serenity.

He continues, 'Dead, that means he has gone to the sky and he is happy. He's thinking about his little boys. He is watching us at the moment.'

Edmond is flabbergasted. He doesn't understand his brother's explanation but he feels reassured because he is with him and he smiles. In no time at all they are both fast asleep.

Captain Rostron immediately sends the list of survivors to Cottam, the radio officer who has been on duty all night. After consulting the crew and Ismay, Rostron decides to turn round and go back to New York. The *Olympic*, still sailing towards the scene of the accident and now not far away, has suggested taking the survivors on board. This would allow the *Carpathia* to go on her way to her destination. The idea, however, is enough to make Ismay shake with terror. He is having a nervous break-down. He won't eat and refuses to answer any questions put to him. The *Olympic*'s suggestion was, in fact, rather nightmarish. How could the survivors cope with the sight of a steam ship identical to the one they had escaped from without them all having a nervous breakdown? The survivors unanimously choose to stay on the *Carpathia*. Before setting course for New York, Captain Rostron sets his mind at rest by inspecting the area where the *Titanic* had sunk. Throngs of sailors scan the surface of the ocean with binoculars. For as far as they can see there are pieces of wreckage and bodies drifting on the water. No one could have survived very long in such cold water. At 8.50am, after a brief service for the dead, the *Carpathia* sails off towards New York.

Three hours earlier, the second-in-command on the *Californian*, feeling worried about a ship having disappeared, had awakened Evans, the radio officer, who then went to the radio room. He heard the following news, sent by the *Mount Temple*: 'Do you know the *Titanic* has hit an iceberg and is sinking?' Evans' distress is indescribable. If only he had gone to bed half an hour later! The *Californian* could have gone to help the *Titanic* in distress. The messages flow in, increasing his sense of hopelessness: he cannot bear to think of the great ship sinking, only a dozen miles at the most, from the *Californian*![3]

Captain Lord establishes contact with the *Carpathia*. Rostron asks him to stay in the waters around the scene of the disaster and to pick up any bodies he finds.

Meanwhile, on board the *Carpathia* everything is being organised. All the passengers are now aware of the catastrophe. Many of them have actually given up their cabins. After a few hours of rest, the survivors are led to their new quarters and the dining rooms are freed, serving as sitting rooms. All the other public areas are transformed into dormitories. Passengers spontaneously give clothes to the survivors, who are comforted by such warmth and generosity.

Bride sleeps for a dozen hours and then, in the afternoon, the Captain begs him to take over from Cottam, who after thirty hours without a break, is starting to crack up. Bride's feet have been frostbitten and he is not able to walk. He is carried to the radio room where he starts working as if he is perfectly healthy. It's a tiring job because the whole world wants to know details of what has happened and there is a huge flow of private telegrams. Above all, a list of survivors is requested but Bride refuses to disclose this. He receives the following telegram from the Marconi company: 'Keep quiet. We will do everything at this end and if you don't say a word until you get here, there will be a large sum of money waiting for you.'[4]

Miss Hays and her adopted children are given one of the finest cabins on the ship. They get to know each other much better the following day. Margaret is on the lookout for any clues leading to the discovery of their mother. The children are definitely from the south of France. They are very well brought up: they have a bath every day and they have very good table manners, even the smaller one does his best.

In the dining room, Mag and the children have lunch with Madeline Astor. Even on the *Carpathia* Madeline is ostracised by the little group of millionaires.[5] Mrs Thayer, Mrs Widener, Mrs Carter and Mrs Smith, sitting together at a neighbouring table, treat her like an intruder. The young widow is badly affected by their attitude towards her. She sticks up for herself as best she can, but she cannot really cope. Mag suggests she join her little group of friends made up of Mrs Frustrelle, whose husband has died in the catastrophe, and Albert and Sylvia Caldwell, from the Navratils' neighbouring cabin on the *Titanic*. They have been lucky enough to escape from the sinking ship by getting into a half-empty lifeboat on starboard.

Madeline describes the children's father to Margaret: he spoke at least four languages. But he spoke them so well it was hard to know what nationality he was. He was perhaps German. The Caldwells don't know any more than Madeline. When Lolo is asked about his nationality he says his daddy was French. Hoffmann? The name doesn't mean anything to him. Without being asked, the little boy remembers his mother and their pretty house where their grandparents, who speak Italian, also live. He explains their daddy had left their house and came every Sunday to take him and Momon for a walk.

During the dessert course, Captain Rostron comes and sits at their table. With him are some of the survivors who might be able to shed light on the children's father: Jack Thayer, the Harpers, Björn Steffanson, Hugh Woolner, Colonel Gracie and Pierre Maréchal. Mrs Thayer and Mrs Widener say Michel Hoffmann seemed to get along better with Lord Bedford and WT Stead than with anyone else. He was a discreet, witty man who observed everything but didn't say much. He revealed so little about himself in fact, that no one knew much about him other than Isidor Straus had invited him to design ready-to-wear fashion in his New York department stores.

After lunch Lolo and Momon are invited to the bridge where Captain Rostron tactfully questions them. Mag and Madeline go with them. Lolo holds his brother close to him because he's frightened and feels unsure about all these strange faces. Momon bursts into tears. Lolo swallows hard and looks pathetically at Margaret. She takes his hand and at last he is able to reply to the Captain's questions. 'We had lots of friends on the *Titanic*: my godfather, Charles, the old journalist friend of Charles, and then Trevor, Olaus and Mirella. Trevor often took me to the radio room.'

'It is strange,' says Madeline, remembering the incident in the train. 'The first time I saw this child was on the special boat train from London to Southampton. Since the father is French, why did he not get on the *Titanic* in Cherbourg?'

'Yes it is strange,' Margaret remarks. 'I first met him on the *Fécamp*. I wanted to do some shopping in London before I left for New York, that's why I didn't go to Cherbourg to board the ship. Perhaps his father had similar reasons!'

'How did you get to the ferry boat, Lolo? What kind of transport did you take?'

'We got a train. A very beautiful big train where we slept all night and we had something to eat several times.'

At that moment Bride arrives supported by two sailors. Boxhall and Lightoller are with him.

'Oh! What have you done? Are you ill?' shouts Lolo when he sees the enormous bandages on his feet.

'Hey! Little Lolo! How happy I am to see you!'

Lolo runs to him and hugs him.

Lightoller, Boxhall and Bride pool their memories of the Hoffmann family. They had seen Lolo on the bridge of the *Titanic* with the engineer, Andrews, who had put Murdoch in charge of him. Boxhall remembers he and Murdoch had shown the map of the Atlantic to Lolo and had pointed out the route the *Titanic* was taking.

'Yes, and then Captain Smith picked me up!'

'That's right,' says Boxhall 'and Murdoch took him back to his cabin.'

Bride then comes in: 'I never met Mr Hoffmann but there's someone here who knew him well, I think – Mr Beesley. Perhaps he can help.'

There is silence. Everyone looks at Lolo who has become very upset without knowing why: memories come flooding back. He has not consciously suppressed them but this mysterious inner battle has exhausted him. He is deathly pale and without being able to do anything about it, tears tumble down his cheeks. They all feel so sorry for him.

Captain Rostron thinks things over without saying anything. Everyone quietly watches him. He suddenly makes a decision, 'You are a very courageous little boy, Lolo. We're going to decorate you. Only, you mustn't cry! It's a great honour you know! Come along, dry your eyes! Stand up!'

The Captain gives a sailor an order and he runs off. Lolo lifts up his little tear-stained face. Bride takes out his handkerchief.

'Wait a minute, I'll wipe your face.'

Lightoller and Boxhall line up and stand to attention. The sailor has returned and presents an open box to Captain Rostron. He takes a medal out of it and pins it on to Lolo's chest, saying in a solemn voice, 'Lolo, I am decorating you with a medal of courage. Always remember, you must be dignified!'

The Captain, officers and sailors salute him and then break ranks. Lolo, who has not had time to understand what has happened, is carried triumphantly towards the dining room. He is applauded and the ghosts of his lost friends, so upsetting to him just a short while ago, disappear. Soon a wan little smile appears on his face.

Lawrence Beesley is a very sensitive man, perfectly able to imagine how upset Lolo might feel remembering his dead friends. He tells Captain Rostron he will answer any questions he can, even though he doesn't know very much about the children's father, on condition the children are not there. In fact, Lawrence merely confirms what other survivors have said. He knows next to nothing about the children's father, even though they had got on well together.

And so, the day after the tragic sinking of the *Titanic*, the two little Hoffmanns have become the focus of attention on board the *Carpathia*. The story of the little French orphan receiving a medal from the Captain goes round the ship, within several hours. By midnight, the possibilities of the origins and identities of the children fire the imaginations of those still awake in the first- and second-class dining rooms. The next morning Captain Rostron sends a dozen or so messages to Margaret, among which are two adoption offers. The messages have all come from wealthy American passengers who want to help the children financially. Margaret has time to muse over the surprises of destiny. Today she is responsible for these children who two days ago she didn't even know. She decides that from now on, she will be their guardian until such time as their mother is found. She has no difficulty in imagining the pain this poor woman must be going through, deprived of her children, not knowing what has happened to them. Margaret feels such a sense of duty towards her that she quickly becomes very attached to the boys.

AMERICA! AMERICA!

EXHILARATION KNOWS NO BOUNDS as the *Carpathia* enters the port of New York on the evening of 18 April. New Yorkers are out in their thousands, milling around the quaysides. Finally they are going to find out who has survived the *Titanic* disaster and all the details will be revealed. The selective silence of the radio on board the *Carpathia* has excited much speculation. A mass of large black umbrellas makes the quaysides look dismal. Heavy rain streams down overcoats and drips off bowler hats. Cordons of police attempt to control the crowds but they are often swamped by impatient groups wanting at all costs to get closer to the jetty. Women are the main offenders and the exasperated police roughly push them aside. Some of them are screaming hysterically. Their husbands, sons and daughters were staff or crew on the *Titanic* and they have been waiting for three days to find out what has happened to them. They dread hearing bad news.

The ship approaches slowly. She has to be manoeuvred in position alongside the quay. The anxious crowd waits silently. Eyes are focused on the gangways, now being wheeled towards the ship. But once in place, they remain empty apart from small groups of immigration employees, uniformed customs men, and doctors and nurses quickly climbing up and disappearing into the ship. The tension in the waiting crowd becomes almost unbearable. Men and women are fainting. The police cordons are broken by the crowd and force has to be used to establish order.

Bride has asked Captain Rostron to simplify immigration formalities for the survivors as much as possible. Two long hours pass from the time when the health and immigration services board the vessel to when the first survivors appear on the gangways. The long wait has also been difficult for them.

As soon as the Statue of Liberty came into view, little boats overloaded with journalists wanting sensational news, had besieged the *Carpathia*. Each reporter wanted to be the first to send the scoop of the year to his or her newspaper. Armed with loudspeakers, the journalists shouted questions, completely inaudible by the time they reached the passengers. These were terrible moments for the survivors whose nerves were already shattered by the tragedy.

Lolo and Momon standing on the upper deck, stared at the famous Statue of Liberty, made by a fellow Frenchman, and let go of Mag's hand to cover their ears. Only those who had not lost anyone on the *Titanic* are joyful to be arriving in New York. They are eager to let their loved ones know they are safe. Lawrence Beesley for example, who stands near Margaret while waiting to get off the ship, finds it difficult to hide his joy. He passes the time by describing life in New York to the children and Miss Hays is grateful to him. She dreads the moment when they will have to confront these indiscreet journalists and talk about unspeakable experiences.

How on earth can experiences, as horrifying as the ones taking place the other night, be openly flaunted for the media, frantic for sensational news? Aren't the survivors marked for the rest of their lives with loved ones floating unburied in their life-jackets in the middle of the ice, offering their bodies to birds. How can they be replaced? Mothers, fathers, grandparents, uncles, aunts, cousins, friends, all these victims sacrificed in the name of profit. Who can give them back their lives? With all the new hopes of America, these foreigners bringing their talents to the New World, have been sacrificed for a mirage. Is it not a repetition of Icarus's flight? How can one express all this to the press? How can the crowd's curiosity, their eagerness to find out about other peoples sorrow, be anything but insane? Why openly express one's sorrow?

Above all, Mag wants to protect the children from such an experience. She will refuse to speak to anyone on arrival and will hold a press conference the following day. She will do this only on condition she knows the questions beforehand, and can choose which to answer. Since she had plenty of time, Margaret would defend her privacy. Lawrence Beesley has carefully prepared a detailed account of the disaster and will give it to the press, refusing to add anything else.

The American Minister for the Navy sent the cruiser *Chester* to meet the *Carpathia*, to be in radio contact with her as soon as possible. The government is very annoyed by the lack of news. It considers itself to be personally involved in the *Titanic* disaster and wants to be in control of events. It wants information about the catastrophe, the survivors and the victims as soon as possible, at source, before any distortion of the events creeps in. The *Chester* was not able to get in contact with the *Carpathia*, the radio was constantly busy, but they did manage to intercept a message, sent by Bride on behalf of Ismay, to the director of the White Star Line in the New York office. The message was passed on to the Ministry for the Navy and decoded. Its contents were damning for Ismay and the White Star Line because it constituted a suppression of evidence about the disaster. Ismay's message was a request for a ship, the *Cedric*, to be chartered so surviving officers from the *Titanic* could be sent immediately back to England, before they had time to speak about what had happened on the fateful night. Ismay's sole concern is the reputation of the White Star Line. The government feels duped and sends an order for Ismay and the officers to be put under 'friendly' house arrest. They organise an immediate commission of inquiry.

Survivors on board the *Carpathia* form a committee to put together evidence of the disaster, which is basically trustworthy. For example, they confirmed that Murdoch had shot himself in the head just before the *Titanic* went down, and that Captain Smith and the engineer, Mr Andrews, chose to stay with the ship and die. Again, the collection of evidence is damning for the White Star Line.

When the moment finally comes to get off the *Carpathia*, Beesley says farewell to the children and their guardian and leaves on the largest gangway. Mag chooses a more discreet one near the rear of the ship, hoping to escape the hordes of journalists. But flash-bulbs splutter and a host of reporters bombard them. News has filtered through about two little survivors who have not been identified and who are being looked after by Miss Hays. They have immediately been nicknamed 'Orphans of the Abyss'.

'There they are! Miss Hays, would you like to give us a statement, please? What are your intentions regarding the children? Will you put them in your orphanage? Would you like to adopt them?'

Mag curtly replies she will not make any immediate comments and dictates her conditions for a press conference arranged for the following afternoon at her apartment.

On the morning of 19 April, Margaret Hays orders a taxi and takes the children to a branch of Macy's. Here, as in a number of places in the city, flags are at half-mast. The employees sadly lament the deaths of Mr and Mrs Isidor Straus, who were known and loved by all who know them. The same is happening at the Waldorf Astoria, the hotel that John Astor was so proud of; in a dozen Broadway theatres belonging to Harris; under the big top of the Barnum and Bailey circus; as well as in stations where two train companies are mourning their owners, Charles Hays and John Thayer.

The arrival of Margaret and the children goes unnoticed at first. But as soon as one of the salesmen recognises the two little French boys whose photos are in all the newspapers, he immediately informs his superiors who tell the store manager. Two hours later, Lolo and Momon leave the department store laden with clothes, carried in big leather bags, that have been given to them by the management.

Lolo and Momon were very enthusiastic about seeing a big American department store. They were shown all the different sections of the store by a salesman, had chosen what they liked among dozens of articles, and had been passed from the arms of one woman to another. All the women in the ready-to-wear department wanted to see them and kiss them. Then, in the toy department, Momon who was inconsolable about the loss of his miniature model of the *Titanic*, sunk at the same time as the big one, had set his mind on a steamboat almost as pretty. Lolo had chosen a car, a shiny black Chrysler, trimmed with chrome and with a driver in chauffeur's uniform just like he'd seen in the garage on the *Titanic* when he'd been taken there by the steward. While the children were busy being shown around the store, a salesgirl told Miss Hays about the sad story of Mrs Alfred Hess, daughter of Ida and Isidor Straus.

Mrs Hess had taken the special train chartered by the White Star Line transporting journalists to Halifax. The journalists were to be there for the arrival of the of the damaged *Titanic*, towed by the *Olympic*. She thought it very amusing to find herself the only woman on the train. The reporters joked about the unsinkable *Titanic*, the finest ship in the world, having to be towed by her sister, a few months older than she is, on her maiden voyage! Suddenly and mysteriously, the train stopped in the middle of the countryside. It had started to move again around eight o'clock but in reverse. There were rumours about the *Titanic* having sunk, but nobody had any faith in them. Around midnight, at the station, much earlier than the majority of others relatives had any news, Mrs Hess learned of the death of her parents and the heroic behaviour of her mother.

After the magic jaunt at the department store, Mag suggests the three of them have a taxi tour of New York. Lolo is amazed and can't believe his eyes: the buildings here really are like their funny names, skyscrapers. He has to stretch his neck to see the tiniest patch of blue sky up above the tall buildings.

After seeing the business area at one end of Manhattan, the taxi goes to Greenwich Village where, according to Lolo, the houses look a little like those in Nice – no doubt because their scale is more human. Lolo and Momon soon find themselves on familiar territory, in a French restaurant, where everyone puts themselves out to please the 'Orphans of the Abyss'. Finally they get back in the waiting taxi. Margaret doesn't care about the cost of anything. Lolo had been dumbfounded the evening before when a stylish servant had served him from a golden serving dish!

The young woman and the children cope quite well with the journalists. But what a relief when they leave! They have a nice evening talking among themselves. Momon seems more mature. He is expressing himself better, gradually using correct words rather than his 'baby talk'. Mag congratulates him. Their mother will be very happy to see how her baby has become a big boy!

Their mother – that is the only issue now. Margaret, in pursuit of any clue as to her whereabouts, never stops turning the conversation round to the subject. The children enjoy remembering their familiar world. It reassures them and helps to put recent memories behind them. Nevertheless, Lolo often talks about his daddy. He starts sentences with: 'When Daddy was here...'

When saying a prayer for his daddy that evening, he bursts into tears and Margaret, feeling very moved by his sadness, holds his hand until he falls asleep. She then goes to her room and starts writing down pieces of the Hoffmann puzzle into a large notebook.

She reads, rereads and classifies the huge amount of mail received during the day. The telegrams have come pouring in, one after another. More than thirty adoption offers in the space of twenty-four hours! Strange, she says to herself, are there so many couples in the United States without children, who are in need of affection? Or is this rush of offers rooted in self-seeking? The bundle of mail is in a rattan suitcase on which Mag has written the name Mrs Hoffmann, the only person able to take a decision about the contents.

~ ~ ~

Six long hopeless days have passed and no light has been shed on the disappearance of Marcelle's children.

On 21 April she is resting on her bed after yet another sleepless night. It is about eight o'clock in the morning when her mother and stepfather come into her room and open the shutters. Her mother, desperately weeping, puts a copy of *Le Figaro* on her bed.

'Quickly! Turn to page two!' Antonio says in an agitated and commanding tone.

Trembling, Marcelle opens the newspaper and finds a full-length photo of Lolo and Momon on page two, taken in New York, at Macy's department store. The caption says 'Orphans of the Abyss'. Her little ones are safe and sound – they've been found! No, there must be a mistake, how can they be in New York? She breathlessly devours the article, once, twice, ten times! Her heart is pounding. She doesn't even hear her mother's noisy weeping and exclamations. She must be absolutely sure it is a photo of her children before rejoicing. She could not stand it if she was mistaken. She examines the photo closely. Momon is sitting in an armchair holding a miniature transatlantic ship and Lolo is standing up resting his right hand on the armchair, happily smiling. Both of them seem to be in good health.

Marcelle suddenly feels free of the inertia making her feel so empty. She watches her parents crying with joy and her heart feels as if it is bursting with sunshine. She herself has not been able to cry since Michel and the children disappeared. Now, the feelings of relief are so intense she just lets the tears stream down her face.

Having recovered from the initial emotional shock, she reads the following article:

> 'According to the *Daily Chronicle* correspondent, seven babies under the age of two years old have been taken off the *Carpathia*. Nobody knows the whereabouts of their mothers or fathers. They were thrown into the life-boats, probably by their parents who themselves perished. The children's clothes give no clue to their identity.

> 'Two other children, who are French, know only their first names Louis[1] and Momon and are four and two years old respectively. Miss Margaret Hays, one of the survivors, has taken them in. They appear to have been accompanied by a passenger in second class, called Hofmann.'

Le Petit Nicois also devoted its front page to long articles about the survivors from the *Titanic*. Only then was the list of survivors known. While Marcelle gets dressed, Antonio runs to buy the rest of the newspapers published that morning. The children's photos are in most of them. Their mother is being sought. The children's nicknames are misspelled everywhere. That Michel had taken on his friend's name didn't really surprise Marcelle, but why is it written with only one 'f'?[2]

By ten o'clock Marcelle was at the American consulate in Nice, asking for an urgent interview. She was seen at eleven o'clock and at one o'clock, two dispatches were sent. One to Etienne Lanel, the French consul in New York, and the other to the Havas agency in Paris.

Leaving the consulate, Marcelle, leaning heavily on her stepfather's arm (she had refused to allow Rey de Villarey to go with her) starts to shake uncontrollably. Two extremely violent emotions grip her body: the joy of knowing her children are safe and the ghastly knowledge that her dream was true and Michel is really dead.

Now that she is more settled, she feels very ambivalent. The mother in her feels immense joy and is she is prepared to do everything she can to be reunited with the children. As a wife separated from her husband, Michel, she feels her unfaithfulness is the cause of his death. She forgets the reasons for their separation, their different characters, tastes and aspirations. She forgets the unbearable scenes of domestic strife between her mother and her husband. She now feels the old woman gave him no peace. She also ignores the fact that problems with their marriage were not the only reasons why Michel left. He had a great yearning to go to America to re-establish his professional life there and to bring up the children, as he thought best. Poor Marcelle feels completely responsible for his death.

Mrs Navratil goes to the consulate on 23 April to answer questions about the children. Another ordeal awaits her. The consul needs to establish the identity of the 'Orphans of the Abyss' and Marcelle is clearly going to do everything she can to let the truth prevail. She is questioned at length about the children, her husband and her career. She has to reveal what she hoped she could keep to herself: her husband was a kidnapper. She has to give reasons why she thinks Michel took the children. Her pride is hurt.

At the end of a two-hour interview, the consul ushers Marcelle into a small lounge where tea is served. The young woman sees six people gathered there, her parents, the Marquis Rey de Villarey, on whom Angelina has turned her back, Michel Hoffmann and his wife, Emma, who have just returned from their trip to Paris, and a secretary who has been taking notes about the interview.

After pleasantries have been exchanged and sympathy extended to Marcelle for the terrible torments she has endured since her children disappeared, the events are put together in chronological order. Michel's business failure is the focus of conversation. The most astonishing thing is the suddenness with which, even before anything was totally lost, Michel Navratil had filed for bankruptcy and asked Michel Hoffmann to take over. It was real sabotage!

Hoffmann reveals the story of the 'borrowed' passport. Navratil had given no explanation for wanting it. This is the most important element of the inquiry because it explains the choice of pseudonym under which Michel Navratil had travelled. There was a strong physical resemblance between the two men. They had the same first name and they came from the same place.

Finally there is the question about Michel and the children's last day in Nice. The consul asks Marcelle if the children had been given an Easter egg.

'No, not an egg,' she replies, 'but a chocolate hen decorated with real rust-coloured and white feathers. It sat on sugar eggs with yellow marzipan chickens inside them.' This detailed reply along with others, like how Momon has some white scabs on his skin, concur with replies and observations revealed by the children at the French Consulate in New York. Their verbal reports had been sent to Nice the evening before. The consul therefore officially identifies Marcelle Caretto, wife of Michel Navratil, as the mother of the two 'Orphans of the Abyss.' The result of the investigation is immediately dispatched to Etienne Lanel and the Havas agency.

The front-page news in newspapers in Europe and the United States the next day is about the identification of the two 'Orphans of the Abyss' and how their mother has been found. Two days later Marcelle receives one return ticket, in second class on the *Oceanic* to New York, along with two singles from New York to Cherbourg. The White Star Line has sent them. She has to wait patiently for another two weeks because the ship doesn't leave Cherbourg until 8 May. All being well she will leave New York on the return trip to France with the children on 18 May.

The next morning the postman delivers a letter from England. It is an emotional moment for her. The envelope is not bordered with black! It is rather crumpled and the writing is clumsy. The address is very succinct. It reads: Mrs Navratil, mother of the 'Orphans of the Abyss,' Nice, France. Marcelle hesitates before opening it. Finally, with a pounding heart, she does so. Inside is a note obviously written by someone who is not French and a posthumous letter from Michel. Marcelle feels faint. She sits in a chair, her heart beating fast and unable to move for a while, holding the two letters.

She relaxes a little and reads the first letter.

Madam,

You do not know me. I live in London and a friend has translated my letter. I feel very ashamed because without knowing it, I have caused you a lot of pain. Your husband gave me this letter to post but it dropped on the ground. It was raining very hard and the envelope got so wet, the address was illegible. I put it in a drawer and found it yesterday. I opened it and then I knew what unhappiness I had caused you! I saw your name in a newspaper and now know who you are. I am very sad about your unhappiness.

Please forgive me.

Yours sincerely,

The signature is illegible.

After an agonising moment Marcelle realises her three dreams were double premonitions. Michel had really written to her before embarking on the *Titanic*, and now the letter is in her hands. Slowly and religiously Marcelle opens the second envelope. She can see it has been carefully resealed. She takes out the sheet of writing paper with the familiar rounded handwriting and with tears running down her face, reads it.

My Dear Marcelle,

By the time you receive this letter, which will put an end, I think, to your worries, we will have arrived in New York. I'm not trying to appease my guilt. I have betrayed your confidence by taking the children away. I know their disappearance will have been an agony for you. But if I had told you of my intentions you would never have allowed me to take them. I hope your pain has been alleviated by the presence of your friends.

You have become someone else, we do not get along together anymore and I must go.

I am taking Lolo and Momon to America where, as you already know, I want to start a new life. I want to bring up the children myself and when they have finished their education I want them to become my business partners. I will send you our address as soon as I can; it will take me some time to find work and somewhere to live.

I kiss you.

Michel.

Marcelle weeps, taking care not to wet the letter for the second time. The words dance in front of her eyes. She thinks about how much she had loved Michel. But life with him had become impossible, she is sure about that. But what fate had made him travel on the *Titanic*?

On 8 May, Marcelle is pacing the promenade deck of the *Oceanic*. She is pensive. The press with exquisite taste has called the *Oceanic* 'the widow's ship'. The steam ship has just changed course at the 'angle' in order to avoid icebergs. The perpetual movement of the green ocean fascinates her. It is alive and has a mysterious mind of its own. It has taken the *Titanic* down to the bottom of its depths. The eyes of the very young woman (she's only twenty years old) are lost in the open sea. Perhaps Michel's body is resting a long way down there, at the bottom of the abyss. Marcelle, a lonely figure, stands trying to imagine the horror of that icy night. Suddenly the ghostly sounds of thousands of deafening screams seem to echo from the ocean. They are the cries of the hundreds of victims in the icy water. Did Michel scream too? Did he try to swim to a lifeboat? She covers her ears, trying to ignore the noise. Is she going mad? She scrutinises the rough surface of the ocean, her eyes wild. She feels overcome with the desire to jump overboard and join the victims who seem to be calling her. It would be so easy. She would jump and her body would meet up with her husband's, in the deep of the ocean. Her guilt would be expiated. But then she seems to hear Lolo and Momon calling her. The ghostly voices get softer and softer. She stops herself thinking about jumping into the ocean and runs to the safety of her cabin.

Marcelle's heart beats fast as the *Oceanic* reaches Bedloe Island. It is the afternoon of 14 May. The gigantic Statue of Liberty towers about thirty metres above the ship. Marcelle looks at the symbolic flaming torch and thinks of Michel who will never see it. She can already make out the famous skyscrapers on Manhattan Island. Yes this is certainly the New World, but she prefers the old one where her roots are. She has only one desire now: to collect the children and to leave as soon as possible. Two days on American soil will be more than enough for her.

Marcelle's entry visa is automatically given to her as she gets off the ship. She looks for the children. They must be waiting as impatiently as she is. At last they are to be reunited! But a pleasant-looking young woman, whose blond hair is in a wispy chignon, welcomes her. Her green eyes are shining with excitement. 'Mrs Navratil? My name is Margaret Hays!'

Marcelle holds out her arms to her. They stand silently together for a moment, then stare at each other. Such a combination of beauty is unimaginable. One northern, the other southern. Marcelle has a mass of soft dark hair drawn up into a low chignon. Her regular features are a little strained, because of anxiety and her light complexion is extremely pale today. Her looks express a deep interest in life, surprisingly childlike considering the implacable destiny that has touched her family. Mag's friendly smile makes Marcelle feel she has known her for a long time.

'Where are my children?' Marcelle immediately asks.

'Be patient, you will see them very soon.'

Journalists and photographers waiting behind a police cordon a short way off suddenly break through it. Marcelle and Margaret find themselves surrounded, bombarded by flash bulbs, questions being shot at them with reporters shouting above each other in an effort to be heard. It's unbearable. Marcelle looks around with an imploring expression in her eyes, then puts her hand over them and huddles up.

The French consul in New York, Etienne Lanel and Walsh, the director of the Children's Aid Society[3] who kept their distance while the two women met up, march over and beg the journalists to leave them alone. A press conference is scheduled for the following day at four in the afternoon at the Children's Aid Society headquarters. Mrs Navratil won't say anything today. The consul introduces himself, takes Marcelle by the arm and quickly leads the little group to a taxi waiting further along the quayside.

'Since we still have a number of formalities to complete before handing the children over to you,' explains Etienne Lanel in the taxi, 'we thought it better you don't see them until tomorrow. A meeting has been arranged for tomorrow at ten at the Children's Aid Society.'

'What society?' asks Marcelle on the verge of tears. How can she be made to wait yet another day before seeing the children. Hasn't she already suffered enough?

Mr Walsh explains the Children's Aid Society needs to verify everything she says and to publicly compare this with what the children say to avoid risking any error. Marcelle is disgusted with the idea of having to share the intimate moment of being reunited with her children with strangers present. But at the same time she understands the institution cannot risk the children being handed over to an impostor.

During her stay in New York Marcelle is a guest of the White Star Line at the Waldorf Astoria, now owned by Madeline Astor. This evening Margaret says she can see the file she has been keeping on the children. She tells her about the adoption offers coming from all over America. Adoption offers? Absolutely not! Marcelle has no desire to read them, and doesn't even want to hear about them! But yes, Mag insists, she should read every-thing, open all the parcels! It's in the children's interest. There are several offers of money and actual gifts of cash, mostly anonymous. But Marcelle vows neither to read any letters nor open any parcels.

However, once in her luxurious hotel room where a

magnificent bouquet of flowers sent by Madeline, is waiting for her, Marcelle's curiosity gets the better of her. She opens the rattan suitcase Mag has had delivered to her room and the rest of the afternoon passes like lightning. She takes pleasure in reading all the letters, often very touching and they distract her from feeling sad about not seeing the children immediately. One letter, written in French says: 'The sympathy I feel for you and the children is very sincere. I am not just anyone. My ancestors landed in America in 1658. Since then we have remained French at heart and in spirit. My heart beats fast when I hear the word France. It would give me great pleasure if you would consent to see me! May I hope for such a favour? Do not telephone because our telephone boy is really stupid!'

Marcelle finds it incredible. So when she was travelling alone across the Atlantic and going through the scene of the disaster, people were thinking about her sorrow and writing to her! She starts to regret her decision to leave so soon. While thinking about this she opens another letter, written in a completely different way: 'I've followed your agony step by step! You have crossed the ocean and will certainly be in need of something other than simple displays of affection!' Ha! Here's a man looking for a bit of an adventure. That could be amusing! 'If you would like to stay in New York, I am in the position to offer you a job with a generous income in an extremely outstanding place!' He must be a banker or an oil magnate! 'I am of the opinion that the expression of my deep sympathy, aroused by the feelings I have for you, should be judged differently than other communications you receive.' Oh! And why?

Marcelle drops the letter on the floor and laughs nervously.

When she feels less hysterical, she starts reading again. She swears she won't let anyone feel sorry for her any longer. Time passes and her anger rises. At what point will she refuse all the cheques coming in, made out to her!

She feels she is in the process of subjugating herself in favour of her family; she will not accept any gifts from anyone! She doesn't want charity!

After dinner she chats with Mag who has left the children asleep, with her maid as a babysitter. Marcelle asks her many questions about the catastrophe, about the children's reactions, and how much they had suffered. Margaret tells her how Lolo had begun to see everything, to understand everything and how he had begged for the lifeboat to go back so his daddy could be saved. Then she related how he had gradually forgotten about things, partly after he had slept on the lifeboat and later much more, on board the *Carpathia*.

'How did Michel die? Did he drown or freeze to death?'

'He froze to death. The *Mackay-Bennett* found his body five days later. It was floating, thanks to his life-jacket. He was buried in Halifax with about a hundred other people who were pulled out of the water. The other bodies had sunk.'

Marcelle feels relieved. She prefers knowing her Michel is buried in a cemetery rather than having been left at the bottom of the ocean.

On the morning of 15 May Lolo and Momon are trembling with excitement at the thought of seeing their mummy again. With Mag's help they get ready very quickly. On the stroke of eight forty-five, they gallop into the headquarters of the Children's Aid Society accompanied by Mr Walsh, the director. They have to pass a row of reporters cordoned off as a security measure, who, not being able to get any closer, shout at the children, asking them how they are.

'I'm very well thank you, how are you?' Lolo bravely replies as he runs past them.

'Very well!' echoes Momon.

The door of the lift closes, leaving the indiscreet crowd behind them. Mr Walsh leads the children into a big light room on the fourth floor where there are two tables. On the larger table there is a mountain of presents, sent from all over the United States. They will be taken to Nice in a special crate on the *Oceanic*. On the other table breakfast is laid out. In a corner of the room four strangers sit in armchairs, reading newspapers. But nothing distracts the children from their terrible wait. They glance briefly at the table stacked with toys. Where's mummy? Why isn't she coming? Walsh tries to reassure them.

'Just be patient a little longer and she will be here.'

Lolo and Momon are more and more anxious. They go to the window and see a crowd gathering, way below.

'Oh! Oh! There, I see her!' Momon suddenly shouts.

'Where? Where?'

'Down there! She's getting out of a car!'

'Oh yes, I see her too! And Mag is with her! And the man who asked us so many questions!'

Contrary to what might have been expected, instead of running to the door, the children stand still, waiting like two cats five or six metres away. It seems like an eternity before the door opens. The four strangers, called as objective witnesses for the reunion, watch the scene above their newspapers.

Suddenly a familiar figure appears silhouetted in the doorway and behind her, Mag and Etienne Lanel. The children are on the alert, then the figure takes a step as the door closes behind her and the children let out a cry!

'Mummy!' they shout, running to meet her.

Marcelle opens her arms wide and wraps them in an embrace none of them will ever forget. They stay like this without saying a word for a minute which, to those watching, seems like infinity. Marcelle emotionally hugs them to her, almost suffocating them, as Michel had done just before their parting. They've come full circle: daddy has disappeared but mummy has come back. It is here, in the heat of emotion that Lolo whispers the message from Michel for Marcelle, with touching tenderness. Then he murmurs something that has been plaguing him, 'Did Daddy hurt you?'

Marcelle waits for a moment before replying. Then, pulling herself together, she replies in a trembling voice, 'Yes Lolo, he hurt me, he didn't tell me he was taking you away and I've been looking everywhere for you. But now, it's all forgotten because he has been very good with you.'

Four days later, a lone figure, away from the crowds on the quayside, stands staring at the *Oceanic* going into the distance with the three Navratils on board. Mag watches until the ship is nothing more than a black dot on the horizon. She feels the tears rolling down her cheeks and makes no attempt to wipe them away. She relives the terrible time in boat D, the horrifying sinking of the *Titanic*, and hears the courageous little voice of Lolo shouting, 'My Daddy must be saved!' She sees the unhappy lifeboats below the *Carpathia* on that magical morning. For the first time since that fateful night, she is overcome by a feeling of despondency. For as long as the children had been with her she had kept her emotions under control. Now the children have gone forever and her nerves feel frayed. Seeing the children leave is an awful wrench. Only time will heal the pain. Gradually, the memories of the *Titanic*, both happy and tragic, will fade into a corner of her mind.

Paris, 14 April 1997.

The 85th anniversary of the sinking of the Titanic.

POSTSCRIPT

Dear Readers,

The story you have just read (do not begin with the postscript, wait till you have read it all) is a true story. Ever since I was a little girl, my father's sketchy memories about an event that deeply disturbed the story of our family have stimulated my curiosity. It is only by the kind hand of fate that my generation and those following exist. These sketchy memories were reduced to the following: sea sickness during the ferry crossing to Dover on the way to London, a walk along the quayside in Southampton at the foot of the huge side of the *Titanic*, eggs served on a silver platter in the second-class dining room, the hugeness of the promenade deck and lifeboats hung from davits, the message Michel gave to Lolo to give to Marcelle, the little boy's farewell to his daddy who stayed on the *Titanic*, floating ice on the ocean around the lifeboats, the humiliating ascent in a sack on to the *Carpathia*, and lastly, the gold dish belonging to Margaret Hays in New York. I had wanted to find out everything about this story.

The idea of reconstructing the epic story of my grandfather, father and uncle needed a special set of circumstances.

My father received a letter in 1976 from a man called Sydney Taylor. He announced he would be flying over France in a balloon in the near future and if it wasn't inconvenient, he would stop off in Montpelier and visit him. 'You will certainly not remember, my dear Michel,' he wrote, 'that you spent three weeks with your brother Edmond at my home in Boston between April and May 1912. At that time we only knew your nicknames, Lolo and Momon. Miss Hays, a young friend of my parents, left you with my family while she tried to find your mother. You stayed with her for only three days after you had arrived in New York. The rest of the time you were with my family. I was six years old at the time, the eldest of four children. I remember you as if it was yesterday.'

And then there was something else, so incredible I did not include it in the book because it was a case of truth being stranger than fiction and I thought no one would ever believe it.

Sydney mentioned in the letter that, at this time, his family had a babysitter whose surname was Caretto, a young Italian girl from Genoa, who was spending a year learning English in Boston. Does the name Caretto mean anything to you? She was Marcelle's cousin! She was very helpful in establishing the children's identities.

My father, little Lolo in the story, enthusiastically welcomed Sydney's suggestion of paying a visit. He was seventy years old and came out of the sky bringing my father a present. It was a typewritten collection of notes he had put together about the story of Lolo, Momon and Marcelle in New York. He had consulted the archives of the Children's Aid Society and carefully questioned his parents. He had scrupulously noted everything down. Thanks to him, a large chunk of the past came to light for my father and me. The impetus to write the story was there and I set about working backwards, consulting and doing research on what had already been written about the *Titanic*, including newspaper reports written at the time of the disaster.

I wrote the first book about this story in 1981, and Hachette in France published it. It was for adults as well as children. But my father did not want me to write the truth so a lot of details were invented. It was a novel.

It was only after the discovery of wreck of the *Titanic* when my father became very sought after by the media, that he started speaking openly about his mother and father and the reasons behind their separation. That is why I rewrote their story, theis time supplying true names and events. This book is written for children as well as adults.

It is similar to the first book but it is not a novel. It is not a totally truthful biography because I have taken certain liberties with the historical events. Amongst other things, I put the arrival of the *Titanic* at Queenstown as being at 7.00pm when in fact she was there at 11.00am. The change made it more striking for the main characters.

There are, by the way, some missing links in this story, (those who could have provided them are dead), so I had to use my imagination. I did not know my grandfather and, for that matter, only ever met my grandmother and uncle once in my life, just before they died. I have studied their photos a great deal, as well as those of my great-grandparents, Angelina and Antonio and Rey de Villarey, my father's godfather. I often questioned my sister, Michèle, who knows a lot about the family history via our maternal family who knew the grandparents and Marcelle very well. I imagined the rest by trying to put myself in the shoes of those who lived the drama. For example, to describe the splendours of the *Titanic* in detail and to develop the theme of the three Navratils mixing with the three classes of passengers (in reality they would never have had access to first class, even if invited by friends), I invented three characters: Mirella, Trevor and Charles Bedford. All the others really existed, even though I presented some of them in a slightly romanticised way, such as Olaus Abelseth.

I also made up the episode where Lolo found himself trapped in third class. At first, I could not imagine why, since he had access to them, my grandfather had not put the children in the safety of one of the first lifeboats that left. Now, I think he hoped to leave with them and so waited until the last moment.

Bu, in any case, if Lolo had not been imprisoned how could I have described the panic in third class? And who is to say I did not imagine the truth?

The four Navratils in my story are both real and imagined. Real, because with the details to hand, their story is true. Imagined, because I reinvented their characters, particularly that of my father, Lolo, who has never been interested in anything technical or remotely connected with machines. He became a Professor of Philosophy.

Hoping this book gives you pleasure and that you find it moving.

Best wishes,

Elisabeth Navratil,
Onnens, 3 August 1997.

FOOTNOTES

Chapter 1

1   This inaugural voyage of the *Titanic* was advertised as part as a huge publicity campaign by the White Star Line, whose owner, the American financier, Pierpont Morgan, had set up a vast steel empire. Like the sister ship, *Olympic,* built two years earlier, the *Titanic* was financed by American money, but the ship itself and the crew were British. The two ships with their 46,000 tons were, in the eyes of the builder and Lord Ismay, the president of the White Star Line, rivals with the *Mauritania*, owned by Cunard which was 14,000 tons lighter and shorter by thirty metres.

Chapter 2

1   Electricity in cabins on transatlantic ships was still rare.

2   The head of the crew is uneasy about the work allocation amongst his men because the majority of them were only taken on a week before the ship started its voyage and they had not had any experience or training on a ship of such immense size. The Captain as well as his senior officers were equally inexperienced. The White Star Line had thought it unnecessary to give the officers any training for sailing a gigantic ship.

3   One nautical mile equals 1,852 metres.

Chapter 3

1   This boat was later converted into a restaurant and is anchored on the Seine in Paris.

Chapter 4

1   Isidor Straus was a Bavarian who emigrated to the United States with his family in 1854 when he was a young man. He did very well in the business world and returned to Europe in 1863 to buy arms for the confederate army. Then he worked in a shipping office in Liverpool. In 1888, along with his brother, he became a shareholder in Macy's, the department store chain that now exists all over the world. The brothers became the owners in 1896. Director of several banks and a politician, Isidor Straus bcame one of the richest men in the United States of America.

2   The stern is at the back of the ship and the bow is at the front.

3   Presbourg, capital of Slovakia, is now known by its old name of Bratislava.

Chapter 5

1 Dorothy Gibson was a big star of silent movies who disappeared once talking movies arrived.

Chapter 6

1 Twenty-one knots equals 38.89 km per hour.

Chapter 7

1 In 1906 a group of women started a movement to demand suffrage, or votes for women. This movement eventually spread through Europe and to America.

2 Lolo met Madeline Astor in the boat train between London and Southampton. Her husband, John Jacob Astor is the richest of the millionaires on the ship. He inherited his fortune from his great-grandfather who emigrated to America in 1783 where he made a lot of money in the leather business and invested it in property. This is Michel's dream, to become a self-made man. John Astor owns whole districts of New York. Three years earlier he divorced his first wife and became a subject of gossip among high society because divorce was frowned upon. He re-married and his young wife Madeline, aged eighteen, and they are on their honeymoon on the *Titanic*.

Chapter 8

1 Lolo did not see Louise Laroche again until 86 years later when there were only seven *Titanic* survivors left.

Chapter 9

1 Séracs are huge blocks of ice that are formed by the intersection of crevasses in a glacier. During warm weather they break easily and fall off the glacier.

2 Pierre Védrines who had recently broken the air speed record by flying at a hundred and forty two kilometers per hour, which was extraordinary at this time, was killed in an accident three weeks after the *Titanic* sank and his name was added to the list of martyrs who died in the name of flying.

3 We will never know whether Captain Smith had taken notice of previous messages that he had openly stuffed into his pocket without reading.

Chapter 10

1 Murdoch should have been second-in-command but the White Star Line appointed Henry Wilde, thus demoting not only Murdoch, who became first lieutenant, but also Lightoller, who found himself as second lieutenant.

2 An inspection of the hull of the wreck, 3,870 metres at the bottom of the ocean revealed six holes over an area of a square metre. The commission of enquiry in 1912 concluded that there was a fault, 30 metres long, that could have sunk the *Titanic* in 10 minutes.

Chapter 11

1 Nourney is travelling, like Navratil, under a pseudonym: Baron Alfred Von Drachenstedt.

2 CQD were the initials chosen for emergency calls before the introduction of SOS.

3 In all there were 3,343 that accumulated before sinking.

Chapter 12

1 If Captain Smith had not forgotten to hold the lifeboat drill scheduled for that morning, hundreds more passengers would have been saved from the *Titanic*, especially in third class.

Chapter 13

1 Paul Poiret was a fashion designer that had revolutionised women's clothes by relieving them of corsets. His ideas inspired many designs in the 1920s and '30s.

2 Madeline is pregnant.

3 The White Star Line reduced the number of lifeboats for economic reasons. It cost the lives of 1,480 people.

Chapter 14

1 There were 77 children among the victims of the *Titanic*. Seventy-six of them were from the third class.

2 Lorraine was the only child from first class not to survive.

Chapter 16

1 There were 53 children, 101 women and 651 men in the ocean. Six hundred and eighty-five crew and staff, men and women, were fighting for their lives, most of them without life-jackets. McCawley, the gym instructor, had said he could swim better without one. They were to die very quickly.

2 Most bodies were picked up during the following week by ships that had come too late to the rescue. They missed some. Months and even years later, skeletons kept afloat by life-jackets, were picked up by passing ships and buried at sea.

Chapter 17

1 Boxhall would write in his will that his ashes were to be scattered on the ocean where the *Titanic* had gone down. It was done on 12 June 1967.

2 At the time no one thought ill of this but later, during the two commissions of enquiry in New York and London, this fact came up repeatedly.

3 From then on, a rule was introduced saying every ship should have at least two radio officers on board, maintaining twenty-four hour radio contact.

4 In fact he receives $2,500 (12 years salary!) from *The New York Herald* for his exclusive news report. Meanwhile, hundreds of families of less wealthy survivors are deprived of news of their loved ones until the *Carpathia* reaches New York on the evening of 18 April, four days after the drama.

5 The scandal surrounding Madeline continues in the days to come. When John's will is published, it is revealed that she inherits his huge fortune on condition she never remarries. The national and international press gloat over this clause. The 9 May edition of *Le Matin* runs the headline: 'Condemned to Gilded Widowhood!' And even lines such as the following are written: 'God of storms, Adamastor, you have well and truly devoured Astor'.

Epilogue

1 It is probable that when Lolo was questioned about his name on the *Carpathia*, his nickname was interpreted as being short for the first name Louis.

2 This spelling error was to have serious consequences. Michel's body, taken to Halifax, was buried alongside other victims but in the Jewish part of the cemetery, which complicated his identification. Marcelle had to go to great lengths to prove that he was her husband, Michel Navratil.

3 The Children's Aid Society played and important role in the story of the Navratil children. They supervised the meeting between Marcelle and the children, and protected Lolo and Momon from being hastily adopted by an American family. The records about their stay in America were consulted and helped a great deal in reconstructing the events.

OTHER BOOKS FROM
THE O'BRIEN PRESS

BRIAN BORU: EMPEROR OF THE IRISH
Morgan Llewelyn
Illustrated by Donald Teskey

This internationally best-selling author, winner of many awards in adult historical fiction, now turns her hand to historical fiction for children with a personalised account of the life of Brian Boru, from his childhood in the midst of a large warrior family to his final role as High King of Ireland.

Paperback £4.99

STRONGBOW:
THE STORY OF RICHARD AND AOIFE
Morgan Llewelyn

An action-packed tale of the famous Norman knight who captured Dublin and married an Irish princess – Aoife, the King of Leinster's daughter.

Paperback £4.99

GRANUAILE: CHIEFTAIN, PIRATE, TRADER
Mary Moriarty and Catherine Sweeney

The story of the extraordinary life of the 16th-century Grace O'Malley, know as Granuaile – pirate, chieftain, trader, politician. Illustrated with photos, and drawings by David Rooney.

Paperback £4.99